Family Secrets

Ellie McLellan Genealogy Mystery - Book 1

Beth Farrar

Edited by Ronnie Pelletier

Cover by GetCovers.com

First edition published – 2022

eBook ISBN: 978-1-7386664-0-9

Print ISBN: 978-1-738664-1-6

Hardcover ISBN: 978-1-738664-4-7

No part of this book was written by AI - just a human's blood, sweat and tears (and a bit of stress!).

Author's Note: Being a Canadian author, please excuse any double "l"s or wayward "u"s in words, eh. Please do not flag them. Much appreciated.

Also By

Ellie McLellan Genealogy Mystery Series

Family Secrets – Book 1

Family Mistakes – Book 2

Family Promises – Book 3

Contents

To my family, who each support the other in their dreams. You guys are my rock.

Chapter One

"Justin wants to know why you won't go out with him," Sophie whispered to her cousin from her seat across the hospital bed. The room was quiet. The heart monitor machine, attached to Sophie's mom, Jenna, echoed a soft beep.

Here it comes, Ellie thought before whispering back, "I'm not dating. You know that." She looked up from her notebook of a client's genealogy charts and sent her cousin a piercing look, hoping to stop any more conversation about her dating life, or lack thereof.

It had been months since her cousin had mentioned that Ellie should start dating again and sure enough, spring was in the air and Sophie felt Ellie needed a man in her life. To be fair, Sophie had waited over a year after Ellie's husband and daughter's deaths to even broach the subject the first time, but Ellie had closed that down hard and fast. And now it was four years and the last thing she would do is let Sophie know she was missing someone by her side. She'd deal with this on her own.

"You can't be a hermit forever. Mom's worried about you," Sophie continued as if Ellie hadn't said a word. Sophie glanced at her mother with weary eyes. The older woman appeared to be sleeping as peacefully as anyone could who had just suffered a heart attack three days before. The two young women had kept a vigil either alone or together since they'd brought Jenna to the hospital.

"I'm *not* a hermit, and she *doesn't* have to worry." Ellie tucked a stray length of dark hair behind one ear. She tried to hide a bone-weary sigh and closed her notebook. The mid-afternoon sun slanted through the window, winking off the pen Ellie tapped up and down. She forced her fingers to be still. This was not a conversation she wanted to have—not here; not now. Her life was good, everything in its place and calm, and that's all she wanted. Sophie meant well, but the thought of what dating entailed sent a dash of acid straight to Ellie's stomach.

"He's very persistent," Sophie continued, ignoring her cousin's agitation. "Justin's smart, not nerdy at all."

"He's a nerd."

"No, quite the opposite."

"He's a jock?"

"Not quite, just..."

"Forget it, Sophie, not interested."

"It's been four years, Ellie." Sophie gazed over at her cousin, obviously not intending to let this go. "You need to rejoin the living."

"It's not about time," Ellie said slowly, "I don't need the work of a relationship right now." She reopened her notebook and tried to focus on her charts to avoid Sophie's concerned gaze. She recognized the new grey streak in her dark hair when it fell across her face again and decided not to bother colouring it. *I mean really, who would notice.* She jerked it back, and added, "I'm happy on my own with Cali," as if that fact alone would end the conversation.

"Yeah," Sophie snorted. "I bet she keeps you warm at night with all that dog slobber! Don't you miss... you know?"

"Sex? Are you trying to say sex?" Ellie forced a laugh as she stood up and stretched her tired muscles. "Yes, I miss it, but I've got other things I need to do, like help you take care of Aunt Jenna, make sure you sleep sometimes so you can finish your exams, do my own work. I don't have time."

"I know you miss the romance, Ellie."

"Don't know what you mean." Ellie refused to agree—it would only serve to encourage Sophie. She *did* yearn for someone to curl up with at the end of the day, to talk with over morning coffee, to hike with through the woods. But there was no way she'd share that little tidbit. Ellie was just coming to terms with it herself, and for some reason was still fighting the whole idea.

"You read a gazillion romances," Sophie teased as she pulled an elastic band off her wrist and tied her red hair back in a ponytail. "I've seen the covers. The men are all tall, gorgeous and internally flawed, right? They're all waiting for the right woman to stumble into their lives." She drew her hand across her forehead like an old-time heroine.

"Like that exists," Ellie scoffed to show it didn't bother her that Sophie knew about her secret. Losing yourself in a romance novel sure beat the possible heartache of the real thing.

"But you won't consider *any* guy at all!"

Ellie cringed, remembering the one blind date she'd attempted. A total disaster that ended with her walking home in the dark and ruining her only good pair of shoes. The dating scene had changed so much in the past ten years and the thought of it made drops of sweat line her upper lip.

"Leave her be, Sophie," a quiet voice came from the bed.

"Didn't mean to wake you, Mom." Sophie grimaced and reached out for her mother's hand. "You okay?"

"I'll be fine." Jenna took a slow breath and looked from her daughter to her niece. "She's right, Ellie, you need to look after yourself more. We'll be fine."

The knot in Ellie's stomach grew. She put her notebook back in her satchel, promising herself she'd work on her nerves. She couldn't have people thinking she was falling apart, which she wasn't—but *could*, but *wouldn't*—as long as she worked on it.

"Then I'll take this moment to go buy my Flip-Pal scanner." She gave her Aunt's hand a squeeze. "I won't be long."

Sophie walked over to her cousin, bent down, gave her a big hug and whispered in Ellie's ear. "Fine. Subject closed for now, but you don't have to come back, El. Go home and rest. Do something for yourself for a change. Mom will fall back to sleep soon. She doesn't even realize we're here most of the time."

"I know." Ellie hugged her cousin tight. "It would suck for her to wake up alone though."

"You are taking a few days to yourself, right?" Sophie held her by the arm and gave her a little shake. "You promised. I've got this covered."

"I can hear you, you know," Jenna said, sending Ellie a tired smile. "Ellie, I *can* be by myself. I'm not dying, for pity's sake!"

Ellie yearned for a few days to herself, sleeping in, wearing comfy clothes, playing with Cali, but Aunt Jenna had been her rock when her parents had died, and Ellie was danged if she wouldn't be the same in return.

"I need you in tip top shape to look after me," Sophie said, knowing how to get Ellie to agree with her. And she never failed to use it when needed.

Ellie gave in. "Just a few days. Can I get you anything before I go?"

"A fancy iced coffee would be nice." Sophie sat back down and took out a text book to study.

"I'm going back to sleep," Jenna grumbled. "I don't want to see you when I wake up."

***

Ellie left the room and Sophie opened her book, closing it seconds later, unable to concentrate. She glanced at her mother, glad to see her breathing already evened out in sleep. According to the doctor, Jenna would be fine, in time.

It was Ellie who Sophie was worried about now.

She drummed her fingers against the arm of the chair as she tried to think of what would put the spark back in her cousin's eyes. Quite simply, Ellie needed someone.

Chapter Two

Ellie pushed through the hospital doors, sucked in a lungful of fresh air, and rolled her shoulders back and forth to release the tension. The warm breeze brushed her face, and her eyes closed in delight. Spring into summer was her favourite time of year. Flowers and plants had started to bloom along the paths, the snow had finally melted, and anything was possible. She dearly loved her cousin and aunt but sometimes their concern was overwhelming.

She knew Sophie would hound her about getting a man in her life, but she could handle that when it came.

She opened her eyes, and strolled down the street, looking into shop windows at things she had no interest in buying. What she wanted was to hop in her car and head north to her farm, but she would buy the Flip-Pal for her senior's genealogy group and grab that fancy coffee for Sophie first.

She desperately needed some quiet time, yet her days had been jam-packed with people for weeks. And right now, being alone on a crowded street, without having to speak to anyone, was an amazing feeling.

When Ellie's parents had died right after her eleventh birthday, Aunt Jenna had taken her in without hesitation. Aunty Jenna raised her right alongside Sophie, treated her liked a second daughter. Today's news that her aunt would be okay set her inner child dancing, and a grin spread across Ellie's face as she soaked in the heat of the sun. Yes, this was a good day.

Lunchtime crowds were thinning, and the world was calming down to a slower afternoon pace. People lingered in the nearby park, tossing footballs or having picnics near the pond. She heard the shrieks of laughter of excited children, then a flash of red caught her eye.

A small boy, no more than four years old, hair flopping over his eyes, jeans grass stained at the knees, darted between two parked cars and into the street following a rolling red ball. He didn't see the truck turn the nearby corner and head in his direction. He was focused on his ball.

Without thinking, Ellie dashed the last few feet as the truck made the curve. His horn blared as she scooped the boy up and felt the breeze on her neck—the truck missing them by inches.

Time froze.

Everyone within a radius of fifty feet turned to see a young woman holding a screaming boy. A large well-built man raced up and threw his arms around them both before dragging them closer to the sidewalk.

A couple had turned. The woman cried out as the man beside her dashed towards Ellie and the boy.

To Ellie, there was complete silence. To everybody else there was chaos.

The boy stopped yelling and his little arms were tight around her neck. He cried up at the man who still held them tight. Ellie looked up and saw the concern in his eyes for the child. When his gaze shifted to her face, her heart skipped.

"Shh, there," his deep voice crooned to them both. "It's okay. Shh." An old scar ran from his temple to his jaw, wolf-blue eyes bore into hers and he continued to sooth them. He was so tall her neck ached looking up at him.

In a flash, the fear and anger she'd bottled up since the death of her husband and daughter years before came spewing forth.

"Why weren't you watching him?" she demanded. "You don't get a second chance, you know!" Her vision wavered but she refused to let the welling tears fall. Their gazes locked, hers filled with anger and dismay, his confused and anguished.

A camera went off in her face.

The press had found her, again. She turned away and fought to get her panic under control. This was not happening. Not now, not here.

The scarred man pivoted them away from the press, putting himself between them and the surging crowd that was forming.

The other man ran up to them. As he gently took the boy from Ellie, she was surprised to recognize him as Owen Walsh, movie star, philanthropist, all-around nice guy. Or so the papers said. Then his actress wife, Lauren McKee, arrived, breathless, her face white with fear.

The photographers were everywhere.

"Quinn!" A blonde woman plunged forward, her phone aimed at their faces. "What happened?"

The man—*Quinn,* apparently—put out his hand, stopping the reporter in her tracks. "Not now, Diane!"

"But Owen Walsh's son being saved from certain death is a huge story!" Diane scurried around him, raised her phone and took a few quick shots.

"I said no!" Quinn grabbed her arm, lowering the phone.

"You're not off limits, Quinn." She glared at him defiantly. "Not *you* and *not* your family—*or* the woman who just saved your nephew." Before Quinn could step between them again, Diane's eyes shifted, taking a good long look at Ellie. Ellie felt like a deer in the headlights, sure that Diane had sized her up and knew her whole story.

Over his shoulder, Quinn yelled at Owen and Lauren, "In the car!"

Ellie stood frozen, tiny droplets of sweat sliding down her back. She wanted to run but the crowd had closed in around her.

"You too." Quinn nudged her towards a limo that seemed to appear out of nowhere, its door yawning open. She could see Lauren was already inside, hugging her son, her eyes large. Owen took Ellie's arm, murmuring, "We won't leave you out here for these vultures," and hustled her toward the limo.

"Hey! I know you!" Diane called after her and pressed forward, shoving her phone in Ellie's face, snapping more pictures before Quinn could stop her.

"Diane," Quinn warned through gritted teeth. "Don't do this."

Spurred by Quinn's changed demeanor—he was obviously on her side in this mess—Ellie forced herself to move and dove into the limo, sliding as far away from the door as she could get. Her hands shook until she clamped them under her arms.

"This is my job, Quinn." Diane lifted her chin as if daring him to question her.

"This is my family, and you know what that means," Quinn countered before climbing into the limo and slamming the door shut behind him.

The limo was surrounded, and the press scrambled to get photos through the tinted windows as the car moved slowly through the crowd and off down the road.

***

Diane Cooper watched the limo leave and turned to her assistant, Annabelle, who had just arrived with a sophisticated camera in her hands. "This is your chance, Annabelle. I need something big for this."

The young woman took one look at the limo and nodded. "I promised you hiring me would be worth it, Diane, I'll get you what you need."

She grabbed hold of her camera tightly and dashed across the road and between two buildings then was lost to Diane's view.

Diane sauntered away from the remaining horde. She was tired of the entertainment scene, the running after celebrities who were ordinary people with problems of their own. It was exhausting and she wanted something better, something bigger. But for now, this was what she had.

If Annabelle was as talented as she professed, Diane would have her killer story by the six o'clock news.

Chapter Three

Owen and Lauren sat in the seat across from Ellie and Quinn. They all sat in stunned silence, the only sound was the quiet sobs of the boy. Owen cradled his son in his arms; while Lauren wouldn't let go of her son's little hand. As the press threw themselves at the car windows like a pack of wolves, desperate to catch a photo of the group inside, the limo slowly left the reporters behind.

Ellie's nerves were buzzing, a shiver crept up her spine; her skin broke out in gooseflesh as her sweat cooled in the limo's air conditioning. Her life would never be the same again. The press would have a field day if they found out who she was. She could *not* fall back into that pool of agony.

"We can't thank you enough, Miss...?" Owen held out his hand to her, his other arm firmly pressing his son to his chest like he'd never let him go.

"Ellie," she murmured, briefly shaking his hand and withdrawing. "Not a problem. Right place, right time."

"Not many people would have done that," Lauren said, tears trickling down her cheeks. Quinn handed her a Kleenex and she smiled at him.

"I'm so sorry, Lauren," Quinn said quietly. "That was totally my fault."

Ellie blurted, "All it takes is a second." Adrenaline still coursed through her body and she still wanted to yell at him and smack him at the same time.

"I know. 'You don't get a second chance'," he recited, repeating her words and staring at the little boy with hollowed out eyes.

"I lost people close to me," she insisted. "This is not a joke."

"I'm not laughing."

"You'll never recover from that loss." Why was she still talking? She dropped her eyes to her lap, willing herself not to cry in front of these strangers. All the emotions she had been hiding from the past years were close to exploding. Yes, they needed to come out, but please, not here.

Quinn nodded, seeming unable to disagree with her. She noticed Owen and Lauren watching Quinn intently, their expressions amazed. She turned to study the man beside her. He was distraught, his jaw moved side to side as if grinding his teeth. She watched him struggle to relax, to stretch out his legs. He threw an arm across the back of the seat behind her. If she was reading him right, nothing seemed to be helping.

Except for the sound of the boy's easing sobs, the silence in the limo grew.

She looked between Quinn and Owen, and back again.

"Brothers," Lauren laughed shakily through her tears at Ellie's expression. "Quinn is the older, Owen the baby."

"I'm the baby," piped up the boy as he scrubbed the tears from his cheeks.

"You're not a baby anymore, Gavyn," Owen corrected. "You're a big boy. And big boys know they shouldn't run away from us, especially not into a street. We can get a new ball; we can't get a new you."

Ellie glanced furtively at Quinn. He sat silent and watchful, a statue, as if he was waiting for her to explode again. The adrenaline seeped from her bones and with the adrenaline went her anger, leaving her body abruptly limp and heavy. She slumped back in the seat. When her head brushed Quinn's warm arm, she jerked away, reaching down quickly to adjust her sandals to disguise her reaction.

Even under *these* conditions, she noticed him—and she didn't like it. Her wonderfully contained and regulated world was slowly unravelling.

While Owen was movie star handsome, Quinn was craggy and jagged around the edges, with fierce blue eyes, black hair that brushed his collar and a touch of grey at the temples. And then there was that wicked scar that sliced down to his jaw, brushing his upper lip. It must have hurt something terrible at the time.

He returned her gaze. No smile, just a lift of an eyebrow in question, daring her to tell him off again. It seemed that Quinn Walsh had recovered.

Her heart skipped a beat and then started to race. A blush crept up her face as he stared her down. "I'm... I'm sorry I came down so hard...," she began. She hated being flustered. "I didn't mean to..." Why was she apologizing to him?

"You were right." He refused to look away.

She licked her suddenly dry lips and focused on her breathing. It had been four years since her husband died and no matter how often her friend Maggie had reminded her life goes on, she'd never noticed another man like she noticed this one. Not good. Sophie would be doing backflips if she knew.

She could still feel the warmth of his arms from when he had wrapped them around her and the boy. She hadn't felt that safe for a long time. A total stranger had made her feel something she had not been able to do for herself in years.

Life does go on and it had just smacked her upside the head. She stared at him in bewilderment, confused by the situation. Too late she saw him acknowledge her feelings with a tilt of his head. Good Lord, was she that transparent?

His lips moved again but she couldn't hear a word. Her head was fuzzy. Was she in shock?

"Are you okay?" His abruptness startled her. Why was he angry with her? And why did he have a Scottish accent?

The buzzing in her ears grew louder as she realized Lauren and Owen were also speaking to her.

"Are you okay?" Owen seemed to be asking her.

"I think she's in shock," Quinn said. "We'll take her to the hospital to get checked out."

Okay—she heard that comment just fine. "No!" she squeaked. "That won't be necessary. I'm great, really."

"But you..." started Lauren.

"Not a scratch, Mrs. Walsh," Ellie assured her quickly. She had to get back in control of this—escape the press following them; escape Quinn Walsh. Two dangers, one solution.

"I don't know how to thank you, Ellie," Owen said.

She squirmed in her seat, not liking this scrutiny one little bit. "Why does your brother have an accent and you don't?" She blurted out before slapping her hand over her mouth. Where was her filter when she needed it?

"*I* grew up in the States," Owen smiled at her puzzlement. "*Quinn* stayed in Scotland and became a police officer. But my accent changes with my job." He proved it by allowing his Scottish accent to flow. It was a revelation.

"And when Quinn left his job as a police officer and came to live here, he became our bodyguard when we're in Montreal," Lauren explained. "And Gavyn gets to spend time with his uncle."

There was an uncomfortable silence as they all realized how close Quinn had come to losing Gavyn.

"Maybe for insurance purposes," Quinn's deep voice said.

"What?" Ellie looked at him, not following the change in conversation.

"We should get you looked at, just in case, for insurance."

"I'm not going to sue you or anything." Ellie sat up straight, offended. "Anyone would have done it—it was a gut reaction."

"No," Quinn said quietly. "Not *everyone* would have done that. Trust me."

"Anyways, I don't have time for this. I don't want the hassle or the publicity, thanks just the same."

"But we have to thank you in some way," Lauren said.

"If you drop me off at the next corner, I can pick up my car and head home." Ellie pasted a cheerful smile on her face. "That would work for me." No need for them to know she was actually headed back to the hospital.

Lauren glanced at her husband and frowned. "Can we pay her something...?"

"I don't need money, thanks." Ellie caught sight of the cars following them. "Are—are they following us?"

Quinn looked back and shrugged his shoulders. "The Paps are always following us. This is going to be big news. They want your picture for the rags."

"Aw, for fu..." she broke off as she saw Gavyn's eyes glued to her. "Sorry. Look, I don't need fifteen minutes of fame. I just want to head back home, that's all. I'm glad your son is okay, but I've got a dog that needs walking and time's a 'wasting."

Quinn's eyes opened slightly in surprise at Ellie's obvious discomfort. "What are you hiding from?"

"Them." Ellie replied resolutely, pointing at the press cars. "Long story, not important, but I don't want to be involved in this."

"I know how you feel." Lauren sighed and reached over for her husband's hand and squeezed it. "For us, however, it's our job. Are you sure you're okay?"

"Yes." Ellie gave her a second cheerful smile she hoped fooled them all. "Life goes on and time heals most wounds. I don't mean to be rude or flippant, but I *do* have to go. And this is a little too unreal for me."

"Where can we drop you?" Owen tapped the window for his driver's attention.

"Anywhere near the Museum on Sherbrooke Street would be fine."

"Anywhere we drop you, you're going to get mobbed by the press." With a frown, Quinn studied the cars still following them. "We'll drop Lauren and Owen back at their hotel first and let the mob hook onto them. Then I'll get you back to your car."

"Good idea," Owen spoke over his shoulder to the driver and before she knew it, Ellie was staring up at the Ritz Carlton Hotel.

"Stay here." Quinn put his hand on her knee to get her attention. His hand was warm, and he squeezed her knee just enough to reassure her.

"Thank you again, Ellie," Lauren said as she gathered her son in her arms, put her sunglasses firmly on her nose and stepped out to the flash of cameras.

"We'll talk again," Owen said as he moved past Ellie after his wife. "Quinn, get her info. This is not over." He smiled at Ellie as he joined his wife and son.

"Circle a few times and lose as many as you can, then take her to the back door," Quinn told the driver. "Wait there, Ellie. I'll bring my own car around so the press doesn't tag along. Just wait, okay?"

"No problem." Ellie sank back into her seat. She turned her head away when a pushy young woman photographer tried to sneak past Quinn for a quick shot of her. "No problem at all," she muttered to herself as Quinn slammed the door behind him.

Ellie watched as Quinn expertly manoeuvred the Walsh family into the hotel and out of sight. The limo pulled away from the curb and drove off.

The driver drove around for five minutes then turned into a back road behind the hotel, pulling up to the back door. Ellie jumped out and the limo continued down the road and around the corner, out of sight. She ran to the back entrance and stepped inside.

Within seconds another car drove by and slowed down. Press. She squeezed into the shadows near the security guard and watched until the car gave up and moved on.

She waited. Her watch said five minutes had passed and she was not a patient lady. Her toe started tapping and she was getting ready to leave when she looked at the security guard.

He raised a questioning eyebrow.

"I was asked to wait here for someone," she defended.

"Right." He smirked.

Right, she said to herself. Annoyed she'd allowed herself to depend on a man—a man she barely knew—she shoved open the door and stepped off the curb to walk to the hospital. A midnight black Porsche sports car pulled out of the garage and stopped beside her.

Quinn slid out, walked to her side and opened the passenger door for her. Her slight hesitation caused her to stumble forward and he caught her in his arms before she hit the ground. She hesitated, saw the seriousness in his face, then slipped inside. He slammed the door shut, saluted the security guard and climbed back in.

Within seconds they were on their way.

***

Annabelle stepped from behind her hiding place along the back wall of the building and checked the photos on her camera. A smile curled her lips as she stopped flicking through them and focused on the money shot.

Ellie in Quinn's arms, looking like a couple about to embrace in a passionate kiss.

A couple that looked like Ellie and ... Owen Walsh from this angle.

A married Owen Walsh embracing a woman who was not his wife.

Chapter Four

"You don't have to do this, you know." Ellie shifted in her seat. The air conditioning was on low and a cool breeze fanned her warm face, but the nerves in her stomach were making her queasy.

The seats were bucket but close together, the middle console the only obstacle preventing their thighs from touching.

"It's not far to the hospital and I can walk it." She groaned as she realized what she'd said.

"I thought I was taking you to your car?" Quinn glanced at her. "Are you hurt?"

"No, but I have to see someone." She shrugged as if it didn't matter.

"Owen will kill me if I don't look after you," Quinn told her.

"Well, I wouldn't want to be responsible for your untimely death." She forced an amused smile. She could tell he wasn't buying her act but she didn't have the energy to care.

They drove in silence until Quinn blurted out, "So, who are you going to see?"

She hesitated then answered quietly. "My Aunt. She had a minor heart attack."

"Shit."

"Yeah, shit." Ellie tried her calming breaths but him being a hand width away made her lose focus, which ticked her off even more. She needed to get out of this car, sooner than later.

"You're close to your Aunt?" He took another quick look at her.

"Very." Ellie stared out the window. "She raised me when my folks died."

"Double shit."

"Indeed." She liked the sincerity in his voice. "She's like a second mother to me, and my cousin Sophie is like the sister I never had. I'm a cup-half-full kind of person."

"I can see that."

Quinn's phone rang. He pulled it from the holder on his dashboard. "Quinn," he said.

Ellie looked at him and started fidgeting.

He continued his conversation.

She took loud, deep breaths, her hands clenching the armrest.

"Hang on a second," he said to the person on the other end. "What's wrong?" he asked Ellie.

"You know," she started quietly, "talking while driving is really bad. In fact, it's deadly and against the law now."

"I know, but I'll be quick."

"I'm sure that's what everyone says before they die."

"I'll call you back," he said to the person on the phone and ended the call.

"Thank you," she whispered.

"You're welcome."

"Ah, here we are." Ellie sat up straight, grabbed her purse, ready to bolt the minute he stopped.

"Let me park and..."

"Not necessary." She could feel a feverish sweat starting at the crown of her head. "Just drop me at the front door."

"No, I'd rather make sure you're okay."

"I'm fine."

"You don't *look* fine." He spotted someone leaving a slot and pulled in after they'd gone.

Ellie started to unlock her seatbelt, but Quinn covered her hand with his. She froze.

"I don't know if you're upset from what happened with Gavyn, or about your Aunt, but I need to see you up to her room," he spoke softly.

Ellie felt a sudden sense of calm wash over her. He *was* sincere and his calm was something she hadn't felt in a long time. She liked it. She wanted it. And it scared the hell out of her to allow another person even an iota of control over her.

"Okay," she said slowly, deciding to see what happened. "Thanks."

He held her hand a moment longer, gave it a squeeze and then let go.

Ellie popped off the seatbelt and stepped out of the cocoon of the car. She headed to the hospital front door but could feel Quinn behind her.

Quiet. Solid. A stranger.

***

It was supper time at the hospital and food services staff were pushing the food carts down the hall, stopping at each door to deliver the daily bread, or in some cases only cups of strawberry Jello.

Ellie walked past them to her aunt's room, Quinn at her side. She didn't know how she felt about him still tagging along. Good in a way, having his strength beside her, but also annoyed that a stranger was getting in her business. Especially a stranger who made her pulse race when pulse racing was not on her agenda for the foreseeable future. She hesitated when she reached her aunt's room and looked back at Quinn.

"I'll wait here," he said, casually leaning against the wall beside the door, looking like he could stay there for hours. "Take your time."

"You don't have to wait," she said softly. "I have no idea how long I'll be."

"I'm free for a while." He smiled at her and nodded his head towards the room, motioning her to go in.

Ellie looked across the hall at the nurse's station and saw them staring at Quinn and whispering amongst themselves. Right, he'll be fine. She pushed the door open with one last glance at Quinn. He smiled at her encouragingly.

***

The minute the door closed behind Ellie, one of the nurses sidled up to Quinn and smiled.

"Aren't you Owen Walsh?" she smiled broadly, not shy at all.

"No," he said, returning the smile. "People make that mistake all the time."

"But you're a dead ringer for him." She stepped a little closer, as if coming in for a better look.

Quinn pushed himself away from the wall which forced the nurse to step back quickly. He was tired of people assuming things.

"Janice Reynolds." She held out her hand.

"Quinn. Nice to meet you, Janice." He shook her hand but didn't give his last name

"Is that your family?" She nodded toward the room where he could plainly see Ellie, and another young woman talking with a nurse.

"No, just friends," he said. "Is she going to be okay?" He craned his neck to see Ellie's aunt lying quietly in the bed.

Janice hesitated, "Her heart's a bit weak but there's no reason she can't recover, with rest." She looked like she wanted to stay and chat, but a call from one of the other nurses had her moving back to the station.

Quinn reached out and put his hand on her arm. "Is there any way you can let me know her condition going forward?" He poured on the Walsh charm, not even sure why it should matter to him. Except when he looked through the door, all he saw was the worry on Ellie's face.

"It's against the rules."

Quinn took out a business card and handed it to her. "Give me a call if she takes a turn for the worse. I don't need details, but a heads up would be nice."

Janice looked at his card. "I'll see what I can do. If I'm on call that is."

Quinn gave her a smile that made her stand a little taller. "That would be great, Janice. Thanks." What was he doing? He never used his looks on women, ever. Golden rule and he made no exceptions. So why was he doing it now?

"No problem. Gotta go." Janice walked away, putting a lot of effort in her exit moves, which were wasted on Quinn. He paced the hall, stretching his legs and wondering what the heck he was getting himself into and why.

***

Ellie had turned from her aunt's nurse to see Quinn hand a nurse in the hall his card and notice the nurse's reaction.

He moves fast.

And why that should matter in the least bothered her. In fact, it ticked her off to know it *did* bother her.

Chapter Five

D r. Wong entered Aunt Jenna's room at double speed, his white coat swirling like a cape behind him. He was a small man, but efficient, kind, and someone they trusted.

"Sorry," he said, "It's been a crazy day." He checked Jenna's chart and ran his finger down the page.

Sophie looked at Ellie and down at her notes. They had a few minutes before the doctor was ready to fill them in.

Sophie had been trying to take her mind off her mother's condition for hours. School work was the ticket, though she wondered how much she would retain. She was studying to be a geneticist and having Ellie as a genealogist was an interesting crossover.

"So, my blood is B and Mom and Dad are both A's. Did you mark that in the charts, Ellie? Wait, that can't be." Sophie shuffled her papers, looking from one to another, a frown on her face.

Ellie took out a pen and started to jot it down on a scrap piece of paper, her mind wandering out to the hall and Quinn, still waiting for her.

"That's impossible," Dr. Wong said as he adjusted the tube leading to Aunt Jenna's nose. "Two A blood type parents cannot make a B blood type child."

Sophie looked down at her notes to double check. "But both Mom and Dad are A types and I'm a B." She looked up at the doctor with a question in her eye.

"Either you've got something wrong or you're adopted, dear," the doctor said. "Your mother will be all right though." He looked from Sophie to Ellie. "She needs to keep calm, so we're going to keep her here for a bit. But you two should go home and rest. I'll be checking on her all night."

He patted Sophie on the shoulder and left the room as quickly as he had entered.

Ellie and Sophie were quiet for a minute. They looked down at Jenna then at each other.

"There's got to be a mistake." Ellie rose from her chair and hunkered down beside her cousin's chair to examine the records. "Sophie, there's a mix-up here. Where did you get this information from?"

"Mom and Dad," Sophie began, gazing over at her mother. She caught her mother watching her through slitted eyes. The beeps from the heart monitor had picked up their pace. "This is Dad's blood type from his surgery before he died, and this paper shows Mom's blood type as it was taken yesterday. I'm studying this stuff, Ellie, I *know* this can't be right."

Sophie took the paper back from Ellie and stood up. "Mom?" she turned to her mother's still form on the hospital bed. "I know that my blood type is B because I donated last month. This is right. How can that be?"

Her mother stared at Sophie; her small hand gripped the sheets until her knuckles turned as white as her hair. The heart monitor beeps quickened again. "I've always loved you," Jenna struggled to say. A tear eased out of her eye and slid down the side of her face, disappearing into her hair before she turned away from her daughter.

"Mom, what's going on?" Sophie asked, alarmed. She turned her mother's face towards her. "What happened?" she whispered.

The heart monitor rang loudly.

"Sophie," Ellie grabbed her arm, "this is not keeping her calm!"

Seconds later doctors and nurses flew into the room and herded Ellie and Sophie into the hallway, closing the door tight behind them.

They stood outside the door, their bags clutched to their chests, scared.

"What happened?" Sophie's eyes were wide with fear and confusion. "Ellie, what's going on?"

"Just hold on, Sophie." Ellie took her cousin's cold hand in hers and watched through the window of the room. "Let's wait till they get her stable and then they'll tell us."

"Something about the blood types set her off."

"There must be a mistake." Ellie couldn't look Sophie in the eye so turned from the room to pace the hall. Blood types don't change. People can't have children with blood types that were genetically impossible.

Quinn approached them. "Is there something I can do?"

Ellie jumped in surprise; having forgotten he was still there. The last thing she wanted or needed was a stranger involved in their business. "No, we're good, thanks." She gave him a shaky smile. "You don't have to stay."

Quinn took a step back but didn't leave. He was good at being quiet, in the background, and that's obviously what he intended to do.

"There's no mistake and you know it," Sophie's voice rose. She grabbed Ellie's sleeve. "Does this mean she's not my mother? That Dad wasn't my father?"

"I don't know." Not only was Ellie confused, but she was getting worried.

Being a genealogist by trade she knew how families were connected. Not only by blood. Never only by blood. A family consisted of many parts, brothers, sisters, aunts, uncles, step-families, generations.

But this was different. Sophie had been raised as Aunt Jenna and Uncle William's child. Everyone knew that. There had never been a question about it. Until now.

"Am I adopted?" asked Sophie in a strangled voice, dropping into a chair in the hall. "This is unbelievable."

"Don't jump to conclusions." Ellie sat down beside her. "We don't know anything yet. You know how I feel about proof. Let's not assume anything."

Quinn stood across the hall from them and waited. Ellie threw him a glance that didn't linger. He had become part of the wall, like a statue.

The door to Jenna's room opened and Dr. Wong came over to them. They stood up slowly, expecting the worst, hoping for the best. Sophie reached for Ellie's hand and held on for dear life.

"We've got her stabilized, but she has to be kept very quiet. Her heart is still recovering," Dr. Wong said.

"What happened?" Ellie tightened her grip on Sophie's hand. Both their hands had gone cold.

"We're not sure. We'll run more tests, but you can go in and see her." He reached out to Sophie and squeezed her shoulder. "Don't worry, Sophie, we're doing the best we can. She should pull through this and you'll have her home before you know it."

The women watched Dr. Wong walk away. Neither said a word. Neither wanted to move.

"That was all my fault," Sophie said softly. "I guess having a secret like that revealed would send anyone into shock. And with her heart..."

"Sophie." Ellie's voice was firm, "Until we know something concrete, it's not a possibility. We'll look into it and then decide what to do. Let's go see her." Ellie turned to Quinn, gave him a brave smile, and led Sophie into the room.

***

The curtain had been drawn against the afternoon sun in Jenna's room. The nurses had almost finished their work, and talked quietly amongst themselves, filling out charts and adjusting the I.V. drip.

Sophie sat back down beside the bed and took the older woman's hand and clasped it between her own. She lowered her head and rested it on the bed beside her mother.

Seeing her cousin like this was alarming. Sophie was such an optimist. Now she looked beaten. "Sophie," Ellie murmured, touching her shoulder gently. "Go get something to eat. I'll stay."

Sophie surprised her by standing up abruptly and giving her a quick hug. "It's like the doctor said, she'll be fine. You go home and walk Cali, she must be bursting. I'll grab something to eat later and I promise not to spend the night here."

Ellie searched her cousin's face and saw a cascade of emotions. "I'll be back tomorrow."

"No" Sophie replied firmly. "You're off for a few days. I'll do my homework here and keep you posted."

"If you're sure." Ellie reached hesitantly for her bag. When Sophie made no protest, she turned to go.

"Who's the hunk in the hall?" Sophie called out in a strangled voice as Ellie reached the door.

Ellie wasn't fooled. Still, she turned a smile back to her cousin. Sophie needed a distraction and maybe this would help. "I'll tell you all about it when you come up to my place. Bring your records and we'll figure this out."

"I'll be by tomorrow," Sophie assured her.

Ellie took a last, confused look at her aunt then left the room. The doctor said Aunt Jenna would be okay. But would Sophie?

Chapter Six

Quinn waited for her in the hall. "How is she?"

"She'll be okay, as long as she's kept calm." Ellie looked around and saw the nurse staring at them.

"What now?"

She blinked up at him with confusion. "Pardon?"

"What do you want to do now?" he asked.

"Oh, I'm going home." She headed down the hall. He fell into step beside her.

"I'll take you to your car." He didn't seem to want to let her go quite yet.

Ellie stopped dead and he swerved to avoid bumping into her. "Not necessary, thanks. My car is just outside. Thanks again for all the help." She held out her hand for a handshake. Dismissive. Final.

"I should be thanking you. You saved my nephew's life." Quinn took her small hand in his. She knew her hand was cold and trembled slightly. Maybe, if the gods were good to her, he wouldn't notice. "You sure you're okay?" He kept her hand in his.

"Yes," she said a little breathlessly. He wasn't the only one making no move to disconnect. His large warm hand wrapped around hers felt like a hug. Like safety. As if clearing a fog, she slid her hand from his, took a deep breath and a step back. "Again, thanks. Gotta go." She all but ran from him in the hallway, bypassed the elevator and took the stairs at a run, not stopping until she plowed through the front doors into the fresh air and evening sun.

Quinn turned back to Ellie's aunt's room. He stopped outside the door then quietly pushed it open and stepped inside.

Sophie looked up at him, seemingly surprised at his size and height. He was used to this. "Hi," he said quietly.

"You're a big one—bet you hear that a lot. Hi."

He nodded. "Ellie just left and I wanted to know if there was anything you needed."

"Who are you?" Sophie eased the sharpness of her question with a smile.

"Quinn." He held out his hand. "Quinn Walsh. Your sister...."

"Cousin."

"...*cousin* saved my nephew's life this morning and I wanted to make sure she was okay."

"Dang!" Sophie let out a breath. "This has been some day!"

Quinn waited. His police training taught him that most people hated silences and felt a need to fill them. He was right. Sophie started talking.

"Come with me." With a determined expression, Sophie stood up, headed out of the room and found a couple of chairs down the hall.

Quinn sat beside her, not saying a word. Waiting.

"I'm sure Ellie will be fine." Sophie turned to him in her seat. "She's been through a lot in the past few years and this is not something she needs right now."

"This?"

"Just a little family mystery," she said, "but I'm assuming there was some press involved with saving your nephew?"

"How did you know?"

"Ellie has that haunted look again." Sophie took a deep breath. "Look, I'm not sharing her story with a complete stranger. You'll have to ask her yourself and good luck with that! But she hates the press. Avoids it like the plague."

"She took off pretty quickly a few minutes ago," Quinn said, remembering the frantic look in Ellie's eyes. "I just want to make sure she's okay."

"Is that the only reason?" Sophie smiled at him.

Quinn shrugged his shoulders. "What other reason could there be?"

"Jeesh!" Sophie blurted out. "Some people are so dense." She stood up and Quinn stood up with her. "I've got to go back to Mom." Quinn opened his mouth to speak but she put up her hand. "Ellie will be back in a day or so." Sophie left Quinn in the hallway and returned to her mother's room.

Out of options, Quinn turned to go. Why was it so important to see Ellie again? It was like an uneasy itch that needed scratching.

Chapter Seven

Ellie drove home with her mind in a blur. The day had exhausted her, had thrown her from her quiet safe life into multiple chaotic situations. Saving Quinn's nephew, Gavyn, had finally reached the frozen core she'd worked daily for years to protect. She hadn't saved her own child, but she *had* saved someone else's.

Her eyes teared up and she lifted her foot off the gas pedal as she realized she was driving too fast. When she got lost in the past, her present went out of focus and that could be deadly.

She needed to stop and see her best friend, Maggie. Maggie always had a way of calming Ellie down. The Cozy Corner Café would be quiet this time of day. A perfect place to relax for a few minutes before heading home.

Ellie took her exit off the highway and struggled to organize her thoughts. Her hands compulsively gripped the steering wheel but she felt the phantom heat from Quinn's hand enveloping hers.

She caught the smile that crept up her lips and tossed it away. She did not need distractions like Quinn Walsh in her life.

Not now.

Not when things were finally getting into a rhythm she could live with.

***

Ten minutes later she pulled into the parking lot of the Cozy Corner Café.

The Café was a tearoom, pastry shop, essentials grocer, library, and quaint meeting place where locals and tourists alike stopped to rest. It was also the main hub for all the "tiny house" seniors' homes that were spread out behind it.

Ellie's best friend, Marguerite—or Maggie—Williams, owned *The Cozy*, as it was known to its fans, and lived in the rooms above it. She'd arrived in Ellie's Sociology class in university, caused a ruckus while debating a point with the professor, and they had been the best of friends ever since.

Maggie was serving an elderly couple of ladies as Ellie walked in. Ellie waved at Shirley and Ruth Cotter, two of her senior genealogy group members.

The aroma of fresh coffee and just out of the oven baked goods hit Ellie's nose. She closed her eyes and breathed deeply. Comfort food—cookies if her nose was reading the delightful aroma correctly.

"I know that look." Maggie laughed as Ellie walked over to the nearest table. Maggie bent to give her a big hug. Most people had to bend down to Ellie. It used to bother her, but she'd gotten used to it.

She sank down on the chair with relief.

"Rough day?" Maggie asked as she went behind the pastry-laden counter to pour Ellie a cup of tea.

Ellie groaned and hung her purse on the back of her seat. "You have no idea!" she said quietly. The Café was where she let her guard down. This was a home away from home, a safe haven. She slumped slightly in her seat and sighed.

Maggie debated between a chocolate éclair, a mini-brioche, or a macaroon, but finally pulled Ellie's favourite, a huge chocolate chip laden cookie from the basket and placed it on a plate. With goodies in hand, she put them in front of Ellie, pulled her long skirt around her legs and sat down across from her. Maggie had curly reddish-auburn hair that she held back with an antique bone clasp that had belonged to a grandmother from France whom she'd never met. She treasured it. While Ellie was slim and tiny, Maggie was taller and full-figured, and they often laughed at how such outwardly opposites could be so similar inside.

"Not too busy right now?" Ellie asked.

"No." Maggie looked affectionately at the two elderly women sitting at a table on the other side of the room. "Shirley and Ruth are planning their next book for their club, though I think Shirley can't wait to get to her next landscaping client. And most everyone else is heading home for supper."

"A cookie is not supper," Ellie chided even as she bit into the heavenly dark chocolate delight. Her shoulders sagged a little more but this time with relief. "I'm so glad your mother passed down her pastry skills to you. These are wicked good."

"Thank you." Maggie crossed herself in remembrance of her late mother. "I call those Ellie cookies."

"The hell you do!" Ellie laughed. "You call them the money cookies. Everyone loves these."

"True, but I did tweak the recipe for you."

"You're a good tweaker," Ellie joked.

"I've been called many things, that not being one of them."

"Add it to the list, dear." Ellie took a sip of her tea and sighed. "That's so much better."

"You know I can only be patient so long, Ellie," Maggie muttered, sitting back in her seat and eyeing her friend. "What the heck happened to you today? You look like your life exploded."

Ellie sat for a minute, staring at the tabletop trying to figure out where to even begin. She drew an invisible map across the placemat with the tip of a finger. "I think my life *did* just explode," she finally said, looking up at Maggie.

"You met a guy!" Maggie declared.

"Yes, I did, but that's not the half of it," Ellie said.

Maggie leaned forward in her chair, surprised she'd guessed correctly. "And? Details, details!"

"It's not really about him. I saved his nephew from being hit by a truck."

"Oh, wow!"

"Exactly."

"Press?

"Lots."

"Why?" Maggie took Ellie's hand and held it tightly, slightly worried by how cold it felt.

"Because the nephew is the son of Owen Walsh and Lauren McKee. And the guy? He's Owen's brother."

"Oh, sweet mother!" Maggie sat up as if struck.

"You see the problem?" Ellie asked wearily.

"Were any pictures taken?"

"Yes, the press was right in our faces and I think one of them recognized me."

"Crapola."

"You have a way with words, Maggie!"

"I take it there's more?"

"Hell, yeah. The more is Owen Walsh has a brother who's almost an identical twin. His name is Quinn and he acts as their bodyguard when they're in town."

"Oh, ho! Now we're getting somewhere. Tell me everything, from the start."

"I was coming out of..."

"Wait!" Maggie stopped her. "Let me get some coffee, I think I'm going to need this!"

As Maggie came back to the table, the elderly ladies got up and put their empty cups on the counter.

"We'll be going now," said Shirley. "We're done for the day. See you tomorrow."

"Thanks, Shirley." Maggie smiled at the two ladies. "Have a nice evening."

"Goodnight, Ellie," said Ruth quietly. She slowed down as if wanting to say more, but when her sister bumped her from behind, she simply added, "Take care of yourself."

"I will, Ruth." Ellie smiled back at her favorite of the sisters. "See you tomorrow for our class?"

Ruth nodded and her sister answered abruptly, "Yes, yes, of course!"

Ellie wondered what new drama Shirley was concocting. Ruth shook her head and shrugged her shoulders at Ellie, hiding a tiny smile as she headed for the door.

As the door closed behind the sisters, Maggie braced herself against the table and said, "Okay, hit me!"

Ellie laughed at Maggie's attempt to humour her. "So, I was at the hospital..."

"I thought you were taking some time off for yourself!"

"Starts now," Ellie said quickly, not wanting to get into that topic again.

Maggie smiled at her. "I'll believe it when I see it."

"Do you want me to continue?" Ellie asked in a mock huff.

"Ellie!" called Daphne, Maggie's assistant from behind the counter. "You're famous!"

Maggie looked over her shoulder to the TV Daphne was pointing to. "Oh, no," she said quietly.

Ellie turned and looked at herself on the newscast and felt her stomach drop.

There she was holding Gavyn, Quinn holding them both tightly, a grim look on his face.

"Turn it up," Maggie called to Daphne who ran to do so.

"We're not sure of the identity of the heroine of the day," came the voice over of the reporter as the video unfolded, *"but we'll have that for you by the late news."*

Ellie watched the video as it showed Quinn pulling her and Gavyn back from the road, the Walshes racing in, and Quinn rounding them all up for the quick evac into the limo. Ellie saw her white face and look of terror.

"Oh, Ellie," Maggie whispered. "Not again.

"They'll know who I am soon," Ellie said, trying to look calm. "Diane Cooper was there."

"Oh, for pity's sake!"

"She couldn't put a name to my face then, but..."

"Okay, forget about Diane "the Shark" for a minute, who's the guy?" Maggie pointed to a paparazzi picture of Quinn standing behind the Walshes on a red carpet.

"That..." Ellie took a deep breath and let it out slowly. "That's Quinn Walsh, brother and bodyguard."

"He can guard my body any time!"

Ellie turned from the TV and the piercing eyes of the man who made her heart race.

"There's more, I can see it in your face." Maggie nudged her arm on the table. "Spill it."

"Yes, well," Ellie began, fidgeting in her seat.

Maggie frowned. "I've never seen you fidget before, Ellie. How bad was it?" When Ellie failed to answer right away, Maggie tried another tactic. "What happened when you got in the limo?"

"We took the Walshes back to their hotel and Quinn drove me back to the hospital."

Maggie waited. And waited. And smiled.

"Stop it," Ellie protested, trying in vain not to return the smile. "It's not funny. You know the press is going to drag everything back up and I don't have the strength for that."

"You're one of the strongest women I know, El," Maggie said. Again, she waited.

"What?" Ellie asked in exasperation.

"It's not the press who will bother you," Maggie pointed back to the TV. "It's him. Hunk of the month."

"That's such an uncool thing to say, Mags." Ellie tried to look put out but felt a grin creeping up her face.

Maggie cocked her head and said, "You do know your face gives you away every time, right? You're blushing, you're smiling. Something happened in that limo." Fortunately for Maggie, she knew when to stop pushing. "Okay then, so what happened at the hospital?" she asked innocently, taking her ever present cloth and wiping the table in front of them. Ellie knew Maggie was trying to take some pressure off her and was grateful for the effort.

"Well." Ellie scrambled to get back on track. "He came up—"

"This guy was at the hospital too?" Maggie stopped wiping; her expression astonished.

Ellie sent her a warning look. "—to the room and..." she slowed and scowled, already back at the hospital in her head. "You know what? He flirted with a nurse, right there in front of me!"

"And this bothers you because?"

Ellie looked at her and let her jaw drop in surprise. "I have no clue!"

Maggie smiled knowingly at her.

Chapter Eight

Ellie drove in through the gates of her property and parked. She went back and locked the gates tight for the night. Her knuckles were white and her grip on the bars of the gate bit into her fingers, but she stood there and looked up the highway. That's where they'd come from. The vultures. The press.

But they wouldn't get in tonight.

She got in the car and drove up to the house. The sound of her door slamming brought Cali running. She was a four-year-old, golden-brown retriever who always made her smile. She danced around Ellie's legs as if she were still a puppy and Ellie braced herself so she wouldn't be knocked off her feet.

She spent the next few minutes sitting on the front porch, rubbing Cali, getting her face licked, soaking in the healing properties that came from a human/animal bond.

"Okay, come on." She stood up. "Playtime."

Cali bounded ahead of her, racing back and forth across the path that led to the barn and the forest beyond. With a sudden sliding stop, as if she were on an icy pond, she turned and raced back to the house to get her toy.

Ellie took it from her and wound up as if getting ready to pitch a baseball, then let the toy fly. Cali took off and caught it before it hit the ground.

This workout continued all over the property until they'd walked every path, past the treehouse, the swimming pond, through the woods proper and back to the house.

Now Ellie felt calmer. Now she could breathe easier.

The low sun spiked through the treetops, casting shadows on the trail and off into the forest beyond. The air was quiet, warm enough to be comfortable, and the forest smells surrounded her with their heat-infused aroma.

She unlocked the front door, dropped her bags inside and fed Cali. Her own meal was a bowl of leftover pasta she reheated in the microwave and ate standing at the sink.

Dishes washed and racked, she turned on the TV and sat at the kitchen table to work.

She loved her job as a genealogist, the combination of finding people and being a detective never got old. She also wrote a monthly genealogy column for a local newspaper and had published a couple of "how-to" books for beginners, focusing on writing their own personal stories.

The case she was working at the moment was interesting. She was helping Tess, one of the seniors in her group, find out what her grandfather's occupation had been. Tess knew he'd had many different jobs over the years, but she wanted to know if the rumours that he had owned a theatre in the town where her father had been born were true.

Ellie spread the papers out before her. She made notes of everything Tess had told her about her grandfather, where he had lived, and even second-hand stories she'd heard about him.

There were census returns to look through, telephone directories, if available, and the town's own history. Plenty of sources to start her search with.

As she got up to make herself a cup of tea, the TV caught her attention and she halted mid-stride. She was on the news again.

This time a close-up of her in Quinn's arms, holding Gavyn. Her eyes were wide with surprise and fear.

And then they said her name.

Chapter Nine

A furry nose, hot doggy breath and a wet tongue woke Ellie up the next morning. The sun was streaming in her window.

"Uh, no." She rolled away from Cali and the light, and buried her head under her pillow. She opened one eye, squinted at the clock on the bedside table and groaned again. "You're like a horrible alarm clock that never gives up."

The dog bounded on to the bed and stepped over her.

Ellie sat up with a start and gave Cali the evil eye.

Cali jumped off in one leap and sat beside the bed, head hung down in shame. She knew better. The bed was off limits—unless Ellie forgot to get up at the normal breakfast time and feed her.

"All right, all right." Ellie swung her feet over the side and stood up. Cali danced around her as she stretched and yawned.

Her "day off" was starting nicely. If only she didn't feel guilty for not being at the hospital with Aunt Jenna, it would be perfect. She'd spent the evening outside with Cali, focused on nothing more than getting through the hours until bed. And then sleep had only come around midnight.

Cali dashed out of the room and when Ellie didn't immediately follow her, she ran back and stared at her, held tilted to one side.

"Do you mind?" Ellie headed to the bathroom. "A girl's got to do what a girl's got to do." She turned back to Cali and pointed her out of the room. The dog took off and Ellie could hear her claws clicking against the wooden stairs leading down to the main floor.

When she finally walked into the kitchen, Cali was sitting by her bowl. Quiet, hungry, impatient. Ellie fed her and waited for the lick of thanks Cali always gave her before diving into her food.

Ellie downed her usual glass of morning water and glanced at the thermometer on the wall. It was a cool start to the day. She put her glass in the sink and grabbed a work jacket from the coat rack. Her raggedy comfy jeans would do for the morning walk, and she slipped into her running shoes before hitting the button to set her coffee brewing at a slow perk. By the time she opened the back door, Cali had finished eating and sprinted ahead of her into the yard ahead. She knew Ellie's morning routine.

Ellie pulled up the collar on her jacket against the cool breeze. She turned her face to the sun, seeking the slow heat, and let the growing warmth seep into her bones. She knew by noon, it could be hot enough for shorts.

Dew dotted the grass as she made her way towards the barn, and the birds flitted in the trees above. Beyond that, silence. Just the way she liked it. This was her joy. Every morning she could walk her 25 acres was a good day. Her route rarely wavered. Through the woods, over the bridge, past the treehouse, and into the apple orchard. Without fail, this calmed her.

After an hour she returned to the house to have breakfast and wait for her cousin. Hopefully, Sophie would have found the records were wrong, and everything was fine.

Because if the doctor was right and Sophie wasn't Aunt Jenna's daughter, life was going to get complicated for all of them.

***

Sophie slammed her car door shut, grabbed her folder and marched up to the porch.

Ellie opened the door before Sophie reached it, took one look at her cousin's face and said, "Glass of wine?"

"It's 11:00 in the morning, Ellie." Sophie gave her a quick hug and they headed for the kitchen.

"You look like you need something strong."

"There's something seriously wrong, El." Sophie dropped her folder on the kitchen table and sank onto a chair. The windows were open and a warm breeze wafted the flowered curtains above the sink. Sophie drew a deep breath of the fresh air and sighed.

Ellie opened the fridge and took out the grape juice, filling a glass from the drainboard. She put it in front of Sophie. It wasn't wine but Sophie looked like she needed something.

"Thanks." Sophie drank it all down.

"What's the problem?" Ellie sat across from her, dreading what was to come.

"I've checked all my documents." She opened her folder and pulled out a bunch of papers.

"What's this?"

"The bloodwork—*everyone's* bloodwork." Sophie passed Ellie the papers.

"You know I don't understand this technical stuff." Ellie looked anyway.

"Okay. Short story? I can't be Mom and Dad's daughter." Sophie's eyes filled with tears.

"Wait!" Ellie sat straighter in her seat. "You're 100% sure? No possibility of error?"

"None," Sophie whispered. "I checked all their medical records. Mom's had tons of blood tests over the past days and I have Dad's records at home. They're all the same results."

"And yours?" Ellie did not want to believe this. "You're sure your own are right?"

"I know my own." Sophie stared at her. "I donate regularly."

"Okay, just hoping there's a screw up somewhere."

"*Hoping*?" Sophie's voice started to rise. "How do you think I feel?"

"Sophie..."

"No! This means that Mom and Dad aren't my Mom and Dad! Who are they? Why am I with them? Who are my real parents?"

"Slow down!" Ellie reached over and grabbed her cousin's flailing hands. "Slow down, take a breath. We'll work this out."

"Am I adopted?"

"I've never heard that. Now we don't know the truth yet, but is there a possibility that one of your parents had an affair?"

"Not a chance!" Sophie was adamant. "They were so much in love. No."

"A DNA test would help," Ellie said softly.

"Oh, gosh," Sophie whispered. "Can you imagine me asking mom for that? Especially in the shape she's in? But there are tons of stories of people raising other people's children. You think someone is your sister and they're actually your mother."

"We just don't know," Ellie said.

"Then who am I?" Sophie blinked furiously, but tears slid down her cheeks. "This is crazy! I feel like everything I believed about my life is false!"

They sat in silence, hands clasped, until Sophie's breathing calmed. "Can you help me, El?"

"How?"

"You're a detective. You find things out."

"I'm a genealogist, not an actual detective."

"But you do find people, research people's pasts, find links. If that's not detective work, what is?"

"Yes, I guess that's exactly what I do."

"So, you'll help me?"

Ellie hesitated then jumped in. "Look, I think it's really important you find out the truth. You might need to know your family history for medical reasons one day. Now, neither of us believes Aunt Jenna did anything wrong, so there has to be a logical explanation. And, Sophie, what if there's someone out there looking for you?"

Sophie screwed her eyes closed with the seriousness of what they were about to do. "Geeze Louise, I could have a whole other family! Let's see if we can find anything." Sophie wiped her wet cheeks with her palms. "I want to know the truth." She looked up at her cousin with resolve. "No matter what we find, I need to know."

"We'll need a plan..." Ellie was already thinking of a research strategy.

"Oh, not again." Sophie motioned to the TV on the counter.

Ellie turned the sound up when she saw Diane's face appear on the screen.

"... *Ellie McLellan,*" Diane was saying. *"You may remember her family was killed by a texting driver, and Ms. McLellan fought for the law making it illegal to use cell phones in cars."*

Photos of Ellie, her husband and daughter filled the screen and Ellie jerked as if she'd been slapped. The shock was physical.

"Oh, low blow." Sophie went to turn it off.

"Wait." Ellie was frozen. "There's more."

"And now," continued Diane on the newscast, *"we find it was the very same Ms. McLellan who heroically rescued Owen and Lauren Walsh's son, Gavyn, from a terrible accident. We will have more on this story once we have spoken to Ms. McLellan."*

Ellie slumped down in her seat and groaned.

"You're not going to talk to her, are you?" Sophie asked as she turned off the TV.

"Of course not—but she's a digger." Ellie sat back and rolled the tension out of her shoulders.

"What if she tries to find out about us, about Mom, or what Mom might have done?" Sophie's face turned white. "I don't want the whole world knowing about this."

"Sophie." Ellie went to her and put her arms around her. "Diane won't get any information from me. Nothing."

"Okay, okay." Sophie returned the hug and stepped back. "We can do this."

"Now, if I can get through a client's phone interview in an hour, I'll be amazed," Ellie tried to make light of it.

"Postpone it," Sophie said.

"No, it's good for business, and I like this lady." Ellie paced restlessly and ended up at the kitchen sink. The view out the window didn't have the usual calming effect.

"Do you want me to stay?"

"No, thanks." Ellie returned to the table and picked up a file. "I want to review a few things before the interview."

"Then I'm heading back to the hospital to work on my paper and study. We'll get through this El, together."

"I know." Ellie reached up and gave her cousin a quick kiss on the cheek. "One day at a time."

"How about one hour at a time?" Sophie smiled at her.

"Getting close to one minute these days." Ellie gave her a shaky smile. "I've got a few ideas already and we'll talk about what our plan should be going forward."

"Call me if you need me." Sophie headed for the door but stopped and turned. With an abruptly wavering voice, she asked, "What do I even call her?"

"She's still your mom. No matter what we find, she's still your mom. Remember that."

"She'll always be Mom," Sophie repeated, nodding in determined agreement. She blinked rapidly, clutched her bag under her arm and escaped out the door.

The kitchen was suddenly deathly silent except for the steady *snick, snick, snick* of the rabbit wall clock. Ellie watched the comical rabbit's nose twitch in time to the seconds passing, then down at her files before simply laying her head on the desk, exhaustion overwhelming her. "Minute to minute," she mumbled against the papers and let her eyes drift closed.

Chapter Ten

"You're quiet," Lauren said to Quinn as they stepped from her trailer. She wore a 1920s flapper dress. She loved the clothes she got to wear in this movie. They walked past the trailers parked up and down de Maisonneuve Street in Westmount. Period cars hugged the sidewalks as they crossed Wood into the camera zone. From here on down the crossing streets had been blocked off to the public.

"Don't have much to say," Quinn finally replied.

"I want to get in touch with Ellie," Lauren glanced up at him. Like his brother, Owen, Quinn towered over most people. Their whole family were giants, except their mother who was as tiny as a pixie.

"Why?"

"To make sure she's okay." Lauren grabbed his arm. "Slow down there, Q, I can't walk as fast as you and your long legs!"

"Sorry." He slowed down and looked at her. "I'm sure she's okay."

"You're not curious about her?"

Quinn kept his mouth shut and Lauren smiled.

"The news has her…" he started.

"Ms. McKee!" shouted a voice from the cross street. "Can I have your picture?"

Quinn watched the young man approach from the barricade, camera in hand. Clean clothes, pleasant smile, calm demeanour. The guard had let him through and then turned back to the crowds beyond as the young man reached them.

"Sure." Lauren hesitated before stepping over to him and putting on her "photo" grin. It was usually Quinn who gave the okay for fans to approach and this threw her. She waited while the camera was held up, she smiled, and the shot was taken.

The young man grabbed her arm. "I really love your movies." He moved too close. "I'm a huge fan! How is your son? Were you worried?"

Quinn stepped between them and pulled the man's hand from Lauren's arm. There was a mark on her skin and Quinn glared at him. Quinn signaled to the security guard who had let him through. "Move him along," Quinn growled to the shamefaced guard. "Bad call."

The young man stumbled away from Quinn's angry face, right into the hands of the security guard who pulled him past the barricade and away from Lauren.

"That was—"

"Unacceptable!" Quinn fumed. "He shouldn't have got to you."

The security guard returned but avoided catching Quinn's eye. "I'm sorry, sir. It won't happen again."

Quinn eyed the guard's humiliated face. "Do you think you can manage walking her to the house?" He pointed to the building where the scene was to take place. The man nodded, obviously afraid to say a word and bring more attention to himself.

"Quinn." She leaned into him and whispered. "Find Ellie for me. They'll find her and I need to know she'll be okay."

"I think they already have."

She gave him that raised eyebrow she used on her son when he had disappointed her. Quinn hated that look, but this time he deserved it.

"After you get Gavyn back to the hotel, check into her, please," she insisted. Without waiting for an answer, Lauren turned on her high 1920 French heels and sauntered up the road, pulling her character around her like a cloak as she neared the cameras.

Quinn strode over to one of the tech trucks and leaned up against it. Before picking up Gavyn, he wanted to do a final look see at the area and make sure the extra security was all in place.

A woman from the food service brought him a cup of coffee and lingered for a minute, hoping for some kind of interaction, but Quinn gave her no notice.

She was on his left side and got the movie star view. He finally turned to face her dead on and thanked her for the coffee. Her jolt reaction to the scar running down his face was exactly what he expected. Sometimes being brutal was the fastest way to handle people. Either they accepted him or they didn't.

If they had a knee-jerk reaction to his scar and stayed in his space, even though he could tell it made them uncomfortable, that's when he knew they were users. If they didn't react at all, he'd consider them.

But then again, not everyone fell into his preconceived rules.

He hated being rude, but he had to block out the way people, especially women, treated him. He ignored those who shied away from his scar. It exhausted him.

He watched the crew adjusting lights on the outside of the house for the next scene and tried to focus on the crowds around him, taking another look around. The only thing front and center in his mind was trying to figure out why Lauren wanted him to find Ellie. It made him curious and cautious at the same time.

Ellie hadn't reacted at all to his scar. In fact, she had shown little reaction to him in any way. Which was both interesting and refreshing. He pictured her bravery at snatching Gavyn off the road, followed by the fear of the press surrounding them, her concern about her aunt and the way she had forgotten he was there.

Was that it? Because she ignored him? Did *that* intrigue him? Hell, yeah. It felt great not having to respond to someone's expectations.

But Lauren was right, the press would get to Elle. He had to get there first.

Gavyn ran out of his mother's trailer and down the road to Quinn.

"You were supposed to wait for me," Quinn said sternly. They had to be careful with Gavyn. He had the energy of an energizer bunny, always on the move, and he'd talk to anybody.

"I'm finished!" The young boy pumped his arm in the air like he'd seen his favorite football players do. And then he pumped it one more time.

Quinn couldn't help but grin at Gavyn's enthusiasm. He loved this kid. He wondered if he was ready to... "Whoa, there!" he called out, whether to stop his own thoughts from heading down a crazy path he didn't want to follow yet, or to stop his nephew from ploughing into him--he wasn't certain.

"Can we go to your house?" Gavyn turned adoring eyes up at his uncle and reached for Quinn's hand.

"We do have that chair to finish sanding." Quinn pretended to consider it.

"I did one leg on my own." Gavyn squared back his shoulders with pride.

"You did indeed." Quinn stopped to give another guard instructions for the next hours, before taking Gavyn's little hand and heading to his car on a side street.

The movie shoot would last till supper, which meant he had babysitting duty until Lauren and Owen finished the day's shooting when their car would return them to the hotel.

"Come on, pop tart," Quinn said, using his favorite nickname for his nephew. "Let's go do some sanding."

Gavyn charged ahead, dragging Quinn behind him.

Chapter Eleven

Ellie was supposed to be on her "days off", but she'd come to town to buy the Flip-Pal Scan for the Seniors Genealogy Group she had forgotten to buy on Tuesday when their lives had turned into a circus. And she refused to come all this way and not sneak in and see her aunt.

She parked on the street by the hospital and took out her phone, compelled suddenly to research her biggest fear before heading in. She quickly Googled the statute of limitations on kidnapping in Canada. None. Kidnapping was something right up there with murder, and so it should be. This train of thought sent her mind trailing down paths of what could have happened, what might happen, and what she didn't want to happen. Worst case scenarios danced through her head, her aunt being taken away by the police, locked up in prison, dying alone.

She shook her head in disgust at herself. She lived by facts, proof, documents and eye-witness accounts, but sometimes those things were not available. Sometimes she had to use common sense to piece things together. Right now, her common sense was telling her Aunt Jenna wasn't capable of kidnapping anyone. But this time it was her own flesh and blood at stake, and she wasn't looking forward to what she might find, and she needed to look at every possibility.

She strode into the hospital and walked slowly past the nurses' station. Nurse Janice was on duty and dashed out from behind her station. "Ms. McLellan." She put her hand on Ellie's arm. Elle couldn't help noticing Janice's anxious breathing.

"She's doing well today." The nurse smiled at Ellie. "Had a rough night but she had a good sleep this morning."

"Thanks," Ellie answered uncertainly before moving towards the door of her aunt's room, completely aware of Janice's stare following her. Ellie stopped and returned her gaze. "Is there something else?" The nurse made her uncomfortable. Not the shiver down the spine kind of uncomfortable, but the twitch at the back of the neck kind. The red flag kind.

"No. Ah... Enjoy your visit. Take your time."

Ellie nodded and resumed her path toward her aunt's room, stopping at the door to look back and consider the nurse. Nurse Janice had never shown interest in Ellie before—why the sudden interest now? She watched the nurse return to her work, talking on the phone, turning away as she spoke.

Ellie opened the door to her aunt's room an inch, peered inside and saw Jenna lying in the white hospital bed, alone. No Sophie by her side to get upset at Ellie for turning up when she was supposed to be taking time for herself.

She gave herself a mental shake. Straightening her shoulders as her aunt had taught her to do when events in her life got difficult, she walked into the room. Jenna was sleeping, her chest gently rising and falling at an even pace. The only sound was the beeping of the machines.

Ellie sat on the chair by the bed. She stayed there for twenty minutes, silent, trying to piece together the puzzle in her head. "Aunt Jenna," she finally murmured. "I don't know what happened, but we've got something strange going on here. Can you hear me?"

Jenna didn't answer. She hadn't expected she would.

"Sophie is torn up." She knew her aunt couldn't hear her, but she had to say this, get this off her chest, throw it out into the ether, even if it was just a barely audible whisper. "Aunty—the blood work says Sophie can't be your child, that it simply *isn't* possible. How can that be?" Tears welled and she rubbed her eyes hard to stop them.

"I'm not sure what's happening. I don't know what to do for her." Ellie sat still for a minute. "I guess life is never what you imagine it will be. Things were going so well. Safe. Quiet. Everything in its place. But that's never true, is it?" Ellie concluded, reaching out to her aunt, taking and tenderly stroking the gentle, soft hand that had soothed her so often as she'd grown up. What she knew of Aunt Jenna and what she knew of bloodlines did not equate. Reluctantly, she went on, compelled to say it all, keeping the words so quiet they were barely a puff of air in the room. "Sophie wants me to find the truth. I don't care what the truth is, but I can't let her believe she's not yours if it's not true. Back to blood doesn't lie. If she was adopted..." Ella stopped, shaking her head in confusion. "But why lie about such a thing, Aunt Jenna?"

Placing Jenna's hand carefully back on the bed, Ellie took a deep breath and stood up. "You're like my second mother, and I couldn't bear it if something happened to you. I will find out what I can and we'll deal with it later. It's going to be okay. I love you."

Ellie bent over and kissed her aunt on the forehead.

"It's going to be okay," she repeated to herself as she left the room.

As the door closed behind her, Jenna let out a soft whimper as the tears escaped her eyes and slid down her cheeks.

Chapter Twelve

Quinn set Gavyn to complete the sanding on the last leg of the chair while he started to work on his motorcycle. But once the cover came off the motorcycle, Gavyn lost interest in the chair and rushed over to sit on a stool beside his uncle, a few tools in his tiny hands.

"Finished your sanding already?" Quinn joked.

"Can we go for a ride?" Gavyn had a one-track mind when it came to the gleaming machine in front of him.

"I don't know if your Mom will let you on the bike just yet, Gav," Quinn replied, straightening up. "Wrench, please."

Gavyn stared hard at the tools in his hands and after considering them all, held the wrench out to Quinn.

"This one?" He smiled up at his favorite person in the world, besides his parents.

"You're getting good at this." Quinn took the tool from him with a nod.

"But I want to ride," Gavyn said, a whine creeping into his voice.

"I'm sure you do." Quinn stared at him. "But what would your mom say?"

"Not yet, it's too dangerous." Gavyn had heard that phrase too many times.

"It's more about your size." Quinn hunkered down beside the bike and looked at a pipe. "Come here a minute, Gav, I need your help with this."

The boy bounded off the stool and ran around to his uncle's side.

"Down here." Quinn motioned him to squat down beside him. "See that little piece of twig in there? The one beside the pipe? I can't reach that with my big hands, but I bet you could."

"Because I'm small?" Gavyn sounded irritated.

"Exactly! Right now, you being small is a big help. One day you won't be able to help me like this, but you'll help in other ways."

"I can ride when I'm bigger?" Gavyn's eyebrows rose in hope.

"Absolutely!" Quinn smiled at him.

Gavyn reached in where Quinn pointed, and pulled on the twig.

"Gently, Gav," Quinn said, "Tug it gently, so it doesn't break off."

The boy focused his attention and gently twisted the twig free. He held it above his head like a trophy. Quinn picked him up and twirled him around, marvelling at how great it felt to be an uncle. What would it feel like if he held his own son?

As Gavyn squealed with delight, Quinn's phone buzzed in his pocket. He put Gavyn down and answered it, smiling down at Gavyn who watched his every expression as he spoke on the phone. The kid didn't miss a thing. Quinn hung up and asked, "Want to go get ice cream?"

Gavyn's eyes lit up. "Chocolate with sprinkles?"

"Come on, sprinkles it is!" Quinn closed up the garage, opened the door to his everyday car and strapped Gavyn into the car seat in the back. He wasn't removing the car seat until Gavyn was big enough to sit on his own.

"And we might see Miss McLellan again too," he casually mentioned before he closed the door on Gavyn's wide-eyed look and got into the driver's seat. He did up his seatbelt, started the car and pulled out into the traffic. The hospital was a five-minute drive, and the traffic was in his favour.

"The pretty lady who saved me?"

"The pretty lady who saved you," Quinn confirmed, grinning at him in the rear-view mirror.

"I like her," Gavyn told him.

"Me too, Gav."

"Are you going to marry her?"

"What?" The question startled Quinn. He was simply wanting to see her again, with no future plans in mind beside buying her an ice cream.

"She likes you too," Gavyn informed him solemnly.

"How can you tell?" Quinn was curious what a four-year-old could see that he hadn't.

"She looked at you when you didn't look at her." Gavyn looked at Quinn as if he should know this.

"Well, I don't know about marrying her, pop tart—I don't know her that well, but let's see if we can get to know her better."

"Good. And she can have ice cream with us!"

"If she wants to."

"Everyone likes ice cream."

Quinn smiled to himself as they reached the hospital. He certainly hoped she liked ice cream. It was the only excuse he had for seeing her.

***

"The ice cream is over there." Gavyn tugged at Quinn's hand and tried to drag him along the road.

Quinn stopped at a bench outside the hospital and sat down. "We have to wait for Miss McLellan and find out if she wants to come with us."

Gavyn climbed up beside him and watched the cars pass by. "What if she doesn't like ice cream?" His worried frown broke Quinn's heart.

"Then we'll invite her to keep us company."

Gavyn thought about it and nodded. He glanced over at the front of the hospital and jumped down. "There she is!" He was halfway across the lawn before Quinn even stood up.

"Gav! Wait a minute!" Gavyn looked at him over his shoulder but didn't stop until he screeched to a halt in front of a surprised Ellie.

"Gavyn, where did you come from?" Ellie asked.

"He's with me," Quinn confessed.

Ellie grinned as he tried not to look guilty.

"Will you come for ice cream?" Gavyn took her hand. "It's this way." He tugged her along.

"Whoa, Gav." Quinn touched his nephew's shoulder to stop him. "You have to get an answer first. Miss McLellan might be busy."

"But it's ice cream!" he protested, as if that alone explained everything.

"Well." Ellie tried to look serious. "Ice cream. That's a tough one."

"With sprinkles," Gavyn said quietly, as if sharing a secret.

"Sprinkles?" Ellie squeezed Gavyn's hand and nodded. "I don't see how I can say no."

"Uncle Quinn?" Gavyn grinned. "Miss McLellan wants sprinkles too."

Quinn glanced at Ellie and saw an exhausted woman. Her eyes were shadowed and red, as if she had been holding in a good cry. Her shoulders slumped and her smile was weary. Maybe this wasn't the best time to ask. "You sure?"

Ellie's face brightened. "I'm sure. It's just what I need."

Gavyn led them to the corner and down the road to the ice cream parlour. Quinn refused to think too hard about the small group they made, a unit, a comfortable group of like-minded people, that's all. The warm feeling in his chest and the catch in his breathing surprised him. Quinn ordered the cones, and they took them to sit on the grass in a nearby park.

Gavyn chatted about the motorcycle his Uncle Quinn was building and how he would ride it one day. "When I'm bigger," he whispered to her.

"I know how that feels, Gavyn," Ellie said. "I'll never be bigger than I am now. My cousin used to call me a shrimp."

"That's not nice!"

"But I can't do anything about it so why get upset?" Ellie licked the ice cream running down the side of the cone and caught Quinn staring at her. He quickly looked away, making a business of putting his wallet away one handed.

"Are you big enough to ride the bumper cars?" Gavyn asked.

"Barely." Ellie laughed. "I love bumper cars!"

"Could she go on your motorcycle?" Gavyn asked his uncle.

"She could." Quinn loved the image that sprang to mind. Nice... "I think she's big enough."

"You could hold her so she doesn't fall," Gavyn said.

Ellie sputtered out her ice cream and Quinn let out a whoop of laughter. "I could hold her, yes."

"Or I could hold on to you," Ellie blurted. "What I mean is I would be on the back and..."

"You have to sit behind Uncle Quinn," Gavyn stood up and shoved the last of his soggy cone into his mouth. He wiped his hands on his napkin and dashed off to put it in a garbage bin.

"Yup, you do." Quinn could not take his eyes off her.

"I don't feel safe on motorcycles."

"I'll go slow," he offered, shocked when the words left his mouth. It was so obvious neither of them was sure exactly what he'd meant—and it was all right. They smiled like goofy teenagers.

"Come on, Uncle Quinn!" Gavyn ran up and hugged Quinn's legs from behind. "I want to do more work."

Quinn finished his cone then pulled Gavyn over his shoulder and tickled him.

"You can come too, Miss McLellan," Gavyn gasped between giggles.

"I would love to, Gavyn," she answered, her exhaustion returning to her delicate face as she wiped ice cream from her fingers, "but I have work to finish."

"Can I see you again?" Quinn asked.

"Things are really crazy right now..."

"He's very nice," Gavyn piped in looking at her from over Quinn's shoulder.

"I'm sure he is." Ellie was clearly flustered. "Can I... can I get in touch with you?" Quinn could feel the brush off coming and all that warm stupid teenage happiness he'd been enjoying drained away. He wasn't a teenager anymore.

She surprised him again when she held out her hand. "Can I have your number?"

"He lives over there." Gavyn pointed back towards the mountain.

Quinn dug out his wallet and handed her a card.

Ellie looked at it and grinned. "Bodyguard?"

"And he makes tables and chairs," Gavyn added.

"I might need something like that," she admitted.

"Furniture or a bodyguard?" Quinn asked her, warmth instantly restored. Man, this reminded him of the first time he'd asked a girl out, terrified and excited at the same time.

"Both," she tucked the card in her back pocket and Quinn noticed how well her jeans fit before dragging his eyes away. He swung Gavyn down to the ground and took his hand.

As they reached their cars, Ellie hugged Gavyn. "Thanks for the ice cream!"

"Uncle Quinn needs a hug too," Gavyn informed her.

They hesitated a moment, then Ellie reached up for a quick hug.

He paused before letting her go. Her head reached his shoulder and her hair tickled his chin. She was skittish in his arms and he was afraid of spooking her.

"Yes, well." She let her hands slide down his arms and gave his hand a parting squeeze. Was she reluctant to let him go? This possibility made Quinn infinitely happy. She said, "Again, thanks for the ice cream, guys."

"Our pleasure," Quinn said as she turned to walk away. Gavyn looked from one to the other, his expression puzzled. It was plain to see the child was certain something was missing. "How about dinner?" Quinn blurted. They both froze, Ellie blinking rapidly. Neither was used to banter and while they'd slid into it like a comfy pair of jeans, they were both startled.

Out of the corner of his eye, Quinn saw Diane approaching, a young woman fiddling with a camera at her side. Exactly what no one wanted—ever. "We're out of here!" He scooped Gavyn into his arms and grabbed Ellie's hand, pulling her along with them.

"What?" she asked, though she *did* run beside him.

"Press."

"Damn!" She glanced all around, searching for the cause of possibly more pain and stress she would have to overcome. "Where?"

"Coming from the south." He guided her towards his car. "Quick, inside. Don't look at them."

He strapped Gavyn into his car seat and jumped into the driver's seat. Ellie hadn't thought twice and was now buckled in and sliding down below the window. Even with the car windows tinted, she wasn't taking any chances.

Quinn pulled away as Diane reached Ellie's window.

Diane stared at her and Ellie cringed at the look on Diane's face. A predator stalking her prey.

Ellie was no one's prey, he thought —not as long as he had anything to do with it.

Chapter Thirteen

Quinn drove quickly through the network of streets to lose anyone following and pulled into his garage, closing the garage door behind them remotely as quickly as possible. They all sat in the dark, in silence for a long moment.

Finally, Quinn climbed out. "Out you come, little man," he announced with what Ellie knew to be forced cheer for the boy's sake. He opened the back door and unlatched Gavyn from his seat. Ellie watched in amazement as the boy bounced out and disappeared through the door leading into the house. She envied Gavyn's youthful acceptance of life.

She however, remained in her own seat, unable to move.

Quinn ducked his head down and peered into the car. "Ellie?" he asked. "Come on lass, I'll get you a cup of tea."

She wasn't sure what to do. This whole situation was out of her control and it made her lightheaded. And very angry.

He walked around and opened her door. He held out a hand to help her out.

"I need to go home," she murmured uncertainly.

"No one knows you're here. You're safe with me." His words washed over her like a warm evening breeze. He took her hand and helped her out, then led the way through the door where Gavyn had disappeared.

"Oh, my," Ellie whispered as she stepped through and looked at the kitchen surrounding her. Her fears eased at once, replaced by a warmth that enveloped her like a wool shawl around her shoulders. She sighed with delight.

"Lovely, isn't it?" Quinn went to the sink, filled the kettle and set it to boil on the stove.

"It's so old-fashioned!" Ellie took a step further in and made a complete turn to take in every aspect of the room.

"You don't like it?" Quinn frowned.

"Gosh, no!" Her glowing face surprised him. "This is so amazing. I *love* it."

"It belonged to my Gran. She didn't want to change a thing. Kept it like this on purpose."

"But it doesn't look old, just old-fashioned." She rested against the back of a wooden chair. "Know what I mean?"

"Absolutely."

She loved how he fit the large room perfectly. He reached up to get two cups from a cupboard, and the pattern of the pastel flowered curtains above the sink drew her eyes. The appliances were older, and the counters were broad wood planks. The table was handmade and home to a few placemats and a small vase with real daisies. A rotary phone hung from the wall. "This is so you," she said. "I could imagine you living here a couple of hundred years ago."

"With a kilt?" he joked.

Her heart flopped inside her chest—just a little as she pictured this man standing before her wearing a kilt. The vision was... unsettling to say the very least. "Well, maybe not here in Canada, but you never know." She grinned at him.

"I'm told I look rather grand in a kilt," he told her with a mischievous smirk.

"Oh, I'm sure you do," she answered playfully. She couldn't help the smile that stayed on her face as she continued to take in the room. "Is the whole house like this?" she asked.

"Oh, aye, to a point." He filled the teapot with boiling water and brought it to the table. He followed with milk and cups. "I'll give you a tour later. Have a seat."

Ellie pulled out a chair and sank onto the needlepoint cushions. She took the cups and poured for them both.

Gavyn raced into the kitchen, sliding to a stop in his stocking feet. "Is it milk and cookie time Uncle Quinn?"

Quinn raised one eyebrow in question. "Slippers?"

"It's fun sliding," Gavyn explained.

"I know, I slid down that hall myself last week."

"No!" Gavyn exclaimed. "Did you tell Mom?"

"Nope." Quinn motioned to the hall. "Get them on and then you can play with your Lego. You just had ice cream so it's not cookie time."

"But you're having..." Gavyn's face fell when he saw only tea on the table. "Okay." His shoulders slumped as he left the room. But they heard him take off again once he was out of sight.

"Slippers!" Quinn called after him.

Gavyn ran back, grabbed up the slippers by the door and raced away laughing.

"You're very good with him," Ellie said.

"He's easy to be with," Quinn stirred a spoonful of sugar into his tea. "Gran would lecture me if she saw me doing this."

"Why?"

"She believed tea should be savoured for its natural flavour."

"Your Gran must have been something." Ellie took a sip of her tea then added a touch of milk.

"She was great!" Quinn's eyes sparkled. "Smaller than you, had a wicked sense of humour, and loved hockey!"

"What more could you ask for?" she asked with a laugh.

"Exactly!" he agreed with her. "Do you like hockey?"

"Been a Habs fan since I was fourteen. I used to sneak a radio under the blankets to listen to the games!"

"We should catch a game sometime."

"Summer just started, Quinn," she reminded him.

"Winter will be here before you know it," he countered with a smile.

"I'm living every summer day right now, thank you very much." She put down her cup. "Winter is a whole other animal."

"Not a favourite?"

"Quite the opposite. I love to skate, toboggan, and build snowmen."

"I love snowmen too!" Gavyn came running back into the room and stopped beside her. "I build big ones and Uncle Quinn puts the heads on top."

"Do you build a lot of them?" Ellie loved the joy in his eyes.

"No." He rolled his eyes. "We don't have snow at home."

"Home base is Los Angeles," Quinn explained. "But they come here around Christmas."

"And we build snowmen," Gavyn reminded him. "Can you build snowmen with us?"

Ellie looked at his eager face and remembered her daughter at this age. Her jaw clenched. The pain was not as bad after four years, but every so often it stabbed her in the heart. Like right now. "I just might do that," she made herself answer lightly, running her hand across his hair. "A big one?"

"Really big." Gavyn remained in place, as if he knew she needed the connection.

"Well." Ellie stood up, taking a step back from them both. "I've got to go."

"Where's your car?" Could Quinn want her to stay?

"Not far—I can walk," she said when he opened his mouth to continue. "I *need* to walk, Quinn."

"Fair enough." He smiled. "Say goodbye to Miss McLellan, Gavyn."

"Ellie," she said to the little boy. "You can call me Ellie."

"Are you coming back?" he asked with the innocence of a child.

"We'll see." She gave him a quick hug. He hugged her back, the feel of his small arms around her neck breaking her heart.

"Goodbye!" he called as he ran out of the room.

"Well, the simplicity of youth."

"Are you sure I can't drive you back?"

"I'm fine." She fought the weariness that abruptly threatened to overtake her by favouring him with a brilliant smile. "Thanks for the tea." She picked up her purse and headed for the door, but he got there first and opened it for her. They stood awkwardly, waiting for the other to say something. Ellie broke the spell by turning to leave.

"Wait!" Quinn reached for her arm. "Wait," he said again, softly.

She waited.

"I suck at this."

"At what?"

"Asking someone to dinner, which I kind of already did, but failed to nail down the details."

"Yes."

"Yes?"

"I'd love to have dinner with you."

"When?"

"I need to check my schedule first," she dug into her knapsack and took out a pen and paper. "Here's my phone number. I feel like I'm in high school!" She laughed.

"Glad I'm not the only one."

"I doubt you have trouble "nailing down" a date." He was messing with her.

"Oh, women can be forward," he assured her, his tone uncharacteristically tentative. He raised his hand to his scar. Did he realize he had? Her heart ached for him. He added dryly, "Only after they know I'm Owen's brother. Not before."

"Stupid women!" Ellie threw her hand over her mouth. "Sorry. I sometimes don't have a filter!"

"I like it." He moved closer.

"Good, right, well!" Ellie declared with cheerful conviction. She backed away and reached for the handle of the open door to steady herself before stepping outside. "Got to run, hate driving in the dark and Cali gets antsy when I'm not home on time."

"Cali?" Quinn frowned.

"Talk to you soon." She waved at him and fled more than walked down the path to the road.

"Who's Cali?" came Gavyn's voice from behind the door.

Chapter Fourteen

With dirty supper dishes still on the kitchen table, Ellie tapped her pen against the pad of paper in front of her as she tried to come up with a strategy to help Sophie. It was proving more difficult than she originally thought. She knew how to find a person and the steps to begin a search, but dozens of "what ifs" flew through her head. This was so very personal.

She used mind mapping in her day-to-day life, and the visuals helped her make connections her brain might not have seen otherwise. There was no reason not to use it here. She drew a circle in the middle of the paper and wrote "Who is Sophie?" inside it. Ellie would need to work backwards and find the people who had known Sophie when she was young. She drew a line to the side and within another circle she wrote "Talk to Aunt Norma". Another line to a circle with "DNA test".

Cali's barking from the porch shattered her concentration. The noise in the otherwise quiet evening startled her, and she dropped her pen. The tone of the bark made her run to the door, then freeze at the sight before her.

Cali stood in the driveway between the house and an intruder. Her hackles were up, and she circled a slim young man. He was dressed casually but carried the tools of his trade, a camera. He took a quick shot of the house as he tried to ignore the menacing dog.

"Hey!" Ellie stepped out. Cali picked up on her anger and move towards the man, growling low and deep in her throat.

The man took a shot of Ellie and raised a hand in a welcoming wave. "Hey there," he smiled in an "I'm your best friend" kind of way that sent a shiver up her spine. She knew his type. "Can I talk to you for a minute?"

"You're trespassing," she yelled. "Get off my land now or I'm calling the cops." She picked up a baseball bat resting against the wall.

"I only wanted to talk," he insisted, his creepy smile still plastered to his face. "Give you a chance to tell your side of the story."

"There *is* no story." She jumped off her balcony and walked slowly towards him, bat in hand as Cali advanced on him. "Cali," Ellie called to her.

"You can't set your dog on me." He had the nerve to be insulted, as if he had every right to trespass on her property and invade her privacy.

"I'm giving you this one chance to leave, now, with no problems," she told him, keeping her voice level and quiet.

He started to raise his camera again.

"Don't you even think of it!"

Cali inched closer to him and bared her teeth.

He eyed the dog, glanced at Ellie and her bat and backed up. "This isn't finished," he declared. "This story is huge and there'll be tons of press here before you know it."

"You're not moving very fast," she said in wonder as Cali got close enough to snap at him.

"You wouldn't dare let it touch me." He stopped in his tracks having apparently gathered whatever courage he had left. Cali barked as she reached him. The man wasn't stupid and continued walking backwards, keeping Cali in his view.

"If I see you again." Ellie swung her bat for emphasis. "I won't stop her. You've been warned." Cali's growl was deep and insistent.

His courage gone, the man turned and took off down the road, Cali close behind.

Ellie called after him, "She won't leave you till you're off my property." She watched as they turned the corner in the road and could still hear Cali barking.

She knew Cali wouldn't hurt anyone unless Ellie was being threatened. Cali understood Ellie's voice and the tones she used, but Ellie wasn't taking any chances this time.

She waited until Cali went silent and came loping back through the woods to her side.

Then she waited until her heart stopped pounding.

"Good girl" Ellie bent down and patted her best friend. She spent a few minutes feeling the warmth of the fur through her fingers and the dog's calming presence.

They headed back to the house, but Ellie worried her refuge was not as secure as she had hoped.

By the lay of the land, people could only come up by her long driveway. It would take some serious crazies to climb the rock wall or wade across the stream. The woods behind the house were deep and accessible only from her property or another property, miles down the road. The path to the highway, while hidden and disguised to outsiders, might be the one weakness she had. She'd have to set up an alarm.

The intruder was right. They *would* be back.

Chapter Fifteen

Wednesday evenings at the Cozy Corner Café were Ellie's favorite night of the week. This was when her group of seniors met to discuss genealogy and devour the special treats Maggie made specially for them.

The meetings started at seven and lasted about an hour, depending on the topic, and ended with time left over for everyone to ask Ellie questions.

When Ellie arrived in the back room of the Café to see her group of seniors sitting around the big table, waiting, it lifted her spirits. The sun was low in the sky, sending streaks of light through the large window and across the floor around them. While some seniors had smiles on their faces, others looked grumpy and not pleased to be here. Shirley had the most uncomfortable expression, while her sister, Ruth, beamed at Ellie with pleasure.

Ellie loved teaching genealogy, especially to people who were interested, and her specialty was teaching people how to write their own personal history stories. "So," she said, plunking her briefcase on the table, "who managed to fill out any of their Timelines?"

"How are we supposed to remember what we did when we were five?" grumbled Lennie Dickens from his seat beside his wife, Tess.

"I doubt you could remember yesterday," his wife shot back at him.

"Tess!" came the shocked response from Doreen who sat across the table, knitting needles silenced for the moment. She never knew whether the other couple were serious or kidding with each other.

Lennie and Tess were tiny in frame and liked to snipe at each other, usually in jest, sometimes in annoyance, but always in love. They were both nearing ninety and patience was not always a strong point for them. Lennie loved shocking people with his comments, but he turned back to Ellie and waited for her response.

"Actually," Ellie began, "I didn't think many of you would manage to get more than your date of birth, marriage, and children's vitals."

"Then why ask us to?" Phil Richards asked. He was a quiet man, tall, slim, and a bit shy, but he listened to everything she taught them and soaked it up like a sponge.

"She was getting the juices flowing," Doreen said. For Phil to even talk during these get-togethers was amazing. He needed to be coaxed most of the time and Doreen was delighted at his progress.

"I doubt many of us have had juices flowing for years," Lennie grunted.

Ellie failed to hide her grin at his comment. "In a way, the Timeline is to start you thinking," Ellie explained.

"I've done a lot of thinking," said Tess. Lennie gave her a look of surprise, as he hadn't thought she was taking this seriously.

"What have you come up with?" Ellie asked her as she sat down and pulled out her own Timeline.

"I *do* remember most of the big events of my life, my first day of school, when my mother died, getting married, my children, but the bits in between are a bit fuzzy."

"Exactly!" Ruth said. "We've all lived long lives, and so much has happened."

"I want you to focus for now on getting those big events documented." Ellie took a stack of papers from her folder and passed them around. "When you're ready to go deeper, use these elementary questions to get started."

"That a good idea," Phil mumbled to himself.

"Here's a tip." Ellie had their attention. "As you go through the big events, little events will pop up—things that happened either before or after those big events."

Ruth shook her head. "I'll never remember it all," she muttered.

"What is the biggest event you can remember, Ruth?" Ellie asked her. Ellie watched her friend take a deep breath and stare off for a minute. Ruth's sister, Shirley, fidgeted in her seat as if to tell her to get on with it.

But as Ellie watched Shirley, it occurred to her that maybe Shirley wasn't trying to hurry her sister along, but nervous about the answer Ruth might give.

Ruth looked at her fingers and fiddled with a small ring on her right hand. "Oh, I'd have to say during the war."

"That's a start," Ellie encouraged. "Write what you remember during the war. No one has to see this but you. You don't have to share any of your memories with anyone, unless you want to."

"Then why do this in the first place?" Lennie asked. Tess shook her head at his lack of enthusiasm.

"Because some memories are wonderful things," Ellie replied.

"And some suck." Shirley got a laugh with that one.

"Yes, Shirley, some do," Ellie agreed. "You might want your children or grand-children to discover who you were, what you did, what your hopes and dreams were."

"Not while I'm alive—I don't want them knowing everything!" Lennie said.

"Who will see your story, Shirley?" Phil asked quietly.

Shirley jolted at being put on the spot. "I don't have children, so probably no one."

"I don't have children either," Ruth said, "but that's not going to stop me from remembering."

"This *will* be personal," Ellie conceded, trying to get them back on track, "but it can be fun, too. I spent last weekend drawing the floor plans for the house I grew up in, my first apartment, and the house I lived in before the farm. It brought back a lot of memories and I made tons of notes for other things to look into along the way."

"Some are not good memories," Shirley muttered stiffly, shifting in her seat.

"No," Ellie agreed, saddened that the older woman's outlook was so glum. "But like I said, you don't have to write everything down."

They all looked at her, waiting for her to continue.

"Okay." She took a deep breath. "Let's start with the progression of your life."

"Sounds like the Lion King to me," muttered Lennie. Tess leaned into him with a comforting nudge.

"Start with where you first lived. Maybe draw a floor plan like I did. Where did you go to elementary school? High school? Did you finish school, and if not, why not, and what grade did you finish at? Who were your friends at school, favorite teachers, hated teachers, favourite subjects, that kind of thing."

"Gosh, that's a long time ago," said Gracie.

"It is, but once you start, you'll be surprised what comes up," Ellie assured them. "You can ask friends and family about things if you're not sure of the facts. They may have other memories you've totally forgotten about."

"How long do we have to finish this?" Ruth asked.

"As long as you want," Ellie answered. "That's why I say fill in your big events throughout your life and then go back to the beginning. And I was going to suggest that we have a special meeting on Saturday after lunch and start looking through photographs to jog your memories. So, I want everyone to bring a few pictures and I'll show you how to scan them."

"Is the press going to bother you now?" Ruth asked quietly and out of the blue.

Everyone froze. They'd obviously all seen the news reports of Ellie saving the movie star couple's son, and the big man holding her safe. They were curious as teenagers but too polite to ask questions.

Ellie gathered herself and faced them. "Yes. I had one walk up the driveway, brazen as can be, expecting me to talk to him. And he was taking pictures of the house and everything."

"Oh, no!" Ruth shuddered.

"It's okay." Ellie shrugged her shoulders as if it didn't bother her. "Cali scared the heck out of him!"

"I knew that dog would come in handy," Phil said. He had brought Cali to her door a few weeks after her family had died. Cali was from one of his own dogs' litters and he had hoped the puppy would comfort her.

Ellie patted his gnarled hand on the table. "Indeed, she has, Phil. The press might come here, nosing around again, though, and I'm sorry about that."

"Not a one of us will speak with them!" declared Tess. She sat up straight and braced her shoulders back as if that alone would keep them at bay.

"Not a one," everyone echoed.

Ellie looked at the faces of these wonderful people who had become her friends and believed they would bite off the leg of the next reporter themselves.

Chapter Sixteen

Quinn parked in the hotel underground lot and checked for press. He'd surprised one sorry fellow the week before as the guy hid behind an SUV. The man had taken off, his camera bag smashing against his hip, when Quinn approached him. Sometimes having a scary persona was a good thing.

"Who you looking for?" Gavyn piped up from his seat in the back.

"Just making sure no one will pop out and take our picture." Quinn opened his door and then Gavyn's. He reached in and unbuckled the boy from his seat and swung him down to the ground.

"I don't like them." Gavyn snuck his hand into Quinn's and held on tight as they headed to the elevator.

Quinn pushed the button. "Me neither."

Gavyn was quiet. The elevator doors opened, and Gavyn jumped in and watched them swoosh close behind them.

"What's bothering you, Gav?"

Gavyn looked up at him. "Why do people follow us?"

"Because your parents make movies."

Gavyn grabbed Quinn's hand again. "But I don't."

"I know, but you're their son." Quinn hadn't realized how upset Gavyn was by the media attention. He'd never shown it bothered him before, treating it almost like a game, making faces at the press when they got caught out in public.

The door opened and Gavyn dragged him down the hall to his parents' room. Quinn knocked a quick three taps and Owen swung it open a few seconds later.

"Daddy!" Gavyn shouted. He raised his arms and Owen scooped him up in a bear hug.

"Hey there, Gav." He looked over his son's shoulder at Quinn. "Have fun?"

"The camera people found us," Gavyn whispered.

Owen raised his eyebrows at Quinn. "Where?"

"We had ice cream with the pretty lady," his son said.

"I ran into Ellie at the hospital." Quinn shut the hotel room door behind him.

"Hey, sweetie," Lauren called out before turning the sound down on the tv. She reached up to catch Gavyn as Owen dropped him into her lap. "Is that an ice cream moustache you have?" Lauren looked questioningly to Quinn. "Ellie?"

"He ran into her at the hospital." Owen gave Lauren a knowing look.

"Did he?" Lauren smiled.

"Cut it out," Quinn said.

"And the camera people came, and we had to go to Uncle Quinn's house," Gavyn informed them importantly.

"Indeed." Lauren looked at her husband sideways.

"I said cut it out," Quinn said.

"Gav," Owen said, "why don't you go play with your cars for a while."

"Yeah!" Gavyn jumped off his mother's lap and ran into a nearby room, slamming the door behind him. It quickly opened again and his head popped out. "Sorry," he said before closing it again slowly and quietly.

"So." Lauren patted the seat beside her. "Come and tell me all about it."

Quinn stood his ground, for a minute. Then he sighed and slumped down beside her. Once Lauren got her teeth into something, you'd better tell her the whole story in one shot, or it would be a long night. And she was in her comfy clothes, which meant it could be a very long night.

"We ran into her at the hospital and…"

"What were you doing at the hospital?" Owen enjoyed interrogating his brother.

"We were going for ice cream and—"

"She *just* happened to be there," Lauren provided, playing along.

"Okay," he closed his eyes. "I found out she was there, and I wanted to see her again. There. Satisfied?"

Lauren grinned. "You have no idea."

"It's like pulling teeth, right?" Owen asked him.

"Worse," Quinn said.

"Why?" Lauren asked. "You obviously had some kind of connection yesterday. She's quite cute."

"Not your type at all," Owen stated, contradicting his wife.

Quinn shifted in his seat. "I don't have a type." He hated talking about his private life, even with his family. No—*especially* with his family. They were all busybodies.

"Oh, hell, yes you do!" Owen whooped. "Tall, blond, slinky and not always able to read."

"That's so nasty, Owen." Lauren shook her head at him.

"And not true," Quinn added.

"Obviously not if you have a hankering for Ellie." Lauren patted his hand. "She's tiny, brunette and looks rather smart."

"And there she is now!" Owen grabbed the remote and turned the volume up on the tv.

The news item showed them all in the park the day before when Ellie had rescued Gavyn. A shot caught her holding Gavyn and Quinn putting his arms around them both.

"Shit," Quinn said.

The news reporter revealed that the mystery woman was Ellie McLellan, a young woman who had lost her husband and daughter to a texting driver four years before.

"Oh, how sad," Lauren said.

Quinn stared at the screen. The press had dug up some film of Ellie right after the loss of her family. Her devastated face flashed across the screen just as she threw a cup of coffee at the cameraman.

"Good for her!" Owen said.

The news clip finished with speculation as to her relationship with the Walsh family and more details would be available in the later newscast.

"Damn," Quinn said under his breath. "They'll hound her."

"If they catch you with her, they'll hound her more," Owen said.

"No." Lauren sat back. She was thinking. It was one of her superpowers to analyze patterns and link things together. "It would actually be a good thing for people to see her with you, Quinn."

"And bring her more press?"

"I doubt you'd let them near her."

"She needs a bodyguard, dear," Owen said.

"I've got that job already, thanks," Quinn replied.

"Take the mystery out of everything," Lauren continued. "Don't have them searching for the story, give it to them."

"I doubt she'd go for that," Quinn said.

"Well, you need to ask her, don't you?" Lauren raised an eyebrow. "What better reason than to go check up on her."

"I'm taking her to dinner."

"When?"

"Don't know, haven't set it up yet." Quinn felt antsy and cornered. "I just saw her a couple of hours ago."

"Don't want to appear too anxious," Owen joked.

"I don't want to appear anything," Quinn shot back, standing abruptly. He opened Gavyn's door. "See you later Pop Tart!"

"Bye, Uncle Quinn." Gavyn jumped up at him and Quinn draped him over his shoulder and walked to the door, as was their normal routine.

"Hey," Owen called after them, right on schedule, "you can sell him to the circus if you want!"

"No!" Gavyn laughed. "Down, down!"

Quinn walked from their room and down the hall, the boy still on his shoulder. When the doors to the elevator opened, he dropped Gavyn to the floor and watched him scamper back to Owen who waited at the hotel room door. Gavyn scooted under his father's arms and disappeared inside.

***

Owen looked at his brother, shook his head and grinned. He knew Quinn was interested in someone and he was looking forward to watching his brother travel that road.

The doors to the elevator closed as Lauren came to his side.

"He really likes her," she marvelled. "Finally."

Chapter Seventeen

Ellie took extra time that morning with her routine. She walked every acre of her land to check for ways people could sneak in. Except for a direct approach up her driveway and the semi-hidden path across the highway past the treehouse, the property appeared safe.

And yet she didn't *feel* safe.

She spent an hour camouflaging the path, leaving a small space for Ruth to slip through. Ellie wiped the sweat from her forehead, enjoying how physical exercise diminished some of her anxiety. Cali had a way of knowing when Ellie was bothered, which was now, and the dog bounded around, trying to get her attention and all the extra loving that came her way. It was as if Cali could tell by the nature of Ellie's pat how she was feeling.

Mid-morning found Ellie back inside the house as the temperature began to rise. She was ready to focus on a client's work she had promised to deliver by the following week. But Ellie couldn't settle and shifted back and forth in her seat at the kitchen table. It wasn't the ideal spot to work, but the atmosphere in the room usually pleased her. Not so much today. She got up and put on the kettle, thinking movement was the answer. And a cup of tea.

Back at the table she tapped her fingers in a restless rhythm. Papers lay scattered in front of her in no discernable order and the laptop's screen showed a blank white page. Heaving a loud sigh, she leaned back in her chair and stretched her arms above her head. The knot that had formed in her stomach earlier wasn't easing one little bit, a common occurrence when she felt she had lost control over her life.

The kettle whistle startled her, and she jumped up to make the tea she had totally forgotten about. Another coping mechanism she'd acquired since the death of her family. The process of making a single cup of Earl Grey. It usually helped. Usually was becoming a foreign word to her.

The view outside her patio door made her pause. To one side grew the deep trees of the forest and to the other lay a field leading to the swimming pond. The sun glinted off the water in the distance and she knew it would be warm enough for her to swim in later.

Ellie forced herself to pick up the client's wish list and promised herself a dip in the pond as a reward later.

She always asked her clients to prepare a wish list so she knew what they wanted to find out about family members. With that wish list, Ellie could develop a plan of attack the client would go through on their own, following the suggestions Ellie laid out for them. Detective work and mysteries had always intrigued her, but she realized today was not a day for client work as she thought only of solving the mystery that might rip her whole family apart. And they were the only family she had left.

Ellie sat forward and typed a wish list. Not for the client, but for her.

Was Sophie Aunt Jenna's daughter?

If not, who were her parents?

Where did Sophie come from?

How did Aunt Jenna get her?

Did Aunt Jenna steal her? Why?

How could I find this out?

Sophie's own documents answered there was a problem. Ellie demanded documentary proof of every piece of information she used, when available, she would have to get her own copy of the blood work.

Since when had this become a case?

Since her aunt had raised a child who might not be biologically hers and only a trio of women now knew this fact.

Ellie turned off the computer and grabbed the paper with the mind map. For this type of work, she preferred the weight of a pen in her hand. She drew more lines out from the circle in the middle of the page and added the questions she wanted solved and possible ways to solve them. This was her best chance of dealing with the situation calmly. Treat it like any other case. Try to stay distant until all the facts were known.

The mind map grew. Branches shot off with the plan she created. Research, people to interview, data to confirm. The initial question in the middle of the page was the most important to her. If Aunt Jenna had taken Sophie, could she go to jail?

A mental flash of Quinn's face popped into her head. He used to be a cop. She could ask him a hypothetical question. Her need to get concrete information warred with not wanting him to know what might be happening. That would bring him too close, and give him access to her family circle too quickly for her liking.

Ellie felt the heat of a flush creep up her chest to her face. She hadn't reacted to a man like this since her husband, and she'd truly believed she never would again.

She didn't want to. Or did she?

Ellie finished her tea and put the cup in the sink. Working in the garden or walking with Cali would help her mind sort through what little she knew and the possible steps to take. She went barefoot and let the door slam as she headed out into the sun.

The phone rang behind her but she didn't stop.

***

Diane kept the phone to her ear and glanced at her boss. He stared at her, arms crossed, waiting for a response.

"I *will* interview her," Diane said emphatically, totally aware of the single drop of sweat trickling down her neck and further along her spine. Her boss kept his office cool to the point of cold, no matter the season. He said he worked better that way. But if she was sweating in these circumstances, it meant she wasn't in charge of the situation, and that was intolerable to her.

"When?" Her boss didn't move a muscle. The tension between them was high and she knew he'd heard the gossip about her trying for his job. He didn't believe she had enough experience, and she knew he felt she was overstepping. The work atmosphere was horrible but she was determined not to get fired because of it. When she left, it would be on her own terms.

"I'm doing an on-camera update in a few minutes. I sent Josh up there yesterday."

"You sent someone else?" The words were quiet, slow, and full of meaning. Diane snapped her phone closed and stood straighter. She knew she'd messed this up. It wasn't like her not to go full throttle on someone herself, but she was tired of constantly being in the field. Tired of the confrontations, the doors slammed in her face, the "no comments", the disgust she saw on people's faces.

"I'm going up there later myself." She headed for the door hoping he would let it go at that.

He did. And that unnerved her more than anything. There were younger reporters snapping at her heels, eager for even a tenth of the exposure she got. With her job on the line, any feelings she may have had for intruding on Ellie McLellan at this point had to be buried and ignored.

She left the room, head held high, ignoring Annabelle by her side. To have someone witness her boss's comments had been humiliating and Diane never left anyone unscathed when she was feeling vulnerable.

Chapter Eighteen

Ellie walked into the Café a few hours later and saw her face on the TV screen above the counter. It was a replay of the earlier report, with a few new pictures.

Maggie caught her expression and turned off the TV. "Not quite the way to start a day, eh?" Maggie tried to joke with her.

"You have no idea!" Ellie slumped into a seat at the nearest table and looked at the cookies in the display case. "I'll have a double chocolate chip, please."

"Oh, Ellie." Maggie shook her head and reached for a carrot spice muffin instead. "We'll not let this blip mess up our health."

"*We* won't do anything! But *I* would like a double chocolate chip!"

"You'll hate me in the morning." Maggie set the carrot spice muffin in front of her and watched her friend reach for it.

"You're worse than..." Ellie didn't finish her comment.

"A mother?"

"You'd make a good mother," Ellie conceded.

Maggie sat across from her and drummed her fingers impatiently on the table.

"What?" Ellie asked, knowing full well what was coming her way.

"He's a very handsome man, Ellie."

"Indeed, he is."

"Have you given up on living?"

"I live."

"It's been a while, Ellie."

"It's been three years, ten months, seven days. Do you want to know the minutes?"

Maggie was quiet for a moment. "You're allowed to be happy."

"Mags, I am very content. My life is full. I've got my genealogy business, my family, my friends—who sometimes butt in where they're not welcome," she pointed out meaningfully.

"I'm not taking offense at that." Maggie poured her a cup of tea. "If someone doesn't push you back into the world of the living, you'll stay exactly the way you are."

"But I'm happy this way."

"But no man," Maggie reminded her.

"Why does everyone think you need a man to be happy? And I don't want a man."

"What if the man wants you?"

"I'm not ready for that."

"You do know when you talk about him, your eyes light up?"

"Who?" Ellie asked innocently.

"Now I'm getting pissed off at you, El. You know who. Quinn the magnificent."

"I never said he was magnificent."

"Then what is he?"

"Big. Cute."

"Cute?" Maggie snorted her tea.

"Okay. He's really handsome. But if you heard me before, I'm not looking for a guy right now."

"Why not?"

"It's too soon." Ellie stumbled on her answer, not quite believing it herself anymore.

Maggie pushed the point, "Almost four years is not—"

"That's enough!" Ellie sat back and folded her arms across her chest. Conversation over.

"For now," Maggie said.

Daphne walked in from the kitchen and flipped the TV back on. It flickered to life to show a clip of Ellie surrounded by the Walsh clan as she was being ushered into the back of the limo.

The camera returned to Diane. "While we can only imagine how Ms. McLellan feels after having lost her own family to a texting driver, we hope she knows how much everyone thanks her for saving the son of Owen Walsh." Diane's tone was dripping with false sincerity.

"I hope to have a follow-up interview with Ms. McLellan in the next day, though she appears to be keeping company with Owen Walsh's brother, Quinn, and has been hard to track down. Stay tuned for more on this story."

The news item changed, and Maggie turned down the sound.

Ellie stared at the TV. "Keeping company? Here we go!"

"They'll come here, won't they?" Maggie asked.

"Already have." Ellie got up and gathered her things. "One courageous idiot braved the wrath of Cali. Pretend you don't know me if they come snooping. I'm locking the gates."

"Maybe you need a bodyguard!"

Ellie looked at her friend, "Maybe I do."

"How's the renovation going?" came a soft voice from behind Ellie.

She turned to see Ruth, followed closely by Shirley, who looked anxious she would miss the conversation. Ellie hadn't seen the sisters when she came in but smiled at her favourite of the sisters, not that she should have favourites, but she had a soft spot for the quiet woman.

"Starts tomorrow." Ellie said.

"Who starts work on a Friday?" Shirley grumbled.

"Ellie's cousin, Pete, makes his own hours, and it's only a preliminary meeting," Ruth said as she gathered her light sweater tight like armour around her slim shoulders. She wasn't afraid of her sister, but Ellie knew Ruth preferred not to get on Shirley's bad side, and sometimes it paid to keep things to herself.

"How do you know that?" Shirley never liked being the second one to know anything.

Ruth looked sideways at Shirley, obviously wanting to say more to Ellie but not with her sister close by. Shirley had a way of overriding her younger sister. She was never far away and took charge of any conversation she could.

"Let's not bother Ellie now, Ruth." Shirley tried to take her sister's arm, not waiting for an answer to her question. But Ruth moved smoothly away. For an older woman, she still had her wits about her and was steady on her feet.

"It's not a bother, Shirley," Ellie said, not breaking eye contact with Ruth. "You're welcome to drop by any time and see what Pete's doing. Nothing drastic, just fixing the downstairs bathroom for now."

"Oh, no!" Shirley blurted. In a rush, she said, "We wouldn't dream of bothering you now. Your plate looks quite full." She nodded towards the TV. "Come along, Ruth, I have a meeting with Sarah from the Tiny House Haven Community. She wants me to spruce up the landscaping for her." This last was aimed at Ellie, with a slight toss of her head, as if showing that she was a busy person as well. This time she *did* grab her sister by the arm and almost manhandled her out the front door.

As they reached the exit, Ruth turned and winked at Ellie. That was their code. Ruth would be visiting Ellie in the next day or so when Shirley was off working with her landscaping clients. Shirley's new hobby had turned into a lucrative job, not only bringing money into the house, but giving Ruth time on her own.

Ellie winked back.

Chapter Nineteen

The late afternoon heat shimmered as Sophie opened the gate at the bottom of Ellie's driveway. This was their new routine: Ellie would unlock it, leaving it closed for Sophie to get in, and Sophie would lock it tight when she left.

Sophie needed an Ellie pep talk before heading back into town. She'd brought her class notes to study while she sat in the hospital chair by her mom's side, and with her final exam scheduled for Monday, she worried about being able to concentrate.

She parked in front of the house and stepped out to the sound of the low buzz of lazy insects. Everything else was still, the world felt heavy and slow. She slammed the car door, and the noise startled a flock of blue jays in a nearby tree. Running lightly up the few steps, she knocked once at the screen door and walked in.

Wet licks and a wagging tail from Cali greeted her enthusiastically.

"Down, you furry beast!" She gave the dog the required patting and then pushed Cali away. She slipped out of her shoes and walked barefoot over the cool tiles to the kitchen table where Ellie sat.

Ellie looked up and asked. "Tea?"

"Nothing, thanks." Sophie looked over the paperwork scattered on the table. She reached for a family chart and studied the names. Ellie watched Sophie's eyebrows go up then settle back down in defeat. "Here I am, the only child of Jenna and William. I guess this isn't right anymore."

"Sophie," Ellie murmured. A headache had started at the base of her neck and was now waltzing up along the right side of her head and into her temple. She blinked a few times, trying to moisten her dry eyes. Another night of tossing and noting the hours ticking by had added to her stress. "Until we have documentary evidence, you are still their daughter."

"But I might not be, and what if we never find this elusive documentary evidence?" Sophie made air quotes with her fingers.

"I'm looking at this like any other case." Ellie leaned across the table and pulled out a pad of paper. "These are the actions I believe we should follow to find the information we need."

"You sound so formal," Sophie said.

"I'm not taking this lightly." Ellie flipped back a few pages and took out her pen. "We're going to settle this. I've seen people who have complications with their family lines, not knowing who they are and what the truth is. It's something that follows them all their lives. We need to figure this out."

"And what if Mom is a..." Sophie took a deep breath, "What if she kidnapped me?"

"Highly unlikely and we'll deal with whatever we find." Ellie tapped her pen against the pad. "So where exactly were you born?"

"Not here in Montreal," Sophie said. "Dad was working on a project up north and they were living there."

"Up north is kind of vague."

"I'm sorry, Ellie." Sophie looked deflated. "They came home, here to Percyville, days after I was born, and honestly, I was never interested before now."

Ellie raised an eyebrow at her.

"I know, I know," Sophie said. "This stuff is everything to you, knowing where you're from, what time of day you were born, if it was snowing!"

"Really." Ellie squinted at the pain that hit her temple. "You don't have to make fun."

"Sorry." Sophie sighed. "I'm just trying to keep my spirits up. So, where do we start? How do we find out where they were living when I was born?"

"We could ask her, but—"

"No way!" Sophie threw up her arms as if warding off a blow. She went to the sink and filled a glass with water, taking a deep gulp before continuing. "The doctor said she has to stay quiet. A shock like this might kill her."

"Sophie," Ellie said, "the doctor also said she'll probably get better, but she might not."

"Yeah, but it won't be a final blow from me that does it!"

"Okay," Ellie said. "I'm going to see Aunt Norma tonight, she might know something."

Sophie's eyes widened in surprise. "Wow, that's fast."

"You want this mystery solved?"

"I guess so."

"You *guess* so?"

"I do and I don't." Sophie sank into a chair. "What happens if she *did* kidnap me? Would she go to jail? She couldn't survive that! God, I can't do that to her! Maybe I *don't* want to know."

"We'll find the truth." Ellie reached out and held her cousin's shaky hands. "And then decide what to do with that information. Don't assume the worst. "

"Yeah." Sophie nodded her head slowly.

"There's something else." Ellie looked her cousin in the eye. "Do you want to find out who you are, where your family is, and possibly meet them? Maybe there's a family, or mother or father, out there who is still missing you and never gave up hope."

"Geesh Louise." Sophie closed her eyes and held Ellie's hand tight. "I don't believe either of my parents cheated. But oh, God, can you imagine not knowing what happened to your child?"

Ellie's breath caught in her chest. She understood the pain that came with the death of a child. But never having closure over the disappearance of a child? Unbearable.

Sophie eyed Ellie's pad of paper. "Your list sure looks full."

"Just some scribbles, thoughts I've had. My mind map of how to attack this situation."

"Is there something I can do?"

"Go study," Ellie replied, using her mother voice. "That's the focus right now. When you're done on Monday, come back. Let me talk to Aunt Norma and we'll go from there. But for now, all you do is study and pass that exam. That's *your* focus."

"Ellie, I don't know if I can handle whatever truth you find. What if—"

"One step at a time, Sophie," Ellie said.

Sophie stared back at her with anxious eyes and repeated, "One step at a time."

Chapter Twenty

With a quick nap under her belt and her headache all but gone, Ellie rode her bike to Aunt Norma's after supper. The cooler air eased some of the heat of the day from her body. The muscles in her neck and shoulders relaxed, and she settled into the rhythm of pedaling along the back roads with a contented sigh.

She took a short detour to the small stone church that sat at the junction of the highway and the main road of her small town, Percyville. She leaned her bike against the wooden fence that surrounded the graveyard and took the bouquet of wild flowers from her basket and made her way among the tombstones. The ones she was looking for rested at the far end, close to the forest that formed a safe barrier around the back-boundary line.

She dropped down to her knees before the small grave markers and laid the flowers out across the two plots. Her husband, Adam and daughter, Winnifred. With a quick kiss from her fingertips to their headstones she stood up, brushed the newly mown grass off her knees and headed back to her bike.

Aunt Norma lived in the next town over, Morriston, which was connected by the main highway and a lovely series of backroads, lakes and hills. This night Ellie enjoyed the slow pedal down the dirt main road of Percyville, past old homes built too close to the road for today's standards, their porches filled with swings and padded armchairs, with multicoloured flowers overflowing their boxes beneath long tall windows. Overgrown backyards held old cars with waist-high wildflowers growing through the engines, almost burying them from view. She passed the oldest house in the town, now housing the library and historical society, with its ski jump Quebec-styled roof newly painted in bright red and its outdoor signage a work of art in hand carved wood.

The town commons was a huge circle of land that housed a bandstand for concerts and picnic tables. Rue des Pins, to the left, headed towards Aunt Norma's house, while the right curve, down Dawson Lane, led to the lake and beach a quarter mile down the road. This backed a fifty-acre apple orchard which in turn backed onto the creek, leading to Ellie's own property. She took the left turn and waved at Gabrielle and Guy Trudeau as they were closing up their roadside fresh fruit stand for the day. A few customers lingered, leaning against their cars and chatting amongst themselves, everyone waving back at Ellie as she passed. A clawfoot tub painted blue held a significant place of honour in their front yard as a shrine to Mother Mary. This area had been settled by the Scottish and Irish in the early 1800s, still remaining more English than French, but the intermingling of the two cultures created a connection between many, whether by marriage or blood, past or present.

When Aunt Norma's husband died, she'd sold her house in the city and bought a small cabin from an old friend. The garden was her haven, and she grew enough vegetables to get her through the long Quebec winters. She was an enthusiastic canner.

Ellie pulled into the winding driveway five minutes later, setting her bike against a wall under the portico. She'd been throwing out interview scenarios as she rode, how to approach this situation and what kind of questions might get her the answers she was looking for. She gathered her notebook from the front basket and headed to the door. She rang the bell, heard the shuffling of feet, and then the curtain on the door moved. Aunt Norma's tiny wrinkled face peered from behind and lit up when she saw Ellie. Three heavy locks clanked open, and the door swung wide.

"Ellie girl!" cried Norma as she pulled Ellie into her arms, which was a feat as Norma was even shorter than Ellie, and a strong wind could blow her away.

"Aunt Norma." Ellie returned the hug and took a breath of her aunt's hair. Lavender. She always smelled of lavender and it was a smell that brought back wonderful memories.

"Come in, come in." Norma disengaged and grabbed Ellie's hand to pull her into the house. She closed the door and locked it behind her, safety foremost in her mind from living in Montreal for years. She led the way into the living room and motioned to a large old chair by the window. "Can I get you something to drink, to eat?"

"Not a thing, Aunt Norma, thanks. I already ate," Ellie said.

Norma plopped herself down in a matching chair on the other side of a small table. She crossed her ankles, displaying her Yoda slippers. Norma had a fashion sense that made most people shake their heads. Comfort was her guide, but her clothes were always clean, fit her perfectly and somehow came out looking trendy. Today she was wearing red jeans and a blue plaid work shirt with a Game of Thrones t-shirt underneath. Her aunt loved science fiction and fantasy, and sent Ellie books when she finished them, including bold critiques.

"So, tell me how I can help you," she leaned in eagerly.

"I've been focusing my business on working with people and living relatives," Ellie began. "Teaching them how to tell their own stories, and I want to find out more about *my* living relatives while they're still around."

"You mean Jenna." Norma took a deep breath and sat back. "I've popped in to see her after visiting hours. Our secret." She winked at Ellie. "But she looked worse yesterday."

"The doctors said she had a minor heart attack, but she's holding her own."

"What a strange phrase that is," Norma mumbled, "'holding her own'. As if anyone else could carry this weight for her."

"So." Ellie brought her aunt's attention back to the present. "I want to know more about Aunt Jenna and prepare a biography for her and Sophie."

"I'd think you know more about her than most." Norma smiled at her.

"I know about her life when I lived with her, and a bit before, but not her younger years. I'm curious about the years around when Sophie was born. Where was she born?" Ellie asked as calmly as possible.

"Well, that's a good question." Norma leaned back and frowned, as if searching for a memory just out of reach. "She was born when Jenna and William lived up north. He was working on a special project for work—lasted almost a year."

"Do you remember the name of the town?" Ellie's fingers were crossed beneath her notebook.

"No, I don't remember that," Norma mused. "She wrote a lot of letters while she was there, mostly at the beginning, but when she became pregnant with Sophie and after, the letters became few and far between."

Norma seemed lost in thought and the memories didn't appear to be pleasant ones.

"Did the envelopes have a return address on them?" Ellie asked.

"You know what, Ellie," Norma's eyes sparkled with delight. "I still have those letters!"

"You're kidding me." Ellie's heart raced. "Can I see them?"

"Of course, you can, sweetheart, if I can remember where I put them." Norma got up and left the room.

Ellie walked over to the far wall and studied all the pictures of family members that Aunt Norma had arranged. Ellie had copies of most of them, but she made a mental note to ask her aunt for copies of those she didn't.

She could see the resemblance in the faces, the stances, the smiles and even the frowns. The picture of her, Sophie, and Aunt Norma, taken one hot summer day near high school graduation, held a prominent position on the wall. Their smiles were broad and the glasses of beer in their hands were frosty. Aunt Norma loved her beer, and she believed once the girls hit seventeen, a responsible glass was not unheard of. Aunt Jenna had not been pleased.

Ellie stepped closer and looked at the picture. With the rest of the family on the wall surrounding them, she could see clearly that Sophie didn't resemble anyone. Damn!

"Here we go, dear." Norma swooped into the room with a shoebox in her hands. "Come, sit." She patted the seat beside her on the couch and Ellie settled down beside her.

"I kept them all," Norma marvelled to herself. "I must have read them a dozen times during that year. I missed her you know. We were closest in age and I so envied her what I thought was a great adventure with her handsome young man."

She pulled out a packet of letters and undid the ribbon that held them together.

Ellie looked on in disappointment. "No envelopes?" she asked.

Norma flipped through the letters. "Sorry, no. Just the letters. Do you want to read them?"

"I'd love to." Ellie smiled at her. "Would you mind if I took them with me to read through later? There are quite a few."

"Not at all." Norma put the ribbon back around them, and handed them over to Ellie. "Now, tell me what's really going on."

Ellie felt like a deer in the headlights. What could she say? She'd never lied to any of her family before, but she wanted facts before sharing anything.

Norma leaned over and gently tapped Ellie's hand. "I had a feeling something had happened when Jenna was up north. I think it changed her. She never talked about it and seemed to be fine when she came back. She had the baby and all, but..."

"Aunt Norma," Ellie started slowly. "I'm trying to put things together and figure out where they were living and stuff like that, to add some colour to the picture."

Norma watched her closely and sat up straight and huffed to herself, deciding. "Fair enough, love," she said finally. "You always were an interesting little thing."

Ellie's eyebrows rose, but she kept her mouth shut. What did that mean?

"I won't push this," her aunt said. "But if you need help, you come to me. You've been through a lot these past years and it's okay to ask for help."

Ellie held up the letters in their ribbon. "This is me asking for help, Aunt Norma," she said with a shaky laugh. "I want to do this for Aunt Jenna and Sophie."

Norma got up and headed for the door. That's one thing about Aunt Norma, when she was done, she was done. Ellie grabbed her things and followed her. "But be prepared for what you find." Norma gathered Ellie into a good-bye hug. "Sometimes the past is better left in the past."

"Sounds like deep dark secrets." Ellie's stomach clenched as she tried to joke.

"All I'm saying is Jenna changed and whatever changed her happened when she was gone." She stared meaningfully at Ellie. "Just don't let it drag you down. You need the light, laughter, and someone to love you to pieces."

"Where did that come from?" Ellie asked in amazement.

"My heart." Her aunt held the door open for Ellie to walk through.

Ellie headed down the porch stairs and heard her aunt say softly, "And my heart's a funny thing." She turned to look, but the door had closed, and the locks were being bolted shut for the night.

Ellie stood on the walkway and watched as the moon started to crest. Not a sound to be heard except for a few birds flying between the tall trees. The breeze flit across her face and she loved how perfect this evening felt. How perfect it would be if she could bottle it up and keep this moment forever. And how terrible it was that her belief in finding the truth was so strong.

Chapter Twenty-One

Pete Dawson, Ellie's cousin on her father's side, was sitting on her porch when she got back from walking Cali after breakfast. He'd left his truck by the gate and walked up to the house. He had a binder, measuring tape, and a pocketful of pens, old school even though he was in his early thirties.

"Hey." Pete stood up and Ellie walked up a step to be level with him before giving him a bear hug. He'd always been her favourite cousin, mainly because he was quiet, but whip smart and witty. His smile showed blinding white teeth and his brown eyes crinkled at the edges. He was a happy person.

"Hey yourself." Ellie released him and stepped away.

He bent down to scratch Cali behind the ears and became her new best friend all over again. Pete had many things going for him, he was polite, great with animals—and cousins—but he looked exhausted. "Thanks for giving me the job, Ellie. That bulletin you put up around town has my phone ringing off the hook."

"You were in England a long time, Pete, people need to get to know you again. And really, this can wait till Monday." Ellie watched him with Cali. You could tell a lot about a person by how they treated animals and small children. At the moment Cali fit the bill of both for her and he had passed the test with flying colours.

"Today is for figuring out your plan for the work." Pete followed Ellie into the house and towards the downstairs bathroom. "I'll take measurements, we'll talk colours, and I'll go get supplies. Monday I'll start the real work."

For the next half hour Ellie explained what she wanted. They agreed on a price and approximate finish date, though Ellie assured him it wasn't a rush job.

She left Cali sitting at attention outside the bathroom as Pete started measuring. She headed outside to work on her garden in the cool of the early morning.

A bright yellow flash in the forest caught her eye, and she turned to see Ruth making her way towards her with a big grin on her face. Ruth waved with glee and adjusted her yellow sun hat as she left the woods and joined Ellie at the garden.

"How is it Shirley hasn't caught on to your visits after all this time?" Ellie gave Ruth a big gentle hug when the woman reached her.

"She wouldn't believe I could walk over here across the highway, and I like it that way." Ruth grabbed Ellie's hand and pulled her towards the woods. "Come on, dear, it's cooler in the forest."

Ruth was a walker. She lived in the Tiny House Haven community on the other side of the highway, behind the Cozy Corner Café, in amongst the trees. She loved walking around the community's lake and was a curious spectator as each new tiny home was built.

But she loved coming to visit Ellie more. She loved revisiting her childhood home, even though it was no longer hers. She wandered the woods for hours—if she could get away from Shirley.

"How is Pete doing?" Still holding Ellie's hand, Ruth set a slower pace. Ellie sometimes forgot Ruth was ninety-three because the older woman was so full of energy and enthusiasm. "He's a nice young man, isn't he?"

"Are you trying to matchmake someone with him, Ruth?"

"Not at all." Ruth acted surprised. "But I believe he has eyes for a red-haired lady."

Ellie thought for a minute and then snorted a laugh. "You mean Maggie? I knew it!"

"And that's between you and me and the trees in this forest." Ruth had a soft spot for Maggie and would allow no one, including Ellie, to give her a hard time.

The two women walked the acreage, lingering at favourite spots, and ending up resting on the bench by the pond as it was sheltered by the trees at this time of day.

"And how are *you* doing?" Ruth took two dark chocolate chip cookies out of her purse and offered one to Ellie. Ruth was aware of Ellie's weakness.

"I'm doing pretty good." Ellie lied as she bit into one of Maggie's wondrous concoctions.

"And I'm a twenty-year-old model," Ruth scoffed, making shooing motions with her hand. "Tell me the truth."

"You don't have to worry about me, Ruth." Ellie brushed the cookie crumbs from her shorts and stared off at the pond. It was a haven for wildlife, and she kept it wild so animals would be comfortable around it.

"I always worry about you, Ellie dear." Ruth patted her hand and watched a raven land by the water. "I know you're a strong woman, but these people, these nasty press people, well, I just..." Ruth was a mother hen with Ellie.

"I have that under control," Ellie said with more confidence than she felt. "Cali would never let them near me."

"Having a man in your life wouldn't hurt," Ruth said. "Someone to take care of these kinds of things."

"I love you Ruth, I truly do." Ellie smiled at her friend. "But I'll be fine."

They sat for a few more minutes in the morning's quiet. The sun was getting hotter, and the air was humming with insects.

"Time to go." Ruth stood up and stretched a kink out of her back. "Shirley will be home soon and I don't want her to get into a mood."

"You have every right to do what you want." Ellie walked with her towards the highway entrance, past the treehouse with the rung that needed fixing. She pushed aside the branches that hid the path from the highway and helped Ruth the last few steps.

Ruth turned to her before she walked across the road. "You do too and don't forget that."

With a wink and a wave, Ruth looked both ways and then hurried across to the Café. Ellie watched her until she disappeared around the side of the building and headed down the path that led to the Tiny House Haven.

Both women had wanted to say more, but each respected the other not to interfere. For now.

***

Pete had taken his measurements, sealed their contract with a handshake, and left mid-morning. Ellie had a good feeling about his ability to take her main floor bathroom into the twenty-first century. It was a project she and Adam had been planning on tackling before his death, but it took her almost four years to even think about moving forward on it.

Now she faced an unpleasant task. Time to call Uncle William's old company to see if they knew where he was living when Sophie was born.

Ellie wiped her hands on her shorts and picked up the phone. She hated calling strangers, almost as much as she dreaded public speaking, though she no longer felt like throwing up beforehand when those instances did occur. Small gains. She dialled the number.

"Sanders Welding," said a woman's voice "How can I help you?"

"Hi." Ellie's palms needed another wipe. "I'm not sure if you *can* help me, but I'm looking for information about a previous employee."

"Oh, I'm sorry," the woman said. "We don't give out information."

"Actually, it's not about him personally," Ellie rushed to reassure the woman before she hung up on her. "I'm trying to locate where my uncle worked thirty-five years ago."

"That's quite a way back, Miss. We don't have records that far back."

"He was involved in a special project for approximately a year," Ellie said. "I just want to find the name of the town."

"I'm not sure..."

"His name was William Keyes."

"Oh," said the woman, her tone softened. "Your uncle you say?"

"Yes. My name is Ellie McLellan and I'm putting together his family history for his wife, my aunt."

"Wouldn't his wife know the location?"

"Oh, no," Ellie fudged the truth. "I wanted to surprise her with a family history."

"Hmm, there might be someone who can help you," the woman said. "He's retired now, but I can give you his number."

"That would be great." Ellie grabbed a pen and paper to jot it down.

"Give me a second here." Ellie could hear shuffling noises in the background. "Here we go. Jason Turner. 514-555-3233. He was your uncle's supervisor at the time."

"I can't thank you enough, Ma'am," Ellie said. "This is a big help."

"Good luck then," the woman said before hanging up.

Ellie quickly dialled the number for Jason Turner before her courage totally disappeared for the day. A recorded message told her the number was no longer in service. Which could mean he didn't pay his bills, was no longer living there, or no longer living. She opened her laptop and went to the search engine for The Gazette obituary listings. She typed in Jason Turner and set it to check for the last year.

Sure enough, she got a hit. Jason Turner had passed away six months before. According to the obituary he had worked at Sanders Welding for over 45 years. He would definitely have known her uncle.

Dead end. For now.

Chapter Twenty-Two

Quinn had done some research of his own and found old news items about Ellie and the loss of her family. It mentioned the town they lived in, but nothing more. She was not listed in any phone directory, though she had a website offering her genealogical services, with an email address to contact her. With only the name of the town as a clue, he drove there and came upon the Cozy Corner Café. He knew that gathering places such as this could be fonts of information, and the detective in him was eager to put his rusty skills to the test.

He walked in and was overwhelmed by smells of fresh baked pastries and coffee. His stomach reminded him that he needed to fuel the tank.

"Can I help you?" A red-headed woman asked as he eased up to the counter. He looked around, taking in the pastry cases, the craft displays, the wood moulding on the walls, the floor to ceiling bookcases and the comfortable lounging chairs.

"Nice place," he said.

"Thank you." She was looking at him as if she recognized him from somewhere. "Are you looking for something in particular?"

"Actually, I'm looking for *someone* in particular." He turned and focused his blue eyes on her.

"And who would that be?" He sensed she was playing innocent.

"Ellie McLellan."

"And why would you be looking for her?"

"That's my business and hers."

The way the woman stared at him made him fidget. "She's a good friend of mine," she said.

"I can see that," he nodded. "I'd like to talk to her. Thank her again for saving my nephew."

The front door opened and a young couple came in and stood behind him in line.

"Will you be ordering something, sir?" She asked him.

"No, I..." he stepped aside so the couple could place their order. "I'll wait."

They chose their pastries and were soon handed their bagged baked goods. Quinn knew the counter lady was giving him the eye and his nerves made him shift from one foot to the other. He moved over to the bookcases and looked through the collection. He picked out a mystery, scanned the back cover then returned it to the shelf.

The couple were paying for their order when the TV ran another news item about Ellie. It gave further information about the incident and revealed her full family history and where she lived.

"Buggers!" The red head growled at the TV.

Quinn watched her anger build. The report focused on Ellie's husband and daughter who had died in a car accident because of a texting driver.

"That explains a lot," he muttered, adding that piece of information to his data base.

"What does that mean?" Her eyes narrowed to slits. Quinn took a step back.

"I didn't understand why she was so upset when I was on the phone...." He didn't get to finish.

"Devil on a broomstick!" Her hand slammed down on the counter, rattling some cups. "That girl has been through hell, and I'll not have it happen again."

"Look, I just need to make sure she's okay," Quinn said firmly, refusing to back down from her anger.

"And why would that be important to you? She's a total stranger."

It stunned Quinn quiet. "I don't know." He blinked like a tired owl, suddenly unsure of himself. "It just is."

"You don't know why?"

"Hey, if you're not going to help me, that's fine." His hands raised in defeat, he backed away.

She stared at him long and hard and then held out her hand, which he took and shook, surprised. "I'm Maggie. I'll help you all right, but if you harm her in any way, you'll be dealing with me." She poured a coffee and added sugar and milk on the side.

"I know I wouldn't want to deal with you."

"Indeed, you would not," she considered her next move and dove in. "She lives down the road at the bottom of the hill. There's no address or post box, just a chained fence. It'll be locked so you'll have to walk up."

"Thank you." Quinn turned to go.

"Wait." Her voice had softened and stopped him in his tracks. "You'll tell her I said it was okay. She'll understand." She put two large blueberry muffins in a bag with the coffee.

"I didn't realize I needed your approval." He didn't know whether to laugh or be angry.

"Oh, yes, approval definitely. She's like my sister, blood without being kin."

"Fair enough. And I have no intention of hurting her." Why he felt the need to reassure this woman, he had no idea. But her direct stare scared the heck out of him.

"I realize that, but she might not." Maggie grinned, obviously enjoying the effect she was having on him. "Here." She passed him the bag. "Coffee for you and muffins for you both. I doubt she'll have eaten much with all this going on."

"Thanks." He took the bag and opened the door.

"Don't thank me yet." He heard her laugh as he walked out.

Chapter Twenty-Three

Ellie changed into shorts and a t-shirt, as the temperature had been rising throughout the morning. She kept her wardrobe sparse, too many decisions were a waste of time. She strolled into the kitchen and opened the fridge to find something to eat. Lunch was the furthest thing from her mind, and she closed the door in defeat. She felt restless, anxious, and terribly thirsty. After grabbing a glass of water, she cleaned and filled Cali's water bowl.

Ellie needed to keep herself busy, a remnant of the aftermath of losing her family. She could focus on one thing at a time and keep her gerbil wheel of a mind in check. There were good days and bad days, and she knew today would be a challenge. Determined not to waste another minute, she sat at the kitchen table and fired up her computer. There was a blog post due for her Gene Guru website and she didn't want to disappoint her loyal readers.

Ellie had discovered genealogy when her grandfather had given her a box of family photos and a gold signet ring that belonged to his grandmother. But before they could dive into putting names to the faces, he passed away. That memory ached inside her. He had been a quiet man, had fought in the first horrible war, and played the piano like a dream. She regretted not asking the thousands of questions she now had.

Memories made her happy, and no one could take them away from her.

Her fingers flew across the keyboard as she outlined the series of posts she would write over the coming months. She broke the topics into stages, exercises, tips, and photos, and jotted down notes about how she would explain each segment. When the outline was complete and saved, she stretched her arms up and out, hearing a crack in her neck.

She needed to get outside for sunshine and exercise. It always helped.

Cali leapt up as soon as Ellie pushed back her chair, and when the door opened, she dashed ahead onto the path to the field. Playtime. Ellie tossed Cali's favorite toy until the dog fell in a heap at her feet, tongue hanging out, exhausted.

Ellie rubbed the dog's head then sank onto the wide bench at the edge of the field near the pond, swinging her legs up. The warmth of the wood seeped through her t-shirt as she stretched out full. She closed her eyes, took a deep calming breath and let it ease from her lungs.

Cali ran off to the water where she drank enough to fill a camel's hump before returning to sprawl beneath the bench, always by Ellie's side. The birds above danced from one branch to another, chattering to each other. A pileated woodpecker landed in a tree nearby and started his tapping. The sound was mesmerizing, and it lulled Ellie to sleep.

***

Quinn pulled off the highway onto Ellie's road and parked under a clump of trees, making sure his vehicle was hidden from passing cars. He got out and rattled the lock on the gate. Shut tight. Not much security, but better than nothing. He worried it wouldn't deter any of the paparazzi he knew, and he was determined to discuss it with Ellie.

He started to squeeze through the gate as a car slowed and pulled off the highway into the driveway. It stopped dead at the bottom, its engine idling. Quinn eyed the driver, then walked towards him. The man inside hesitated, then backed the car up, turned around, and took off.

Quinn tore his sunglasses off to get a better look at the license plate, but the car was gone.

He waited until he was sure it wouldn't return, then made his way through the gate and up the hill, following the road into the trees.

Quinn took his time, checking out the lay of the land. The woods were quiet. There were small paths leading off in different directions, while other areas were dark with dense growth. The air was cooler under the canopy and he welcomed the change.

He passed a playground with a swing swaying in the breeze. A mini basketball court stood empty, weeds growing through the gravel, the basket netting ripped and dirty. A creek to his right meandered under the road and on through the woods to his left.

He turned a corner and saw a large rust-red barn, its wide doors gaping, dust motes floating in the sunlight. He looked in as he passed. Empty.

Quinn continued on and found an old, two-story house, freshly painted white with deep green window trim. The porch boasted a hanging swing, rubber boots, and various odds and ends.

No one answered his knock on the front door, and he peered through the screen. Nothing moved inside except the curtains in the kitchen window. He looked around and felt a deep calm from everything he'd seen of the farm so far. Behind the house were the beginnings of a garden, and to the side a healthy apple orchard. The sound of a single dog bark in the distance drew his attention, and he headed towards it.

The path by the barn led him to Ellie, stretched out on a bench, fast asleep. Cali saw him and dashed up to greet him. How Ellie had slept through the dog's bark was a testament to how tired she must be. But Cali's dancing around Quinn for a pat made enough noise to break through to her. She slowly opened her eyes, trying to situate herself, and turned her head.

She locked eyes with Quinn and, startled, swung her feet off the bench, and sat up. His sudden appearance had obviously unnerved her.

"Hey," he said.

"Hey," she replied sheepishly. "How'd you find me?"

He held up the bag of muffins and coffee. "She said it was okay and thought you might be hungry."

Ellie smiled and motioned to the bench. "In the house or out here?"

"Pardon?" he sputtered.

"Do you want to eat the muffins out here or in the house?" His reaction seemed to amuse her.

"Here's good." He joined her on the bench. "This is an amazing spot." He looked admiringly around at the open field surrounded by trees, the pond big enough for swimming, and the blue sky with a handful of fluffy clouds slowly passing.

"My refuge." She snagged the bag from him, opened it and pulled out a muffin. Holding it to her nose she inhaled deeply and moaned, "This is heaven."

"The food or the land?" He laughed.

"Right now? Both." She handed him the other muffin and took a huge bite out of hers.

"I was wondering how you were doing." He focused on taking off a piece of his muffin and popping it in his mouth.

"I'm fine, how about you?"

He could tell she did not want to have this conversation with him, at all. But there was the matter of her totally inadequate gate needing to be discussed. "Did you catch the news?" he ventured, taking another bite.

"Yup." She opened his coffee—he didn't protest—and spiked it with two sugars. "Same shit, different day, and excuse my language."

"We don't have to talk about it if you don't want to."

"Great! Don't want to." She took a sip of the coffee and leaned back against the sun-heated rock wall behind the bench. "So, what really brings you here?"

"In the neighbourhood."

"Right." She gave him the side-eye.

"I wanted to see you again, simple." He glanced at her. The sun was in her face and her eyes sparkled. The streak of gray that flew from her left temple to her shoulder fascinated him. She abruptly pulled an elastic out of her pocket and tied her hair back. She'd noticed his scrutiny and was uncomfortable—and that was the last thing he wanted her to feel.

She caught his expression. "Hot, huh?"

He nodded. They sat in silence. The coffee was drunk, and the muffins eaten. Restlessly Ellie looked into the bag, maybe hoping for one more. To break the silence, which was growing painfully long, he announced, "You're right," and rolled up his muffin paper "They *are* heaven."

"Maggie has many talents." Ellie smiled. "Baking is one of them. You didn't have a coffee?"

"It's way too hot," he lied, fighting a grin. But he *was* thirsty.

"What time is it?" She stood up and gathered the remnants of their snack.

He glanced at his watch. "Three-thirty."

"Sounds like beer time to me!" She headed towards the house then stopped. "Do you drink beer?"

"Depends on what kind." He followed her. Anything wet at this point would be a blessing.

"Stella?"

"That's the kind." He walked beside her. Something wet licked his fingers, and he laughed as Cali cleaned the muffin crumbs from his hand.

"She's not usually this friendly with strangers." Ellie watched with obvious disappointment as her "guard dog" became a wimpy puppy when Quinn scratched her behind the ears.

"Guess I'm not a stranger," he said quietly.

She had no quick-witted reply.

Chapter Twenty-Four

Ellie pulled two Stellas from the fridge and held them up. "Glass?"

"No thanks. Bottle's fine." Quinn toured the living room, checking out the various photographs. A grouping near the fireplace caught his eye. It was of Ellie, a man and a young girl, arms wrapped around each other on a beach, all grinning and soaking wet. The family she had lost.

Ellie saw him studying the pictures and a quiver of unease stole through her. And when he hesitated before the collection of romance novels on her shelves she squirmed in embarrassment. "That's my husband, Adam and my daughter, Winnifred, or Winnie."

"You look very happy."

"We were." The usual gut-wrenching pain was absent. Instead a soft ache flowed through her.

"I was married for a while." He turned to her and shrugged his shoulders. "Turns out she didn't want a family and I did."

She had heard every word he said but would need time to process his openness.

"So, what's the *real* reason you're here?" She poured herself a glass of beer and brought his bottle to the kitchen table and sat down. Redirection was one of her superpowers, or as Maggie would call it, defense mechanisms, and right now she needed it.

He pulled himself away from the books and joined her. He took a long swallow of the beer. "Lauren asked me to find you. We *both* wanted to make sure you're okay."

"I'm fine, as you can see." She motioned with her hands around the house. "All quiet."

The telephone's sharp ring broke through the peace and she frowned before reaching to pick it up. "Hello." Ellie hesitated, looked at Quinn and said, "You've got the wrong number."

She hung up but it rang again within seconds.

"Do you want me to take this?" he offered.

"Thanks, but they won't stop." She picked up the receiver.

He motioned to her to hand it to him anyways, wanting to save her from the onslaught to come. She wished she could let him handle this, but if she didn't make her own stand now, the press would never leave her alone.

"Look," she said to the caller. "I've got nothing to say." She listened to the person for a minute and replied, "I'd think twice about that if I were you. I have a guard dog and it's very protective."

Quinn kept his hand out, but Ellie raised an eyebrow at him and shook her head.

"Why *wouldn't* I sic my dog on you?" she asked the caller calmly, as if explaining important instructions. "If you're on my property without my permission, you are not welcome. Read the sign at the bottom of the road. You've been warned."

She hung up the phone with exaggerated calm, turned back to Quinn, picked up her glass and took a good long gulp. She gave him a tight smile and let the silence grow.

"So," he began, "does that happen often?"

"Hasn't happened since..." She trailed off, refusing to get into specifics.

"You handled it well."

"My mom always said you can get more with sugar than with vinegar. But throw in a mean looking dog who will protect me, and it's a win-win for me." As if knowing they were talking about her, Cali drew closer, laying her head in Ellie's lap, sensing her disquiet.

Quinn took a swig of his beer and eyed the dog. "I wouldn't want to be on the wrong end of her."

"As long as *I* like you, *she* likes you," Ellie said.

"And do you like me?"

"I don't really know you, but you're in my house, sitting at my table, drinking my beer, so for now, you're in."

"I'll take it." He seemed quite pleased with her comment.

"So, tell me more about your bodyguard business," she asked. "Do you do it often?" Her gaze brushed over the scar, not stopping to stare but definitely wondering.

"I do it for Owen and Lauren, usually when they're working near Montreal. I went to the Bahamas with them once, but it turned out they were getting me to take a break in a sunny place." He made air quotes with his fingers around the sunny place comment.

"They don't think you relax enough?"

"They don't think I relax at all."

"Do you?"

His eyes didn't waver from hers. "Sure." He smiled suddenly. "I make furniture in my garage."

"Really?" She should have known by how rough his palms were that he worked with his hands in some way. And remembering the texture of his hands made her realize she was drifting and letting him get too close. She couldn't afford to let anyone get too close to her family problems right now, and that meant Quinn as well.

"What?" He'd sensed her change of mood. How did he do that?

"Nothing," she muttered. "Just remembered I have work to do."

"Are you throwing me out?" He tried for light and breezy, but she could see he was awkward. He got up and pushed his chair in.

"No," she stammered. "I—"

"No worries," he assured her. "I have to get back to town." He stopped at the front door and turned. She almost ran into his broad back and had to reach out a hand to steady herself.

He took her outstretched hand in his and held it still. And then he shook it.

She let out a nervous laugh.

"Would you like to go to dinner with me tomorrow night?" he asked. She felt as surprised as he looked for having asked. She now understood how a deer in the headlights felt.

"Oh, I don't do dinners." She tried to pull her hand out of his.

"Just dinner, nothing more, nothing less." He let her hand slip through his fingers. "I've got a favourite Italian restaurant and I'd rather not go alone. And you could drop by and see your aunt while you're in town."

"You've got it all worked out." She wasn't sure if she liked that or not.

"I've got nothing worked out." He shook his head. "I'm winging it here. Give a guy a break."

Why was she making this so hard on both of them? She made one of the few spontaneous decisions of her life and hoped she wouldn't regret it. "Okay, fine. I'd love to."

"Great." His grin transformed his rugged face into that of a kid anticipating Christmas. "Should I pick you up?"

"Gosh, no!" she said with a laugh. "That's a long drive. I'll meet you there and I like your idea of seeing Aunt Jenna while I'm nearby."

"Here's the address." He took out his phone and entered the information. "Sent it—it's on your phone." He started to leave then stopped once more. His face had gone bodyguard serious. "When I parked down at the bottom, by the gate, another car pulled in behind me."

She froze. "Did anyone get out?"

"No." He was watching her closely now. "I walked towards him and he took off."

"It's going to get worse." She sighed. "I was hoping they wouldn't identify me so quickly."

"This is what they do."

"Yup, that's the truth." She managed a weak smile. "Thanks for warning me."

"That lock on the gate is not much of a deterrent and if I can get through the bars... Do you have someone who can come and stay with you?"

"I'll be fine, Quinn. It means they can't drive up. And I've got Cali, and you'd be shocked at how good she is at scaring people!"

"If I didn't understand dogs, I'd agree with you."

"Yes, well, you were a surprise reaction." It unnerved her how fast her stranger-wary Cali had taken to Quinn.

"It's a gift," he said. Right on cue Cali nudged his hand with her wet nose, angling her eyes up as if agreeing with his comment.

"She knows threats," Ellie asserted. "She can hear it in my voice."

"Fair enough." He patted Cali's head. "Call me if you need me. Anytime."

They looked at each other and Ellie felt safe and not alone for the first time in years. With a stranger no less. A stranger who made her want to run her fingers through his hair. Oh, this might not be good at all. She moved toward the door. "So, I'm kicking you out now because I have things to do." She pulled the door open.

"Understood." Quinn didn't even try to hide his grin.

She leaned against the door and jammed her hands into her pockets to still their trembling. She knew he felt the chemistry between them but did either of them want any complications right now? Probably not. Could they fight it? Did she want to?

"Thanks for the beer." Quinn stood before of her.

He was close, she could reach out and touch him. She said, "My pleasure," and shifted back on her feet. Was that a slight shudder? It certainly wasn't cold out.

"I'll see you tomorrow night then." He stepped past her out on the porch. She let out a quiet breath as the screen door closed gently.

It was easier to speak with something between them, easier not to reach out and spook the other. "See you then," Ellie called out as he moved off the balcony.

He turned and waved at her and she watched him until he disappeared around the corner of the road. She grinned in delight. What was wrong with her? She was actually looking forward to their dinner date!

Chapter Twenty-Five

S aturday was Ellie's favourite day because she forced herself to slow down and relax. Cali knew it was Saturday too because it was special treat day.

As Ellie ran her genealogy business from home, she tried to keep her life on a regular schedule, even on weekends. Kind of like before, when she had a family to remind her days off were to be cherished and enjoyed.

With her morning household chores done, and her walk through the acres completed with Cali by her side, she curled up on her comfy couch with a cup of Earl Grey tea on the side table. The windows were open and the fragrance from the flowers in her garden blew in on the gentle morning breeze.

Ellie picked up the box of letters her Aunt Norma had given her and settled back with them in her lap. Cali rubbed up against her leg, received her head pat, then sank to the floor in front of the couch to nap with a satisfied groan.

The letters had no individual envelopes but were tied by a faded red and white ribbon, the kind you might see at the bottom of older kitchen curtains. Ellie picked through the letters, recognizing Aunt Jenna's handwriting.

The first was dated July 2nd, 1990.

"*Dearest Norma.*

I finished unpacking, what little unpacking there was. Mostly hanging up clothes. The house is already furnished, even sheets and towels and plates and cups! You can't believe how tired I am and all I did was put our clothes away.

Will started his new job today, and he was a bit nervous. I believe living here for a while will be good for us. I have to go out later and get more groceries. The company was kind enough to set up the staples for us, but there's so much to buy. Will told me to get whatever I need.

The store is just down the road so I can walk there. Everything is small here, the house, the town, the store. But the house is bright and clean. I like that. Hopefully not too much dusting to do! We both know how much I loved that when we were young (that's a joke).

There's a doctor nearby as well and he delivers babies. Four months to go. Will is worried I'll overdo it. Trust me, I won't. I nap each day. It's such a decadent thing to do, but my body is telling me to rest, so rest I will. I've been walking every day, too. You know how much I love that (that's not a joke!). I'll explore the whole place and draw a map for you. It may not be as good as what you're used to, but it will keep me busy.

I think Will is concerned that I won't be happy here. Already I feel a weight off my shoulders. I wanted alone time. Just us for a while.

I have to go now, darling Norma. I am happy and looking forward to seeing what this little town has to offer.

Your loving sister, Jenna."

The next letter Ellie opened was dated a week later.

"Dearest Norma.

Hope all is well with you back home. Things are going along slowly. I've met a few people but they do keep to themselves. My French isn't that bad, and I speak it as much as I can. There is an equal number of English speakers, and everyone gets along quite nicely.

The store is quaint and has all the necessities. I've been doing a lot of baking and cooking. Some days I'm too tired to do much of anything.

Have been walking every day, well, almost every day. When the weather is nice. The town is bigger than I thought. I've managed to walk to one end and see the houses and stores along the way. There are smaller roads that branch off the main road. Some go up into the hills. I don't know if I'll get that far before the baby is born though.

They have a library here, Norma! I'm so happy. It doesn't cost much, and they have a good selection. I like to curl up in the afternoon with a book and read. Then usually fall asleep! Will came home the other day, and I hadn't even started supper. He joked about it and I managed to put something quick together. You were right, I was blessed to find him.

Must go, love to all, Jenna."

The following letter was over a month later. The tone was changing.

"Dearest Norma.

Wish I was home. I know, what a horrible thing to say. I was so full of hope and excitement when we first came here. Will is working late these days. His job is taking up most of his time, and since he has a specialty knowledge they require, he has to accept the hours. But we knew this before we came and I'm just feeling sorry for myself.

I hate to say it but I'm lonely. The women here are nice but they don't take to making friends easy. There's one woman at the library who is quite lovely and we sit and talk every week. But I have no one to talk to otherwise.

Sorry for being down, but I do miss everyone. I'm sure once the baby is here, I'll have so much to do that I won't have a minute to be lonely. Just tired!

Need to nap, darling Norma. Love to all."

Two months later, the letter was short and to the point.

"Dearest Norma. The baby is big and I'm having trouble sleeping. Walking is harder, and the weather is not helping. I do try to be positive about it though. I have no energy for writing much, I do apologize. Two more weeks and I'll have a baby in my arms. It is such a quiet thing these days. It must be gathering its strength for the big moment! I can't wait to bring the little one home to the family. Love to all."

The last letter was different.

"Dearest Norma. I am days away from delivering and the most wonderful thing has happened. I met a lovely girl named Helen at the hospital a couple of weeks ago. We were both there for check-ups and it looks like we may deliver around the same time. She is staying at Miss Petersen's Boarding House until she has her baby. I feel

116

bad for her because within days of her and her husband arriving in town he headed north to work, and now she hasn't heard from him for a few weeks. I know she's worried and I thank God I see Will every night, even if he's too tired some nights to hold a conversation. At least we can hold hands in bed and fall asleep together. She's very quiet but has a strength in her that I gravitate to. Will is walking in the door. Must go. Love to all."

That was the last letter. From the date on it, Ellie knew Sophie had been born two days later. As Ellie put the letters back in the box, her fingers touched something inside the edge.

She reached in and pulled out a black-and-white picture. It showed Aunt Jenna and another young woman. Both were pregnant and beaming for the camera. The young woman looked tired; Aunt Jenna glowed.

Ellie turned the picture over and on the back was written, *Jenna and Helen, 1990.*

She flipped the picture back over and looked at it more closely. The two women were standing in front of a wooden fence. Behind them was a grassy field as far as the camera eye could see. To the right was an old-style wooden bulletin board. There was a name carved into the wood across the top, but Ellie couldn't make it out.

She went to the drawer by the sink, pulled out a magnifying glass and held the picture up to the light of the window. Ellie stared at it through the magnifying glass and tried to make out the words.

Only the last five letters of the actual name were legible. It read *"ights Park".* This could be where Aunt Jenna had been staying when she gave birth.

Feeling a kernel of excitement flitter across her back, Ellie sat at the table and turned on her computer. She would start with a concrete name. She typed in the name "Miss Petersen's Boarding House" and there was one response. The business had closed in the mid-nineties, in the town of Steller Heights.

Ellie entered Steller Heights into the browser and a whole page of information opened in front of her. She expanded the map that went with the town name and checked out its location. It was a short distance above Mt. Laurier. According to the web page, Steller Heights had almost died out when the local mine closed.

Ellie continued to read. The founder of the town was Matthew Steller, and the park had been named after him. She scrolled through the rest of the information and came to a longer description of Miss Petersen's Boarding House. Back in the sixties through nineties, it was where a lot of the mine workers stayed. Some had lived with various families in the town, but most used the boarding house.

Ellie leaned back in her seat and looked at the picture again. From the information in Aunt Jenna's letter, this must be the boarding house Helen had been living at. But was it just a coincidence?

Only one way to find out. She'd go to Steller Heights herself.

But she'd have to sit on this until Monday when Sophie came up. While Ellie's curiosity was spiked, she refused to tell her cousin anything that would make Sophie lose focus and fail her exam. Sophie was heading for medical school and everyone knew she'd be an amazing doctor.

Besides, Ellie was thankful for the reprieve. She could put this burden down for a short while and wait for Sophie, and they could figure out a plan together.

While part of her wanted to run from her findings, she knew that patience in waiting to solve a mystery was not one of her virtues.

Chapter Twenty-Six

Ellie's knapsack was heavy on her back as she walked into the Cozy Corner Café that afternoon. She waved to Maggie at the counter but didn't stop for a chat as she was late for her seniors' group, and she hated wasting their time.

The first face she saw in the book corner was Ruth. She was sitting quietly at the table, hands folded on a pad of paper, pen by the side. She smiled at Ellie and the whole room brightened. There was something about Ruth that always raised Ellie's spirits. She loved to sit with the older woman, and they could do so for hours, sometimes in total quiet, and agree it had been a wonderful visit.

"Sorry, all." Ellie dropped her bag on the table and looked at her group. "I was doing research this morning and the time just flew by."

"That's happened to me, a lot," Doreen piped up. She pulled out a bright red ball of wool and started a new creation, her needles clicking softly.

"Weren't sure you'd turn up." Shirley wasn't a fan of genealogy but believed she had to go with her sister wherever she went, sure that Ruth would be unable to cope on her own.

"You know me better than that, Shirley." Ellie plastered a smile on her face for a woman who tested her patience more often than not. "I'd never let you guys down."

"Did you bring it?" asked a soft voice to Ellie's right. Ellie turned to Tess. The woman's eyes sparkled and her hands clutched an envelope full of pictures, slides and negatives.

"I certainly did." Ellie pulled out a small machine from her knapsack and placed it on the table. "The scanner," she said as if unveiling a holy relic.

Tess let out a gasp. "Oh, I don't know how that's going to work at all." She clutched her envelope of pictures as if to guard its precious contents against a mechanical beast.

"Wait till you see what it can do," Ellie said. "Did everyone bring at least one slide or negative?" She looked around.

They all held up their envelopes of history, some had single thin envelopes and others had large brown ones filled to bursting with treasures.

"I'll show everyone how to do this for one negative and one slide." Ellie set the machine on the table.

"Could it damage them?" Ruth's eyes were round with worry.

"Not at all," Ellie said. "Ruth, would you like to start?"

"Oh…" Ruth hunched her shoulders and frowned.

"I'll do it." Phil opened his envelope and took out a negative. He handed it to Ellie carefully by the sides. "I haven't seen this face in years! I can't find the actual photo and would love a printed copy."

"You can do that?" Hope shone from Ruth's eyes.

"Indeed, you can." Ellie took the slide from Phil and inserted it into the scanner. "Now I'll show you the easy way, using the defaults of the machine. If, and when, you buy one, you can play with it to get the quality you want for each picture."

Everyone leaned forward in their seats to watch what she was doing. For the next few minutes Ellie took them through the process of scanning and saving pictures onto an SD memory card. "The picture shows up on the image display and it's saved digitally for you." Ellie smiled at Phil.

Phil pushed his glasses up further on his nose and looked down at the image in the viewfinder, transfixed. "That's my Ma." He smiled up at everyone. "This is black and white, but she had blue eyes, look, you can see how pale they were!"

"She was a beauty, Phil." Ruth peered over his shoulder to look at his mother then took a negative out of her own envelope so carefully that it hurt Ellie's heart. She handed it to Ellie. "This one, please."

Ellie handed Phil back his slide and then placed Ruth's negative in the scanner. When the picture showed up in the viewer Ruth gasped and put her hand to her chest.

"What is it?" Shirley moved forward to peer at the image. "Oh, Ruth, where did you get that?" She sounded angry and disturbed at the same time.

"It's mine." Ruth hadn't taken her eyes off the image of a young man in uniform. "It's Jeremy."

"I know who it is," Shirley said sharply. "I thought you let go of that years ago."

"Old boyfriend, Ruth?" Lennie joked.

"Very handsome." Tess admired the young man.

"Yes, he was," Ruth whispered.

"Did you bring a memory card, Ruth?" Ellie asked her.

"No." Ruth looked heartbroken. She refused to look at her sister, likely knowing the scowl Shirley would be directing her way. "Shirley forgot to get one."

"I have an extra one." Ellie ignored the tension between the sisters and put a memory card in the machine and saved the picture. "Here you go. You can open it on your computer and make copies or a print."

Ruth took the memory card and negative from Ellie, replacing them both gently in the envelope and back in her purse. Shirley watched her and shook her head, but Ruth refused to return her sister's stare.

The tension was so obvious Ellie had to break up the uncomfortable atmosphere. "Okay, that's two of you. Who's next?"

For the next hour, they all got to use the scanner and save their images. Each picture had brought forth a story and warm memories, some tears, and lots of laughter.

As Ellie put the machine away, Maggie placed a big pot of tea with cups on the table. She placed a plate of fresh-baked cookies beside them and smiled at the moans of pleasure the men were making. "Now, Phil," she chided the eldest member of the group. "Only one cup, and you know why."

"Because he'll be visiting the loo every half hour!" Lennie laughed. Phil gave him the evil eye. "I'm kidding, Phil, I have the same problem," Lennie assured him. "I watch more late-night TV than I knew even existed!"

Everyone helped themselves to tea and cookies and sat back to talk. They looked forward to these meetings, getting out of the house, chatting and gossiping, and relaxing with people who understood what they were going through in their later years.

Ellie went to the counter for napkins and Ruth stepped up beside her. "Are you okay, Ruth?" Ellie asked her.

"I was wondering..." Ruth began, then hesitated. Whatever the woman wanted to share, it appeared stuck inside her.

"Ruth!" came the loud voice of her sister. "I think we should be going."

"She'll be with you in a minute," Ellie answered, not liking the way Shirley took over everything in her sister's life. Shirley looked taken aback by Ellie's curt response and she stayed where she was. Ellie noticed her eyes never left Ruth. Ellie frowned and asked, "Is there something wrong, Ruth?" She was ready to guard this tiny woman with her own life.

"Maybe," Ruth stared at her and took another deep breath. "Have you found anything in the house since you've been there?"

"Like what?"

"Oh, anything we might have left behind." Ruth took a quick glance at her sister. Shirley held a cup of tea in her hand but wasn't drinking. She caught Ruth's eye but Ruth turned away. "Like pictures or documents or ... letters." The last word was whispered between dry lips, and Ruth's knuckles turned white as she gripped the countertop.

"Nothing yet, Ruth, but I'll let you both know if something turns up."

"Oh, no!" Ruth grabbed Ellie's arm. "Just *me*—just *tell me* if you find anything. *Please.*"

Shirley headed their way when Ruth's voice rose in alarm.

"Of course, Ruth," Ellie assured her quietly. "Only you."

"And I can't tell you how much this newfangled machine is going to help," Ruth blurted out as Shirley reached her side. "I'm sure I'll have a lot of fun with it."

"I didn't say we would buy one." Shirley shook her head.

"I wasn't aware I had to ask you for permission." The sisters stood together, still as statues, Shirley surprised by Ruth's answer and Ruth obviously delighted by her own outburst.

Ruth gave Ellie a smile, called goodbye to the others and walked out the front door. This caught Shirley off guard, and she shook herself into action, calling goodbye to everyone before scurrying after her sister.

"What happened?" Maggie asked.

"I'm not sure," Ellie murmured, watching through the window as Ruth climbed into the car and waved at her. "But I like it."

Chapter Twenty-Seven

Ellie dashed into the Italian restaurant, out of breath. It had taken her half an hour to pick her outfit for the night and another twenty minutes to find the dressy shoes packed away in a box in the attic.

She was a few minutes late, her stomach had butterflies, and she wanted to turn around and bolt. But she hesitated inside the front door, took a few calming deep breaths and let her eyes sweep the tables inside.

There he was.

Quinn raised his arm to draw her attention and gave her a huge smile when she caught his eye. She smiled back, her shoulders relaxing.

The Maître D, experienced and efficient, noticed their interaction, and with old-world manners led her to Quinn's table. Quinn got to her chair before him and pulled it out for her.

People were staring.

She hated being stared at and refused to look around as she took her seat. Quinn's hand rested on her chair for a moment as he helped push it in. It brushed her back, and the heat was a surprising comfort.

"You look great." He sat across from her, crinkles appearing at his eyes from his boyish grin.

"Thank you." She took her napkin off the table, flipped it open and placed it on her lap. Quinn did the same.

"I thought I'd be late." He leaned forward on his elbows.

"Me too!"

"Couldn't decide what to wear," he joked.

"Me too!"

"I think you'd look great in anything. Everyone's staring at you."

She wasn't used to compliments and tried to redirect his attention. "Maybe they're staring at *you*. Do you get that often?"

"It's part of the deal," he said. "People usually think Owen and I are twins. I don't see it."

"Really?" Ellie watched two women at a nearby table whispering and nudging one another. She turned back to Quinn. "Do they..."

"Hi," one of the women had moved so quickly to their table it startled Ellie. "Could I have your autograph?"

"I'm flattered," Quinn said, "but I'm not Owen Walsh."

"Oh, but you are!" The woman made a flapping motion with her hand. "I've seen all your movies! I'd know your face anywhere!"

"I'm sorry, Ma'am." He smiled at her. "Not me. I get that a lot."

"I am so sorry." The woman's face turned pink as she finally noticed his scar and stepped away. "Sorry for bothering you both." She crept back to her seat, whispered with her friend, and continued stealing glances at him.

"That must get annoying." Ellie was amused but Quinn did not look happy.

"You have no idea. But I have to be nice because they usually discover I'm Owen's brother. Once that happens, it's only a matter of time."

The Maître D stopped by the table and handed them each a menu.

"Thank you." Ellie smiled at the older man. He reminded her of Uncle William, which reminded her of Aunt Jenna and what may lay ahead. She shook her head to dislodge the thoughts.

"Sir." The Maître D handed Quinn the wine list. Quinn raised his eyebrows at Ellie. "Would you like something?"

"Nothing for me thanks, a beer on a hot day is my limit."

"Ever?"

"Never acquired a taste for it." She studied her menu.

"I guess we'll both pass, Simon, thanks." Quinn handed the wine list back.

"Very good, sir." Simon accepted it with grace and gave a slight bow before heading off.

"He's quite old-fashioned." Ellie watched Simon's retreat.

"That's what I like about this restaurant." Quinn glanced at the decor of the room. "It reminds me of a farmhouse in here, cozy, quiet, and the food is amazing."

"It's my first time," she said.

"First times are always special." Quinn beamed at her over her menu.

"Sometimes they are," she quipped back.

They sat for a few minutes checking out their dinner options.

"So, how did you get into the bodyguard business?" Ellie started the conversation hoping it would ease her nerves. Take control of the situation and never be surprised.

"I only do it for Owen and Lauren," he said. "It's interesting. And you, what do you do?"

"Wait, I wasn't finished!" Ellie laughed. "What made you go into police work before?"

"I wanted to help people and found myself in the missing person's division."

"That must have been a hard job."

"And that's why I left." He raised his eyebrows at her. "Your turn."

Ellie was sure his story was much deeper than what he'd skimmed over but left it for the moment. "I'm a genealogist," she said. "Most of my clients want to find dead people."

"Not the answer I was expecting, but okay." Quinn grinned. "What exactly does that entail?"

"Well, it would bore some people silly, but I love it." She placed her menu on the table and leaned forward. "I get to untangle mysteries in families, discover lost branches of their family trees, look into histories of old houses, and stroll through graveyards searching for elusive relatives people can't find."

"Sounds like being a detective."

"It is!" She sat up straight and grinned. "And the people I'm looking for never give me a hard time!"

"Living people do?" It appeared as if his cop antenna perked up.

"Living people can be a pain in the patoot."

"Not a fan of living people?" He was intrigued.

"Well, some are okay." She stopped there.

"I totally understand." The connection between them went up a notch.

A waiter appeared at their table, pad in hand to take their order. "Have you decided?"

They placed their orders and sank back into a quiet spot.

"How long were you a cop?" Ellie blurted out, trying to stem any further personal questions from Quinn.

"Started out young, worked my way up and set up a Missing Persons department for a special assignment, then ended up heading it for ten years."

"I can't imagine that would be a fun department."

"No." His eyes clouded for a moment, then cleared, as if a better memory came to mind. "Around that time my grandmother was having problems living alone but didn't want to go into a home."

"And you quit your job to move here to help?"

"It was time for a change." He shrugged as if the whole move across the ocean event was an everyday occurrence. His tone left no doubt there was more to the decision he had made, but now was not the time for answers.

"Wow, that's quite the change." Ellie was impressed.

"I'd visited her over the years, and I've always loved Montreal."

"And your grandmother?"

"She passed away last year."

"I'm so sorry."

"Don't be. She had an amazing life." He stretched back in his seat and smiled. "Now what about you?"

"My life is pretty boring." Ellie nodded her head as if to convince herself.

"Family?"

"Is this where we give each other our histories to see if we pass some test?" she tried to joke, but it came out stiffer than she'd intended. She didn't want to talk about her history right now.

"Something to hide?"

The waiter arriving with their plates saved her from reliving the loss of her family and she grabbed at the distraction. "This looks amazing," She gushed, searching her brain for another topic. "So, ever thought of joining your brother making movies?"

"You're changing the subject!"

"For now."

"Fair enough." He cut into his steak.

"It's all about the timing." She grinned back at him.

"I'll remember that."

They peppered their meal with small talk and by the end of dinner, most of the tension had left Ellie's neck for the first time in a week.

A young man walked up to them and stood by their table. He wiped his hands on his pants. "Sorry to bother you, Mr. Walsh, but I'm a huge fan." He held out his hand.

"And I'm sorry to tell you that I'm not Owen Walsh." Still, Quinn put down his knife and fork and shook his hand.

"You look exactly like him!"

"So I've been told." Quinn shrugged and smiled.

"Sorry." The disappointed fan walked away, shaking his head.

"And that's why I don't want to go into moviemaking." Quinn took his final piece of steak and popped it into his mouth.

"Point taken."

"So, tell me about yourself." Quinn wiped his mouth on his napkin and sat back.

"Not dropping this, are you?"

"I think the timing's good."

"Well." Ellie hesitated, deciding what to reveal. "My parents died when I was eleven and Aunt Jenna and Uncle William took me in and raised me. Sophie is like my sister."

"No other brothers or sisters?"

"Nope, just me. And you?"

"God, don't get me started!" He took a sip of his water. "You've met Owen. We're the only two on this side of the pond."

"Except your Grandmother lived here."

"Yes, she did. She felt more connected to Canada. She came to Montreal on her honeymoon and wanted to stay."

"Did your grandfather want to stay too?"

"He couldn't say no to her. They loved each other more than any two people I've ever seen."

"So." Ellie tried to calculate things in her head. "Your mother was born here?"

"She was." Quinn looked around the room. "But my Da was from Scotland. He came over for a visit. The families were close. He met Ma, and that was that."

"She went back with him?" Ellie finished off her rice and placed her knife and fork gently on the plate.

"She did."

"That must have been hard on your grandmother," she said.

"It was, but she knew what being in love meant."

A commotion at the front of the restaurant caught Quinn's eye.

"So, you and your—how many siblings do you have?"

"Five."

"Five!" Ellie turned to see what Quinn was staring at.

Diane Cooper strode towards them and all eyes were on the reporter.

"Oh, no, no, no!" Ellie jumped up, wiped her mouth on her napkin and threw it on her plate.

"Ellie!" Quinn tried to get her attention. "It's okay. Don't worry."

"You don't understand." Ellie refused to be fodder for the press again. Not if she could get away.

"Trust me." He stood up and met Diane before she reached the table.

"How did you find us, Diane?" He barred her way, not allowing her access to Ellie.

"I've got spies all over the place, and I wanted supper." She tried to move around him but he blocked her.

"Don't do this Diane, not tonight, not here."

"I have every right to talk to her." She put a hand on his chest as if to push him aside.

"You don't want to start a scene here," he said quietly.

"Oh, a scene it shall be if that's what you want." She looked up at him and smiled.

"Don't make this personal."

"This is business." She held her ground. "Big business. The press will be all over her in hours and they know where she lives."

"She'll be guarded," he replied.

"Really?" She considered him. "You willing to play bodyguard for her?"

Quinn refused to answer.

"Are you playing bodyguard already?" A glint came into her eyes. "This would add to the story!"

"Why are you doing this?"

"She's used to the press, Quinn." She looked around him at Ellie who was still standing by her chair, ready to run. "You've heard her story, right?"

Quinn just stared at her, his silence menacing.

Ellie came up to them and took hold of Quinn's arm, felt his muscles quivering under her hand. One look at his face and she could see the anger barely concealed. She murmured, "Let's go, Quinn."

"I want to talk to you for a minute, Ms. McLellan. I'm Diane Cooper." She held out her hand.

"Sorry, no time." Ellie refused to take the other woman's hand.

"You'll have to speak to us sometime."

"No, I *don't*," Ellie hissed, stepping into Diane's space. "You can hound me all you like; I don't have to talk to you. But you do have to stay out of my face and off my property."

***

Furious at Diane, Quinn watched Ellie dart around her and head for the door. It was apparent Ellie was running on adrenaline now and had to escape. She kept her head down, refusing to meet the eyes of the other customers who sat frozen in their seats, watching the drama unfold.

Simon approached Diane. Speaking louder than necessary, he announced, "I'm sorry, Ms. Cooper, but your card was refused for the takeout." Quinn fought back a satisfied expression. It seemed that Simon would not allow Diane to go after Ellie. Good man.

None-too-gently Quinn moved Diane aside and followed Ellie to the front of the restaurant.

"On my bill," he called to Simon as he passed him. Simon nodded.

Quinn dashed out of the restaurant after Ellie to catch up with her. "Ellie, wait."

"I'm not going through this again," she muttered to herself, shaking her head furiously. "Not now. Not ever."

***

Ellie stood on the sidewalk outside the restaurant and wrapped her arms tight around herself. She was hyperventilating and had to consciously slow her breathing. She needed to get back to the country, to where she felt safe. Her phone rang and she saw that it was a message from Diane and swiped the message away. How had she gotten her phone number?

Quinn barrelled out behind her, coming to stand beside her with unspoken support. Together they watched the evening crowds of people walk around them. Snippets of conversation wafted by, couples wondered where to go for supper, which club would have the best music, laughter at bad jokes. And still, Ellie remained silent. What could she even say?

"Can I drive you somewhere?" Quinn jammed his hands in his pockets, and she guessed he was fighting his natural male "must fix this problem" urge.

"Thanks, but no. I'm going to see my aunt before I go home."

"Come on," he motioned to his car. "I need *something* to do."

Ellie opened her mouth to argue, caught herself, shrugged it off and headed towards his car. Diane Cooper was the problem, not Quinn Walsh. He hurried ahead of her and held the door, waited for her to settle in, then closed it. He let the traffic pass on his side before sliding into his seat.

"I don't know all the details, Ellie." He put the key in the ignition and started the car. "But if you ever need to talk about it, I've got big shoulders."

"I noticed," Ellie said without thinking. She couldn't believe the things that popped out of her mouth when she was around Quinn. A heated flush of embarrassment crawled up her neck and face.

He checked the road before pulling out into traffic.

The ride would be short and Ellie needed to change the subject. "So, do you know anything about kidnapping?" She looked at him innocently.

"Huh?" Again, she'd caught him off guard. She watched him rearrange his confused expression and consider her question. She had to give him points for effort. "Ah... Well... Like in *how* to kidnap, or...?"

"No, no!" she said, surprised and grateful for the release of tension. "More like the actual laws."

"*Planning* on kidnapping someone?"

"Not yet." She tried to keep it light.

"What exactly do you want to know?"

"Well, are there any statutes of limitations?" She knew the answer, but she was a glutton for punishment and asked anyway.

"Not with kidnapping." Quinn stopped for a light and looked over at her. "Is this factual or fictional?"

"Just curious." Her palms were sweating, even with the air-conditioning.

"Anyone who kidnaps another person should be locked up forever." His voice was rough and clipped.

"I'm sorry." Ellie put her hand on his arm as the light changed and he headed to the hospital. "It was something I've wondered about. Some TV shows don't show you what happens after." She was chattering, trying to lighten the mood.

"No, I'm sorry. I didn't mean to snap, but I dealt with that for way too long." He pulled into a parking spot at the far end of the hospital. He sat for a minute then turned to her, his forehead furrowed as if something wasn't adding up.

"Thanks for the ride." Ellie blurted. She knew he was about to say something serious and she needed light and airy. She started to open her door, but he was out of the car and around to help her before she could take a step.

"I'll stay and drive you back to your car." He walked towards the hospital, leaving her to follow.

Quinn's strong reaction had surprised her, but considering his background, of course he'd want to see someone prosecuted for kidnapping. *If* that's what Aunt Jenna had done.

And that was something she prayed would never happen.

Chapter Twenty-Eight

The hospital halls were whisper quiet, and the lighting seemed dimmer, but maybe that was wishful thinking on Ellie's part. Lower lighting usually eased her nerves, but she felt the itch of stress creeping up her spine.

Quinn followed her along the hall until they reached the nurses' station. Only Nurse Janice was there, and she gave him a big smile as she moved around the counter and reached out to touch his arm.

"It's so *good* to see you again," she gushed.

Ellie tried to control her eyebrows from shooting up into her forehead before she turned and headed into her Aunt's room.

She closed the door firmly behind her, hoping to lock out the scene outside and keep the quiet inside with her. Without a second thought, she sank into the bedside chair and leaned back. She closed her eyes and let the peace of the room calm her. She was thankful Sophie was home studying and Aunt Jenna sleeping peacefully. The heart monitor gave a reassuring steady beep and Ellie watched her Aunt's chest move at an even pace.

She reached out and gently took her Aunt's hand. It felt cool, slightly rough from years of working outside in her garden and keeping the tidiest house Ellie had ever seen. When times were bad for Ellie, Jenna would always sit her down and hold her hand, sometimes letting the silence between them do the work, other times asking quiet questions that brought Ellie's troubles to light. This physical connection was something Ellie missed every day.

"I wish I could talk to you," Ellie whispered. "I bet you'd set us straight with a quick answer and we'd all be laughing."

Though she fought it, her gaze was drawn to the door window and she saw Quinn step back from the nurse. Janice did not look pleased by their conversation. More drama to avoid.

Ellie stayed with Aunt Jenna for another five minutes, regaining her composure, and reassuring herself her aunt was okay. When she left, she closed the door quietly behind her and nodded at Nurse Janice as she passed. Nurse Janice gave her a curt nod.

Trying to make a quick escape she walked past Quinn without a word and headed down the hall to the exit. She wasn't usually rude but she was so bone weary tired she didn't have many words left. He followed, caught up and passed her in time to hold the front door for her. Back outside, they stood in the cooling night air, the calm broken by the sound of a siren as an ambulance raced into the emergency bay.

"Come on." He walked on. "I'll take you back to your car."

They rode in silence and she could feel Quinn stealing glances at her. "Nothing's changed with my aunt," she told him. "I'm... I'm sure that's a good sign, no news is good news."

He reached out and held her hand in his, giving it a supportive squeeze.

He pulled in behind her car and turned off the engine with his left hand, their fingers still intertwined.

Without warning, he leaned over, cupped her head in his hands and kissed her. For a moment they both froze.

And then the kiss deepened.

Like two kids on a date, restricted by their seat belts, leaning into each other like hungry survivors of a crazy world. Slowly and reluctantly they broke apart.

"Holy shit," he whispered. He ran his hand nervously through his hair. "I'm so sorry."

"I'm not." She beamed at him, unbuckled her belt with one hand, opened the door with the other and jumped out.

She stumbled a bit at her car, completely embarrassed and grinning like a fool at the same time. She fumbled in her purse for the keys, dropped the keys, picked them up, waved at him like a drunken sailor and disappeared inside. She was so embarrassed. He must think her a total klutz!

***

Ellie didn't start her car.

Neither did he.

They sat there, each gathering their wits and breath about them until Ellie finally *did* start her car and eased out into the traffic.

Quinn wasn't so quick to recover. What the hell just happened? He'd never done anything like that in his life. A goofy grin crossed his face.

Why had he never done anything like that in his life? It was amazing!

Chapter Twenty-Nine

The ride home passed in a blur. Ellie kept the window open a crack to let the cool evening air sweep across her heated face. She drove on autopilot, reliving the last moments with Quinn. The kiss. She felt there should be a neon flashing light with a fanfare announcing the event. It had been that good.

And that meant it was that bad.

She'd made sure there was no time for a man in her life. Right now, her priorities were to find the truth about Sophie and Aunt Jenna's relationship and keep the press away from her family in case they got wind of this "situation". Ellie put all things annoying in quotes. It made the "situations" manageable and set them in a place to be dissected when she had the time, or strength, or need. The kiss was a "situation", one she couldn't force in its place because she could still feel the warmth from his lips on hers.

She approached the curve in the road that led to her driveway and slowed for the turnoff. Her headlights illuminated a vehicle parked at the bottom of her drive, the silhouette of a person sitting in the front seat.

She drove past and didn't look towards the car. The press had done the same thing to her when Adam and Winnie died. They stalked her. This guy probably thought she was home right now and was waiting her out.

But she refused to give them even one sound bite for their voracious machines. She'd made that mistake once., but *she* was in control this time.

She pulled into the empty parking lot of the Cozy Corner Café. It was closed for the night, the ground floor dark, but a single light on the second floor assured her Maggie was awake. Ellie parked around the back of the building and walked to the backdoor. Her knock was loud in the quiet country air.

It took Maggie a few minutes but when she opened the door and saw Ellie standing there, she said, "In you come," drew her in, and closed the door tight behind them before pulling her into a hug. She took Ellie's hand and led her up the backstairs to her apartment above. Maggie was a tactile person, something Ellie appreciated in a best friend, because sometimes hugs were exactly what she needed.

The light was low, Celtic music played softly on the stereo and the smell of Ellie's weakness, double chocolate cookies, wafted through the air.

Ellie sank into the deeply cushioned couch and slipped her shoes off. "Oh, that's nice."

"Cookie?"

"You have to ask?" Ellie laughed.

"Milk?"

"Again...?"

***

Maggie set about getting Ellie's snack in silence and watched her friend stretch her back, then curl up into the cushions. It had taken Maggie a while to figure out how Ellie's mind worked, but found it was better to let her speak than ask questions that might send Ellie running. So, silence it was.

In time, as predicted, Ellie opened up. "Aunt Jenna may be a kidnapper, there's press at the bottom of my driveway, and Quinn kissed me."

Maggie froze. "Quinn kissed you?"

"That's what you focus on from everything I just said?" Ellie shook her head. "Mags."

"Yeah, I know." Maggie brought the cookie and milk and put them on the table by Ellie. "Hopeful romantic, so shoot me."

Ellie took a bite of the cookie and groaned with delight.

"Almost as good as sex?" Maggie teased. "And you might get to dispute that if he's as good as he looks."

"It was just a kiss," Ellie snorted. "But a really *great* kiss."

Maggie sat in a chair across from Ellie and stared at her. She watched her friend finish the cookie, down the milk, and sink back with a satisfied sigh.

"Nice dress," she said.

Ellie squinted at her friend, dreading that look in her eye. "We had dinner downtown. It was nice."

Maggie was smart when it came to how skittish Ellie could get. A change of subject was in order. "What's this about Aunt Jenna?"

"Aargh." Ellie rubbed her eyes like a kid not wanting to see the monster under her bed, then dropped her hands in exhaustion. "We found out that Sophie is not Aunt Jenna's daughter. Blood does not lie."

"Dang." Maggie shook her head. "What exactly does that mean?"

"That's what Sophie and I are trying to find out." Ellie took a deep breath. "Mags, no one else knows about this except Sophie and me, and now you. I have to get the facts, not accept *what ifs* and try to make things up to suit us."

"Can I help?"

"Just be here." Ellie stood up and stretched. "And maybe walk me home. I don't want to deal with the guy on my road. I'll pick the car up tomorrow."

"Still can't walk in the woods at night alone?" Maggie joked as she put her shoes on and grabbed her flashlight.

"I don't have a flashlight." Ellie hated people knowing her weaknesses, but this was a big one.

"Fine." Maggie headed for the door, knowing offering Ellie her own flashlight would not matter. Fears were fears and this was a big one.

Maggie followed her out into the night and hid her smile as best she could. Ellie had kissed a boy! Things were looking up at last.

Chapter Thirty

The ring of Ellie's phone sent a jolt of electricity buzzing through her nervous system. She had turned it back on before she crawled into bed, in case Sophie or her aunt needed her. But right now, she was still in bed, the sun barely rising, bed sheets tangled around her legs from a restless sleep. "Hello?" her voice was early morning raw and unused.

"The car is still parked by the highway," Maggie said. "Thought you should know. Don't do anything..."

"Thanks." Ellie slammed the phone on whatever else Maggie was going to say and grabbed her jeans from the bottom of her bed. Her sleeping t-shirt would have to do.

Dashing down the stairs to the hall, she stopped only to slip into her running shoes and call to Cali.

She slammed out of the front door, her anger building to a boil. Ellie was determined to take back control of this whole mess. A good night's sleep depended on it, and she loved her sleep. She grabbed her bow from the balcony, slung her sheath of arrows across her shoulder, and took off along one of the smaller paths from the house, Cali at her side. This was her home, her haven, her safety. She'd let no one disrupt this.

Ellie and Cali jumped the creek together and slowed as they came to the bottom of her road. Ellie motioned for Cali to sit and they stopped behind a clump of trees where they could watch the person in the old car on her driveway.

The sun was behind her as Ellie approached the vehicle, its rays touched the road, sending tree shadows dancing ahead to the car, shining off the windshield in a blinding light.

She pulled up when the car door opened, waiting to see who stepped out. A young woman—a surprise—got out slowly, a camera slung over her shoulders. Was this Diane Cooper's assistant? Ellie vaguely recalled this young face from her first encounter with Diane. The girl stretched long and hard, then rubbed her eyes as if she'd slept here all night. Perhaps she had. She was slim, gangly, and looked barely fifteen years old. When she wiped her palms on her faded jeans, glancing hesitantly around, Ellie could see she was nervous. Good to know.

When she headed towards the gate Ellie stepped out onto the road, Cali by her side.

Cali's deep growl made the young woman stop in mid-stride, as if a deadly game of Red Light, Green Light had begun, and she'd been caught out. Her eyes grew wide with fright when she saw the bow in Ellie's hand and the arrow being confidently strung into it as she strolled towards her.

"No, no!" She held her hands up high in the air, pleading surrender. "I'm Annabelle! I'm Diane Cooper's assistant. I…"

"—was just leaving?" Ellie's soft tone seemed to spook her even more, much to Ellie's satisfaction.

"I only want to ask you a few questions," Annabelle tried to assert herself. "I need to give Diane something, a picture, a comment, something. Please."

"Don't beg," Ellie said. "Don't take my picture, don't ask me a question, and for the love of Pete, stop working for Diane, she'll walk all over you."

"Yeah, well." She made a move to get her camera.

"I'm not kidding." Ellie raised her bow and arrow into position. "You like your car?"

"Hey, stop, stop!" Annabelle's hands shot to the sky again. "I'm going, but if it's not me who comes back, someone else will and they'll walk right up to the house."

"That guy came already. My dog almost took his leg off, and he left with nothing," Ellie informed her.

"Listen, please." Annabelle sounded apologetic and exhausted. "Diane really needs a story with you. The picture is only a back-up plan."

"I don't know what you're talking about." Ellie lowered her bow slightly and looked at Annabelle straight on. "But I had this treatment years ago, and you'll get nothing from me."

"She'll just take it then, and it probably won't be the truth." Annabelle threw her camera on the passenger seat, her shoulders sagging. "Diane is desperate; she needs something big or they might fire her."

"Not my circus, not my problem," Ellie said. "But I appreciate the warning."

"I wanted to be a photographer, like weddings and art stuff." Annabelle shook her head in disbelief at where her life had gone. "This really sucks."

"I bet you'd be great," Ellie said to her. "But right now, you need to leave."

Before climbing back into her car, Annabelle met Ellie's gaze and dared a smile. "Your weapon? That's bad-ass stuff, lady!"

Ellie watched the young woman get in her car and lowered the bow slightly, waiting till the vehicle disappeared onto the highway. Then she raised it and with a yell of anger and frustration let the arrow fly into a nearby tree.

She retrieved the arrow, apologized to the tree, and returned the arrow to its sheath. Her aim was getting better, but no one needed to know she'd never use it.

Cali walked over and plunked down beside her, leaning her heavy warm weight against Ellie's leg. She reached down and rubbed Cali's head.

Bad-ass stuff would keep her safe.

***

Ellie spent the rest of the morning walking the property, checking for spots the press might invade and reinforcing the camouflage she'd set up near the highway.

The small space she'd left for Ruth to enter had not been messed with, and from the road it was invisible.

Lunch had been a quick sandwich, and she gave herself the next few hours to relax. She curled up with a good romance on the couch, drifting between reading and the half sleep that comes in the heat of a warm afternoon with a full belly.

Her phone alerted her to another message from Diane, this one with the header "It's your fault if this goes live". She sat for a full minute before hitting the open button because she believed that forearmed is forewarned. And then she wished she had deleted it.

A picture of her and Quinn behind the Ritz Hotel implied they were in a romantic embrace. And Diane's caption below sent a chill down her back. *Owen Walsh running around with the woman who saved his son's life. How will his wife react to this latest affair?* Below that Diane had written, *Here's the deal: An interview for this picture disappearing. Your choice.*

This time Ellie jabbed the delete button and practically threw her phone across the couch.

Cali's loud barking jolted her out of her stupor. An instant adrenaline dump had her running for the bow and arrow she'd left inside the front door. "That little..." She dashed outside then skidded to a stop. Quinn stood at the bottom of the stairs with Cali leaning against him in total adoration. He raised his arms in mock alarm when he saw the weapon in her hand.

"What are you doing here?" Ellie demanded. Her emotions were mixed seeing him again so soon. Old Ellie was annoyed at him invading her space, especially with the curveball Diane had just thrown her way, and new Ellie was trying to slow her heartbeat and ignore the jig of delight inside her stomach.

"Maggie called me and told me you were having problems with the press."

They stood in silence, each waiting for the other to speak.

Quinn broke the quiet. "Tell me what happened."

"It's nothing." Ellie held out her bow and arrows. "Handled it myself."

Quinn tilted his head, his eyes roaming her cut-off shorts, white t-shirt, bare feet and holding the bow and arrows. "You look fierce." She hoped her flushed face could be explained by her earlier encounter.

"You don't think I can take care of myself?"

"On the contrary." His smile turned into a full-on grin. "I'd be wary of you in this mood."

"Damn straight!"

"What's been happening?" He sat on the top step and waited for her to either tell him to leave or sit beside him.

She eased herself down. "What have you heard about me and my past?"

"I know you lost your husband and daughter and I'm really sorry you had to go through that."

Ellie remained silent. The hurt was easing into more of a dull ache after almost four years.

He tried again. "I know the press did a number on you right after because you went after texting drivers, and I know you hate them with a passion."

"That about sums it up."

He sat still, gazing into the forest beyond her barn.

The wind was picking up, swaying the treetops and sending the scent of wildflowers towards them. She inhaled deeply and let the fragrance wash over her.

"Ellie, they'll be back, trying to get in for that one picture or comment."

"Someone tried this morning, hence these." She held up her bow as if it were her armour.

"Would you actually use it?"

"Not on a person, but I'd take out their car tire, no problem."

"Are you good?"

"I practice, I hit targets, I'm okay." Again, the silence. But this time it was comfortable, like old friends who had never left. "Why *are* you here?" she asked quietly.

"I want to help you."

"How?"

"I could—"

"You're not planning on sleeping on my couch or something, are you?"

"If needed."

"You think I have a press problem now? Imagine if they find you here, sleeping at my place!"

"Ellie, I understand Diane." Quinn looked her in the eye. "Rumour is she's close to losing her job and needs a big story to hang on to it. And this is a big story. If she can combine your past with you saving Gavyn, she's got a winner. And catching us together at supper last night, well..."

"And what kind of story would you and I be to her?"

"Nothing like the fake story they did on Owen and Lauren last year, but who knows how'd they flip the truth."

"Then that's settled." Ellie got up, brushed off her shorts and hid her hurt. "You can't stay. Neither of us wants any more spotlights."

"The next few days will be intense." Quinn stood up and towered over her. "I don't care about my privacy. I'm bulletproof."

"I'm not." Ellie thought of Diane's picture of her and Quinn and how she was planning on spinning it around Owen, and also the possible explosive story looming with Aunt Jenna.

"Then we'll figure something out."

"I'm staying with Maggie tonight, so I won't be alone." She fought with herself to ask him to stay, let him help her handle all this mess, but old Ellie won. "I'll be fine."

He bent down and kissed her on the forehead. "You're a tough little one, aren't you?" He stepped off the porch. "I'll be back and if I have to camp out in the woods, that's what I'll do."

The image of him sleeping in her forest appealed to her. She could manage that.

"And call back this wild dog," he tossed over his shoulder as he headed down the road, Cali right by his side. "She's a terror." Cali looked between Ellie and

Quinn, but when Ellie whistled to her, she ran over to Ellie and sat by her on the porch.

Ellie reached out and ran her fingers through Cali's soft fur. It's amazing where you can find comfort. Quinn reached the top of the road and turned to wave. She waved back, feeling her chest relax and her hope rise.

Comfort.

Chapter Thirty-One

Ellie dried her last supper dish and put it in the cupboard. Dishcloth tossed over her shoulder, she leaned against the counter and stretched. She moved slowly, the heat making her languid and the thought of Quinn coming back in the morning curling a traitorous smile across her face.

"Right," she said to the empty house. "Sleepover at Maggie's. Take dog food, lock up, carry a big stick." Talking to herself was something she had done since a child. Even when met with mean comments by students at school, she had relied on the trick to keep herself grounded when feeling troubled. She'd die of embarrassment if someone walked in on one of her self-help pep talks now, but they centred her.

She packed a bag with PJs and her toothbrush, locked the door and started off along the path into the early evening woods, Cali by her side. Ellie loved hearing the nocturnal animals start their night, and the way the stars skittered across the sky as the night wore on. She could handle dusk with a flashlight, knowing Cali was nearby. What she *didn't* enjoy was the claustrophobic feeling she got when walking through the DARK, the trees close and towering above her.

Cali loved the woods at any time. She darted off the trail after hidden creatures only she could smell, but she never wandered out of eyesight and always returned to Ellie's side to lick her hand and assure her she wasn't alone.

The path wound past the swimming hole, around the apple trees and beside the treehouse.

Ellie stopped and tested the ladder. The bottom rung needed fixing, and she made a mental note to do that the next day. The treehouse held a special place in her heart and she normally made sure it was taken care of. If she closed her eyes, she could hear the excited squeals of her daughter the first time she climbed the ladder to the secret place above. This had belonged to Ruth and Shirley in their youth and Ellie and her husband had refurbished it for Winnie.

Brushing the thoughts away before they completely overwhelmed her, Ellie and Cali continued on and made it to the end of the trail. Directly across was the Cozy Corner Café, the first floor dark, Maggie's apartment above was softly lit, like a welcome beacon.

"Cali." Ellie grabbed the dog's collar and listened for traffic. The bend in the road was deceptive for seeing oncoming cars. She could hear when one was coming from Percyville around the turn or heading towards Montreal from the other direction. Engines had a sound on this road that gave away their location.

Silence. Perfect.

"Now!" Ellie let go of Cali's collar and raced across the highway. Cali dashed past her and didn't stop until she reached Maggie's back door where she plunked herself down and waited for Ellie to catch up.

"Show off." Ellie ruffled her dog's fur and Cali's tail thumped loudly on the wooden porch.

"Door's unlocked," Maggie called softly from above.

Ellie looked up to see Maggie's long red wavy hair blowing in the breeze as she leaned out an upper window. Maggie motioned her in with an impatient hand and slammed the window shut behind her.

That's Maggie. In her ideal world, she'd never have to talk. She loved the silence of nature and would never miss the havoc of human speech. Considering she owned a store that had people in her place more hours of the day than not, Ellie found this an interesting quirk in her personality.

Ellie waited for Cali to do her final night business and then headed inside, locking the door behind her. The staircase was dark as she felt her way up to the flickering light ahead. The walls were thick in this old house and the air was blessedly cooler.

Cali dashed up to the top and chuffed a welcome to Maggie, leaning against the tall woman for the rub she expected.

"You darling thing," Maggie whispered to her, rubbing the dog's chest and behind her ears. "Who wants a surprise?"

Cali's ears perked up, and she sat at attention.

"Mags," Ellie admonished her, "you shouldn't feed her anything at this time of night. I'm not taking her out again."

"Oh, you beast." Maggie laughed at Ellie. "She'll be able to hold herself until morning. It's just a biscuit."

The said biscuit appeared in Maggie's hand, held inches in front of Cali. The dog sat calmly, a brief thump of her tail and then she controlled even that. As if they had made a secret arrangement, Maggie placed the cookie on the floor and stood back. She nodded, and like the lady she was, Cali licked it up and lay down to chew.

"I've never seen her do that." Ellie was aghast. "She's a rude eater. What have you done to my dog?"

"Treated her as she wanted to be treated."

"Oh, pooh, that's nonsense."

"Just as I treat you the way you want to be treated."

"Oh, so now I'm a dog?" Ellie pretended to be insulted.

"No." Maggie curled up on the sofa in the living room, tucking her naked feet beneath her and wrapping her long skirt around her toes. "But you need taking care of as well."

Ellie plopped down on the huge armchair across from her friend and stretched her legs out in front of her. Very unladylike, Aunt Jenna would say, but at this moment she didn't care. Maggie understood her.

They sat in silence for a while. Maggie raised one eyebrow at her, and Ellie decided to fill her in on what she knew.

"I found out where Aunt Jenna was living when Sophie was born."

"How did you..." Maggie started. "Never mind. Genealogy voodoo tricks."

"Logical deductive thinking," Ellie corrected her.

"What happens now? Do you tell Sophie?"

"She's coming by tomorrow to discuss a plan."

"And if you find out something unpleasant?"

"I have to see records, get the facts. I've learned the hard way not to assume anything."

Maggie sat forward and took Ellie's hands in hers. "Aunt Jenna is not a bad person."

"No," Ellie agreed. "She's not, but who knows what a person is capable of when despair hits them."

"Sounding like a Regency novel, are we?"

Ellie decided to ignore the jab. "My gut says there's more to this than meets the eye, but if she *is* a kidnapper..."

"Oh, Ellie, that's such a harsh word!"

"It's the only thing that comes to mind." She sat back, withdrawing into herself and away from the soothing aura of her friend. "I *will* find out the truth, Mags, whatever that may be." She sat back and started picking the skin around her fingers—a major giveaway of nerves.

"What else?" Maggie watched her closely.

Ellie took a deep breath before sharing her new dilemma. "Diane has a photo of me and Quinn in what looks like a romantic situation."

"And?"

"And she's threatening to release it, but she'll insinuate it's proof of Owen and me having an affair. The angle makes it seem possible and I won't put Owen and Lauren through another episode like that. Rumours can kill."

"She's blackmailing you?" Maggie sat forward and grabbed Ellie's hand again.

"Yeah, I guess she is." Ellie clenched Maggie's fingers and then slowly released them. "I can't let that picture get out, and I have to keep Diane out of whatever is happening with Aunt Jenna. It was her assistant Annabelle outside my gate last night and this morning. She claims Diane is desperate for a juicy story."

"So, what are you going to do?

"I may have to give her something about saving Gavyn, and what life's been like since my family died."

"Oh, Ellie, that's so unfair."

"I guess it could be worse. At least I'll control what I give her."

"Speaking of Quinn," Maggie said.

Ellie sat forward and let out a soft moan.

"Oh, that good, huh?" Maggie was intrigued.

"He's coming to bodyguard me tomorrow." Silence. Ellie snuck a look at her friend to see the largest smile and a twinkle in her eyes. "Oh, for pity's sake." Ellie shook her head.

"I didn't say a word," Maggie tried to wipe off her smile. It didn't work. "Is it necessary?"

Ellie's shoulders slumped. "Yes, I think so."

Chapter Thirty-Two

E llie climbed out of the pond and dried herself off with the large towel she'd left warming up on the diving rock. The heat of the mid-day sun was scorching but the water was a cool relief.

Pete had worked all morning tearing out the old bathtub and sink and had trucked the debris off to the dump. He would tackle the toilet and floor next time and then put in the new items—which meant Ellie could choose how she'd redecorated the room once he was done. The fun part. For now, she stayed out of his way by working in the garden, ending up in the pond playing ball with Cali. Pete had the next few days to buy the materials needed and assured her he'd be there Thursday morning to continue. She told him there was no hurry.

Cali clambered out of the pond behind her, shook herself off, and tweaked her head as if listening for something in the distance.

"Come on." Ellie headed back to the house. "Sophie is probably tapping her feet through the porch waiting for us." Cali took off ahead of her and was sitting beside the foot tapping Sophie when Ellie walked out of the woods.

"I should have brought my suit." Sophie smiled at her cousin. "You look cool as a cucumber."

"Where did that saying even come from?" Ellie laughed. "I feel nothing like a vegetable, though the swim did me good."

"How was your night with Maggie?"

Ellie reached into a hanging plant and took out her key. She refused to leave the house unlocked these days, even if she was out walking the property. "She has a way of listening and before you know it, you're spilling your innermost thoughts," Ellie grumbled as she opened the front door and stepped into the quiet house. She missed the sounds of her family living here. Sometimes the loss came out of nowhere and swallowed her whole. At least the pain eased quicker these days, though sometimes it took longer than others. "How was the exam?" she asked as they headed into the kitchen.

"Easy peasy, lemon squeezy." Sophie gave her a thumbs up and a huge grin. "I was worried for nothing. Then again, I could be feeling overconfident and have failed."

"Doubt that."

"So, show me what you have and let's make a plan." Sophie was so focused on her own problems that for once she didn't notice Ellie's sombre mood.

"Let me get changed." Ellie ran up the stairs to the bedroom and peeled off her wet bathing suit before changing into her usual summer uniform, shorts and t-shirt. She took a few minutes extra to towel dry her hair and settle her thoughts.

When she returned to the kitchen, she found Sophie holding one of her mother's—Ellie *believed*, but could not yet prove—letters. "I've read them all," Sophie said. "Who is Helen?"

Ellie sat down across from her and picked up the picture. "I'm not sure. They were both living in the same town when you were born."

"She's tall." Sophie took the picture back from Ellie and brought it closer to her face, hoping the grainy photo would come into focus better. "Is she my mother?"

"I don't know, but I'm heading there tomorrow to see what I can find."

"Why not right now?" Sophie looked up at her, worry and excitement warring for a spot on her face.

"I'm sorry Sophie, it's an hour's drive." Ellie glanced at the clock above her sink that read one o'clock. "And Quinn is coming to bodyguard me, thanks to you."

"What?" Sophie sat back in surprise. "Oh, that's great!"

"I don't want him here."

"But you need someone here, for a while," Sophie reasoned.

"Not a while, *just* for today," Ellie said, anger raising the colour in her face. "I'm only doing this to get him off my back and..."

"But it would make you feel safer," Sophie stated the obvious. "I know you can take care of yourself, and everyone else, all the time, El, but sometimes you have to accept help."

Ellie opened her mouth to talk but Sophie held up her hand to silence her.

"Just for today, okay, let him come, sleep in the barn, whatever. If it gives you peace of mind, great."

"But I'd rather him not know what's happening with Aunt Jenna."

"So, don't tell him," Sophie answered. "It's as easy as that. We don't really know anything yet." She sounded like she was reassuring herself more than Ellie. "And I'm going with you tomorrow."

"No." Ellie shook her head and gathered the mess of papers together. "I need everything to be as normal as possible. We can't have Diane getting curious. She can't find out about this."

"But..."

"Please, Sophie, I need to slip in and slip out, not be noticed by anyone. And *you* are noticeable!"

Sophie smoothed back her red hair and grinned. "Fair enough."

The sound of footsteps on the gravel drive and the way Cali's tail thumped on the floor instead of her growling told them Quinn had arrived.

"I'm glad you left the gate locked," Sophie said. "Any safeguards can't hurt."

"We'll see."

"I wouldn't mind a safeguard like him!" Sophie whispered as she gave Ellie a quick kiss and headed out the door as Quinn reached them. "Take care of my cousin." Sophie gave him a soft punch on the shoulder before heading off down the road.

She took a quick look back to see Ellie and Quinn standing on the porch, awkward as two teenagers.

Quinn dropped his sleeping bag on the floor inside the front door and waited. It didn't take long.

Ellie grabbed the papers from the table. "You really don't have to be here." A picture fluttered to the floor.

Quinn ignored her comment and picked up the picture. "Family?"

She reached for the picture and he handed it to her. "It's my Aunt Jenna, from years ago," she mumbled.

"Is that Sophie she's carrying?" His detective mode triggered the moment he saw how reluctant she was to talk about it.

"We're not sure." Ellie put the papers and picture face down on the counter and turned to face him.

"Not following you." He watched her closely. Whatever inner battle she was waging was making her sweat—and it seemed as if she'd come to a decision. To trust him, finally, he hoped.

"Have a seat." She motioned to the chair across from her and sat down with the look of someone about to lose her best friend.

Quinn sat and waited her out, again. But Ellie wasn't a criminal he was using his tactics on, and he didn't enjoy seeing her in distress. He asked, "Can I ask questions? Would that help tell the story?"

"Sure." She let a brief smile appear and released a deep breath.

"Is Jenna Sophie's mother?"

"Wow! That was a quick assumption." She hesitated then plunged in. "But according to blood tests, no."

"Does Sophie know this?"

"She does now."

"Who is the other woman in the picture?"

"Not sure."

"Is Sophie adopted?"

"Not that I've heard."

Quinn was quiet. He was so hoping this was not what it looked like.

"Did Jenna kidnap her?"

"Don't know."

"Oh, for..." he stopped. His voice had got louder and edgier as the questions continued.

"I'm going to Stellar Heights tomorrow to see what I can find out."

"I'll go with you."

"No thanks. I already told Sophie we can't let anyone think something's wrong. Because there might not be." She tried for a smile and failed miserably.

"But *you* don't think so."

"I'm *hopeful* there's a good explanation." Ellie had never been a hand wringer, but her nasty habit of picking the skin around her fingernails had left her hands looking horrible. She jammed them in her pockets.

"And if Jenna *did* kidnap Sophie?" He saw her eyes flutter closed as she searched for inner strength.

"I'm not even going there, yet."

"There's no statute of limitations on kidnapping."

"We don't *know* anything yet!" Ellie stood up and wiped her wet hands on her jeans.

"If she *did* kidnap Sophie, Jenna could go to prison."

"Not if we don't tell anyone." She threw out the comment without thinking, without believing it or considering it a possibility.

"Not if you don't..." Quinn stood up slowly and gripped the back of the chair so hard it creaked under his hands. "Don't you think Sophie's biological mother has a right to know her daughter is alive?" His voice had gotten loud and Cali let out a low growl and planted herself by Ellie's side.

"Look, we have no facts right now and we're not making any decisions until we do."

"Do you *know* how something like this rips a family apart?" He couldn't control the anger in his voice. "*Do* you? It strips them of *everything*. Never knowing what happened to their child. Are they alive or dead? Is someone hurting them or treating them well or..."

"Stop!" Ellie yelled back. "Stop right now. Why are you assuming the worst?"

"Because I've seen this before—it's what I used to do." He tried to calm his voice. He looked down, searching for strength before scanning her white face again. This wasn't Ellie's fault—he knew that. Softer now, he continued, "You don't have the right to make this call. You don't have the right to protect one person while another person lives in despair."

"I'm not making *any* call," Ellie said. "I have no idea what I'm facing."

"You can't conceal this information."

"I never said I would! I don't want my aunt to go to jail." She finished her sentence in a whisper, anguish causing her eyes to tear up, control refusing to let them flow.

It seemed like hours that they stared at each other, their eyes blaming and pleading and coming to no conclusion.

"This is so messed up!" Quinn stormed to the door and slammed out onto the porch and off into the woods.

***

Ellie watched Quinn leave; his shoulders hunched as if braced against unseen punches. It was as if a storm cloud headed into her forest.

"We don't know anything yet," she whispered as a silent prayer. She refused to believe Quinn would turn her aunt in, but what if Jenna was guilty? Deep down she knew Quinn was right and she would never keep a mother from her child, no matter what. No matter who.

Cali once again tried to comfort her by leaning her solid weight against her leg. Ellie reached down and gave her friend a scratch behind her ears.

It took a few minutes to get a handle on the sinking feeling in her gut, and then Ellie went outside, grabbed her hammer and container of nails and headed for the treehouse. She had a ladder to fix. Smacking something would do her good right now.

Chapter Thirty-Three

Quinn arrived at the Cozy Corner Café, having blindly walked the path to the highway and through the camouflage Ellie had created. He debated turning back, but he needed to ground himself first, and he was thirsty.

He entered like a whirlwind, catching the door behind him from slamming against the wall.

Maggie saw him and pulled a beer out of her fridge and put it before him on the counter.

He looked at the bottle, at her, sat on a stool, and gulped half. "Thanks."

"Rough day?" Maggie asked.

"Your friend doesn't accept help easily." He wasn't sure who he was mad at or why anymore.

"You want to protect her?"

"She doesn't want to be protected." Quinn placed his hand flat on the countertop and forced it to stop shaking. The anger was seeping out of him like a slow leak. He stared at Maggie and let out a long deliberate breath. "Do you have any idea what's going on?"

Maggie frowned. "I think I do."

"Sharing is good."

"It's been a while since someone cared for her, besides family I mean," Maggie said. "She's afraid of being hurt and she doesn't know how to handle it or trust it. And she certainly doesn't trust anyone with her family. Except me, of course."

"Yeah, well." He couldn't look her in the eye, "She's dealing with some serious stuff and I've experienced things from the other side. I know she wants to protect everyone, but I also know she can't. We let our emotions get out of hand and I... I came down on her hard."

"I bet."

"I have to apologize." He twirled his beer bottle between his hands. "This whole situation is a touchy subject for me."

"I'm sure it is." Maggie waited.

He twitched. "Are you a psychologist or something? I never spill my thoughts to strangers."

"Sometimes strangers make the best friends."

Quinn studied her. She looked harmless but she was using his own tactics against him. Quinn saw the TV over her shoulder. "Turn that up, please!"

Maggie looked over to see Ellie on the TV, a red banner racing across the bottom of the screen claiming this was a *Live Report*. A man towering over Ellie with a microphone. A camera had zoomed in on her white face.

"Ah, God, not again," Maggie moaned as she turned up the volume.

The reporter took a step towards Ellie, invading her space and forcing her to stumble backwards. "But you must have felt wonderful saving Owen Walsh's son after losing your own daughter."

Ellie stood at the bottom of the treehouse, hammer in her hand, the lowest rung hanging by one nail.

"No comment!" Ellie's eyes were wide as she backed away, trying to put some distance between herself and the reporter. Cali launched herself between them.

The man reached out and grabbed Ellie by the arm, ignoring the growling dog. "Wait." He spoke fast, "This must be a rough time for you, with your aunt in the hospital and the anniversary of your family's accident, and now saving the Walsh boy. Surely you have some comment." He glanced at the camera with a suitably concerned expression.

Cali barked and jumped at the man.

"Get the hell off my property!" Ellie spat the words at him, raised the hammer and the camera went dead.

Quinn was already out the door and sprinting across the road and into the woods beyond.

***

Quinn burst through the woods, bypassing the meandering path and straight through the trees to the sound of Ellie's angry voice.

"I don't give a flying fig who you are!" She took a step toward the reporter and would have thrown her hammer had Quinn not reached her and eased her arm down. Ellie turned her anger toward him only to lose her breath in a loud whoosh when she realized suddenly she wasn't alone anymore.

Cali had the cameraman's lower leg in her jaws. The man stood frozen, terrified to make a move or say a word. "She was going to hit us, and that dog!" the reporter informed Quinn indignantly from where he stood hiding behind the Cali-tethered cameraman. It appeared as if the guy was under the misbegotten impression they had every right to be on Ellie's private property and Quinn was here to rescue them.

Quinn's furious face made the reporter jam his jaws together with a snap. Quinn moved toward them, hammer now in *his* hand, motioning with it towards the tangled woods that would lead them to the river.

"You have ten seconds," he said quietly.

Pointing back towards the house and what he thought was safety, the reporter whined, "But our car's—"

"Five..." Quinn took another step.

The reporter stumbled back in alarm.

"Cali," Ellie called the dog off the cameraman.

Cali released her grip but kept both men in her line of vision, every muscle of her body gathered in anticipation of Ellie's command to resume an attack.

"This isn't over," the reporter proclaimed in a trilling, trembling voice, trying to look tough but the bead of sweat rolling down his forehead made a liar out of him.

"One..." Quinn darted toward the pair.

They both squealed, spun away, crashing gracelessly through the undergrowth and deeper into the woods, grunting, falling, and swearing as they struggled. The reporter was in the lead, the cameraman dragging behind as he lugged his heavy camera, wheezing with the weight of it.

Quinn reached for Ellie and pulled her into his arms.

"They followed me!" Ellie said, still angry and shaking at the same time. They stood together, both catching their breath, Ellie wiped the tears from her face, embarrassed. "What a ninny I am. I'm not usually a crier."

"Ah, darling." Quinn refused to let her pull away and she gratefully stayed in the safety of his arms and let her breathing slow. "This is such a heavy load for you to carry alone, let me help if I can." He turned her face to look at him and brushed a stray tear with his thumb. "I'm sorry I said those things, and I shouldn't have left you."

Ellie nodded her acceptance of his words and pulled away from him. After a moment of consideration, she surprised him by reaching out hesitantly and tentatively twined her fingers with his. His fingers curled protectively around hers. She murmured. "They'll... they'll do anything for this story."

They stood together for a moment, listening. The sounds of the struggling news team were gone.

Ellie blinked at him brightly. "I'm guessing the treehouse will have to wait for another day.

"Sounds like a plan," he agreed. "Going home now?"

She nodded. They fell in step, beginning the journey back to Ellie's house through the peaceful forest path still hand in hand, Cali quietly padding behind them. Quinn liked the feel of Ellie's hand in his. After several moments, he suggested, "Maybe we should give them something to throw them off track. A story about you saving Gavyn—"

"Ergh!" Ellie stopped in her tracks and stepped away from him, their fragile connection broken. "I don't want to go through that again. You have no idea what they put me through when my family died."

"Ellie." Quinn retook her hand firmly in his and they continued walking. "I know what they're like. I live with it every day, even when I'm not working with Owen." He glanced at her down-turned face, adding, "It's this ridiculously handsome face."

She blurted out a laugh, just as he'd intended. "Indeed."

***

After wolfing down the monster sized ham and cheese sandwiches with salad Quinn put together for supper, they changed into bathing suits and headed back to the pond. Cali was thrilled to have someone else tossing her ball back and forth and by the time they reached the water she dove in after her toy, brought it back to shore and collapsed on the grass beside it, ready for a nap.

Quinn and Ellie swam and raced each other back and forth through the cool water and ended up on twin towels by the diving rock drying off in the late day sun.

Quinn had filled Ellie in on the remainder of his family tree and told riotous stories of misadventures his brothers and he had gotten into when younger. Ellie appreciated that he took credit for the good *and* the bad. "It's not that I was better at climbing a tree than anyone, I scoped them out beforehand and knew which ones would hold me and how quickly I could make it to the top before them. But I guess I shouldn't have put money bets on it. I made a lot of money that summer!"

"Always a planner then?" She admired that in him. Forward thinking, checking out the angles before committing to something.

"Not to say I'm not spontaneous at times." He followed this by leaning over and planting a kiss on her lips before rolling back to his towel as if nothing had happened.

"Goodness, don't let anyone say that!" She wished he'd be more spontaneous.

"Look." He pointed to the darkening sky. "The stars are amazing here!"

Ellie couldn't believe they'd been lying here, chatting about everyday things for hours. The sky was indeed dimming, a slight cool breeze picked up and here they were still in their bathing suits, though now wrapped in towels for a bit of warmth. And yes, they'd moved closer to one another and she could feel his body heat beside her.

"Gavyn would love this," he said quietly.

"Does he make you want to have children of your own?" she asked before realizing what a personal question that must be.

But Quinn answered honestly. "I never thought I would want kids, but I think I do."

The silence between them grew and she wondered if he was waiting for a response of some kind regarding her intentions for children in the future.

"I think I do, too." She sat up in surprise. It was the first time she had even admitted that to herself, having spent the last four years promising herself she'd never let that kind of pain and loss into her life again. But what was living without taking chances?

"I bet you're a great Mom. Everyone deserves a chance to be a parent."

"I know where you're going with that, Quinn." She turned to him and gave him a weary smile. "But I have to find the proof for Sophie on my own. It's the least I can do for Aunt Jenna. Does that make sense?"

"Totally." He brought her fingers to his lips for a gentle kiss. "Just know you've got help if you need it. But right now, you probably need a good night's sleep before your adventure."

He stood and helped her up, retrieved both of their towels and slung them over his shoulder before reclaiming her hand. Their fingers fit together with ease.

When they reached the treehouse, he paused and bent down for the hammer they had discarded earlier in the day. With a couple of strong whacks, he affixed the loose step to the tree then stood back to gaze up at the building above.

"Ruth and Shirley used to play there," Ellie said. "And then Winnie and I used to have picnics and draw marvelous creatures we were sure lived in our pond. You can make out the corner of the pond from up there." Her smile was relaxed, the pain of the memories easing and becoming bearable, almost sought after. Something to welcome instead of hiding from.

It was full dark when they walked into the house. Cali had finished her nightly routine had her fill from her bowl and meandered into the living room to plop down on her rug by the couch. There was a new person in her space and she seemed to enjoy it.

After changing into bed attire, which for Quinn meant a pair of loose shorts, he picked up his sleeping bag and rolled it out on the living room carpet.

"There *is* a guest room." Ellie pointed up the stairs, desperately ignoring his lack of clothes.

"I think I'll stay on the ground floor," he replied. "Just in case."

She didn't want to imagine what the "just in case" might be. She was too tired, and the next day would probably be even more exhausting than this one had been. "Good night," she said softly as she watched him in the low light of the living room. She turned off the kitchen light before she went up the stairs, leaving him with Cali who was already curled up at the foot of his sleeping bag.

***

"Good night." Quinn watched Ellie trail up the stairs from the couch, knowing the chances of him slowing his thoughts this night was slim to none. His nerves were on alert and he'd probably get only a few hours of sleep.

How was he going to let her go on her research trip alone tomorrow? How could he let her out of his sight now?

How could he not trust she knew what was best in her own situation?

Chapter Thirty-Four

Ellie tip-toed out of the house as the early morning sun was peeking through the treetops.

Quinn was lying on the couch, sleeping bag open to his hips, chest bare. One arm was flung across his eyes as if protecting them from any light that might streak through the living room window. She watched him breathe, regular, in and out. He pretended to sleep like a pro.

She went through the mudroom and gently opened the back door, the only one that didn't squeak. As she stepped out into the fresh morning air, Cali dashed off in front of her. Ellie felt secure leaving Cali with Quinn for the day. They'd keep each other company.

She wanted to run back inside and ask him to come with her, for once let someone else help her and take some of the pressure off. But not this time. This was family and something she had to do on her own.

Cali stopped and looked back at the house as Ellie got in her car. Ellie refused to do so. She knew what she would see. Quinn standing in the window. It said a lot that he pretended to be asleep and let her go. It also said a lot that she let him.

***

Ellie pulled into the Cozy Corner Café parking lot minutes later. The store was dark, but the kitchen was alive with light as Maggie went about baking her sought after pastries. The smell drew Ellie through the back door and into the already hot room.

"Coffee's on the counter," Maggie called to her as she pulled out a pan from the oven.

Ellie soaked in the luscious aroma of chocolate muffins. "I need a minute to gather my thoughts," she whispered.

"And another minute to wolf down a muffin." Maggie shook her head knowingly. "I do wish you'd take time to savour these morsels."

"Can't help it." Ellie picked up a coffee cup and stood close to Maggie while the muffins were moved to the cooling rack.

"Five minutes," Maggie said.

"But I'm leaving now." Ellie eyed the chocolate delights and licked her lips. "I could take one and wait till it cooled down?"

"As if you'd wait for anything!" Maggie watched her friend move about the kitchen. "Where's your knight in shining armour?"

"I think he's standing at my living room window cursing he didn't make more of a case for coming with me."

"Brave man."

"Smart man."

"We'll see." Maggie took a hot muffin and placed it into a paper bag and held it out. "Really, though, don't burn your mouth on this."

"You're a peach."

"I saw the skunks running for their lives yesterday." Maggie's serious voice stopped Ellie dead. "They were soaking wet and really ticked off. What did Quinn do to them?"

"He advised them it would be in their best interests to leave me..." Ellie's attention was caught by the newscast on the TV behind Maggie. "Oh, for pity's sake!"

Maggie turned to see Diane on the screen and a quick take away video of Ellie in Quinn's arms at the treehouse. The picture was slightly out of focus and shaky, but it was them.

"They got footage of us anyway, those slimeballs!" Ellie was stunned. "I should have hit him with the hammer when I had the chance."

"Do you want me to turn it up?"

"No!" Ellie gathered her things. "I'm going to Steller Heights to find out what I can about Aunt Jenna and Sophie. I can't let Diane get any closer, Maggie. I don't want her nose in my business, and now she's making things up about Quinn and I. He's going to flip a lid."

"You think so?"

"Look at us." Ellie stared at the TV. "We look like a couple."

"Far be it for me to tell you how to live your romantic life," Maggie started.

"Oh, sure, far be it." Ellie knew what was coming.

"So I won't." Maggie looked her dead in the eye. "But are you sure you want to find out the truth about Sophie? This could open a whole can of worms you might never recover from."

"Sophie needs to know and Aunt Jenna needs to, well, be free of whatever this might be."

"You can't make that decision for her."

Ellie held her gaze, allowing Maggie to see the dread she felt.

"Be careful." Maggie gave her a quick hug and turned back to her baking. "Feels like rain so drive carefully."

Ellie glanced out the window, not a cloud in the sky. But she had learned not to dismiss Maggie's intuition, and to listen to her advice and counsel with both ears wide open. Maggie was usually right, which was very annoying.

Ellie returned to her car, put her coffee in the holder and opened the muffin bag. Not to eat, just to inhale and let it cool faster. She started the car and sat for a moment, settling herself and enjoying the peace of the morning. The birds were flying from tree to tree, singing their good mornings to each other. She watched a lone fox dash across the road into the woods beyond. The day was beginning for everyone.

She drove onto the empty highway and headed to Stellar Heights. Had she been looking in her rear-view mirror, she would have seen the black car parked down the road pull out slowly behind her.

Chapter Thirty-Five

B y Ellie's map calculations, she should be in Stellar Heights in an hour. So far, the weather was holding, no rain yet. Ellie hated to drive in bad weather. It reminded her of the day her family died, the policeman turning up at her door, rain pouring off his hat as he informed her of the fatal accident.

She adjusted her butt in the seat and settled in for the ride. She hit play on her CD player to let Hugh Laurie's latest CD start. This was her favourite driving music and she turned it up until she could feel the vibrations in her bones. Fun, toe-tapping music. Music to chase away painful memories, put a smile on her face and make her want to sing along. If she had a voice, that is.

Music had helped her manage her pain in the past few years. She was getting better at catching herself before she hit bottom and found that choosing her memories and associating them with good times got her through a lot of rough patches.

Ellie followed the meticulous directions she'd written out for herself. The joke in the family was if she had been an olden days' explorer in charge of plotting out the path, everyone would have got lost and died. Sophie had bought her a GPS for the car but Ellie knew it would be too distracting for her. She preferred maps, pen and paper, things she could grasp in her hands over technology.

Half an hour into her drive she pulled into a gas station and took out the map once more. From here she needed to pay closer attention to the directions, so she double checked everything. She'd never travelled this way before and the scenery was spectacular. Only a few other vehicles passed her at this early hour and she felt alone in the world.

She stepped out of the car for a stretch and adjusted the cushion on her seat. Sometimes she hated being tiny. At least her feet reached the pedals.

Ellie pulled a chewy bar out of her pocket and ripped it open. The muffin had disappeared in the first five minutes of her drive, and it had tasted as delicious as it smelled. She knew this break was purely procrastinating before reaching her goal, but she needed a breather. Once she found out the truth there would be no turning back. Everyone's life would change, and lord knows, she hated change. She should probably work on that defect... if she had to.

Ellie looked around the empty station parking lot. Not a person in sight. A sound drew her attention and she shaded her eyes with her hand and glanced up at a flock of birds flying overhead. She watched until they disappeared over the forest.

Ah, this is nonsense, she told herself as she threw the wrapper in the garbage can nearby. Time to face whatever lay ahead. She got back in the car, buckled up, and headed back onto the highway. Three more small towns to pass through and then onto some smaller back roads. Thirty more minutes, if she didn't lose her way, and she'd be in Steller Heights.

As she looked both ways before turning back onto the highway her eyes skimmed over a car parked down the road on the shoulder. It was a blip in her mind and then forgotten.

***

Forty minutes and one wrong turn later, Ellie pulled up at the park in Steller Heights. She sat still, gathering her thoughts and calming the jitters that raced through her stomach. The last ten minutes she had driven through rain, clouds appearing and dropping a steady stream of wet against her windshield, only to end the moment she drove down the road to the town.

She got out, took her backpack, locked the door, and approached the sign. It looked newly painted, startling black and white lettering, looking proud and regal at the entrance to a well-maintained green oasis beyond. She raised her hand and ran it along the wood. The roughness told her the sign was old, carefully hidden under the facelift of new paint.

The land spread out as far as she could see, with a playground off to the right, a baseball field in the far distance, and a pond to the left. Young children played in the park, their mothers standing around the wet benches, chatting together as they kept an eye on their offspring.

An older man stood near the pond, his hands behind his back, his eyes staring straight ahead. From around a large bush came a duck, followed by five ducklings, trailing her like a long tail. The man didn't move a muscle, but Ellie saw a smile creep up his face. The duck family walked within feet of him, never stopping, continuing on and into the water. Once they were all in, they turned and faced him.

He pulled his hands forward and opened the bag he held. He tossed handfuls of cracked corn into the water and laughed as the mother and ducklings swam towards the food and gobbled it all down. When the bag was empty, he held it up to show them there was nothing more. They swam around for a few minutes before sedately paddling away.

The whole scene captivated Ellie.

The old man caught her eye, nodded his head, and turned to walk further into the woods around the park.

Ellie realized she had been smiling since the ducks appeared.

Perhaps it was a good omen.

Perhaps this was a good place.

***

Across from the park stood the town church. The wood building was small and would have held the congregation when built and probably continued to hold the dwindling population now.

Ellie walked over and read the announcement board out front.

Holy Trinity.

Services this Sunday at 11:00 a.m.

Messes ce Dimanche a 11h00.

The church was made of stone and wood; stone from ground to below the windows, with the wood racing up and into the roof above. She ran her hand down the wall near the front door. Ellie loved to feel the texture of things, the temperature of things, the energy of things. This building felt calm, mature, settled.

She walked around to the side, fingers sliding along the wall, following the flow of the building until she reached the back. She dropped her hand and stared in awe.

A graveyard lay ahead, surrounded by a white picket fence. Graveyards were one of her most favorite places to do research. When she told people it was one of her "happy places", she got the strangest looks.

Most of the tombstones here appeared old, some chipped, while others had barely legible writing. She opened the gate and stepped through. The gate, like the surrounding air, was quiet, as if someone had oiled it that very morning.

The only sound that disturbed the silence was the dripping of water drops from the trees circling the graveyard, while the smell of wet newly mown grass filled her nose.

The cemetery itself had a modest layout with the markers arranged evenly. She noticed a few grouped together at the far end, sheltered by a large tree. They drew her.

She walked along the middle path, glancing to the sides as she went. The lawn was well tended and plastic flower arrangements in vases were placed on certain of the graves. The group at the back were small plots with tiny headstones. Children. She read the names and realized none were related to each other. Why would these children not be buried with their families?

Ellie was halfway through the grouping when she stopped short and caught her breath. There before her was a small ivory stone, simple and plain.

The inscription read: *Baby Sophie October 3, 1990.*

The air came out of her lungs in a whoosh. Could this be Aunt Jenna's daughter? Had she stolen someone's child and named her Sophie after her own baby died?

Ellie shook her head in disbelief. She normally wasn't one to let her imagination get away with her like this. She needed proof. Her gut clenched, and she hoped this tiny child wasn't who she was looking for. Reluctantly she took out her camera and snapped a picture of the tombstone of Baby Sophie. To keep herself centred and on track, she had to treat this like a case for a client. Gather information and confirmation. Don't make assumptions.

The rain started again, a soft drizzle, but enough to slip along Ellie's neck and send a shiver down her spine. Ellie turned away from the tiny headstone to the church and saw a smaller building attached off the back. A faint light burning in the window beckoned her.

She left the graveyard, closing the gate gently. When she reached the door, it flew open and an older woman smiled out at her. A bight blue sweater was tied around her neck, strands of long wavy grey hair caught in the folds.

"Come in, come in!" She held the door wide for Ellie to step inside. "What a day to be a taphophile!"

Ellie closed the door behind her and smiled back at the grandmotherly woman before her.

"A taphophile?" she asked.

"Someone who loves being in graveyards." The woman motioned for Ellie to follow her. "Lots of people do it. They find graveyards to be calming places."

"I totally agree! But actually, I'm looking for a particular grave and I believe I found it." Ellie crossed the threshold into the room beyond.

It wasn't a huge space but one wall held nothing but shelves and books and binders. A fire crackled in a grate on the far wall and a large worktable sat in the middle of the room. Two comfy chairs flanked the fireplace. A desk stood in the corner, piled high with papers and a small laptop.

"Have a seat, Miss?"

"Ellie." She held out her hand to shake the older woman's. "Ellie McLellan."

"Geraldine Harold." The woman shook her hand. She had a warm, firm grip. "But everyone calls me Gerry."

Ellie sat in one of the comfy chairs and Gerry brought another cup to the small table and put it down beside her own.

"Tea?" she offered.

"Thank you, yes." Ellie gratefully accepted and welcomed the warmth of the cup in her hands. She inhaled the aroma of the tea then took a sip. Heaven.

Gerry took the other seat and studied Ellie for a minute. "Did you find who you were looking for?"

"I think so." Ellie looked thoughtful. "I found a tombstone that might be family. Baby Sophie, out by the back wall."

"Ah, yes, the poor little ones," Gerry whispered.

"Why are there so many?" Ellie asked the question that had been bothering her. "And why are they not with their families?"

"Most of those children are from people passing through who didn't settle here, or who moved away. A lot of people moved away. Early on they thought it a good idea to rest them all together."

"That's a nice thought," Ellie said. "Would there be any records of them, or who their parents were or anything else?"

Gerry placed her cup in its saucer and jumped up from her seat. She was spritelier than her age led one to believe. "We've got the original church records here." She walked to a shelf and looked back at Ellie. "Do you remember the year?"

Ellie pulled out her camera out and brought up the picture she had taken of the grave. "Baby Sophie, October 3, 1990".

Gerry ran her fingers across a few old books and settled on a newer one. She removed it and brought it back to their chairs. Ellie tried not to get too excited. Sometimes what appeared to be an easy answer ended up as a dead end.

Gerry opened the cover and turned the pages. She slipped on a pair of glasses hanging from a chain around her neck, started to read and found the entry near the beginning. "Ah, here it is," Gerry said. "Baby Sophie Keyes, died at childbirth, oh, poor thing." Gerry looked up at Ellie. "Poor mother too. Let me see," she continued reading. "Mother Jenna Keyes and father William Keyes. Is that who you're looking for?" She looked at Emma's stunned face over the top of her glasses.

"Yes," Ellie whispered. "But that can't be right."

"It's the wrong information?"

"No, yes, I don't know!" Ellie looked startled. "May I?" she asked Gerry, who nodded her understanding. Ellie put her tea on the table beside her and picked up her camera. Gerry held the book open for her to snap a picture of the entry.

Ellie's shoulders slumped, her mind racing. She needed more information. "Is there a library in town?" she asked Gerry.

"Indeed, there is." Gerry smiled at her. "But it won't be open for..." she stopped to peer at her watch, "...about ten minutes from now."

Ellie looked at her watch. It read 3:12. How unusual to open a library at 3:22! She looked quizzically at Gerry.

"I open it when I feel like it," Gerry laughed. "Usually Saturdays and Sundays it's opened at regular hours but if you need to look for something, we can go over now."

"That's really generous of you, Gerry." Ellie was amazed by the kindness of people, especially strangers.

"Not at all." Gerry got up and put on her coat. "Sounds as if you have a mystery you want to solve. Which is a lot more interesting than filing!"

Within minutes they had locked up the church hall, crossed the street past the park and entered a newer looking building.

Stellar Heights Library the sign read.

Gerry opened the door, turned on the lights, and ushered her in.

Chapter Thirty-Six

Ellie stopped short when she entered the building. The lights were bright, like a welcoming warmth that circled the room in a hug.

"Come along." Gerry bustled in, shrugged out of her coat, dropped her keys on the main counter and turned to Ellie with a grin. "Where to start?"

Ellie glanced around and spotted the microfilm readers. That could mean old records. "Do you have any newspapers for this town?"

"Oh, yes," Gerry smiled. "What year would you like?"

"I guess about the time Baby Sophie died, so October, 1990?"

Gerry took a minute to think, hand raised to her lips, eyes narrowed in thought. "Those we have in paper form," she decided out loud and headed to a large cabinet at the back of the room.

Ellie followed behind, walking between rows of bookshelves. She reached out and ran her fingers along the spines of the books as she passed. The coolness of the leather made her shiver.

"Here we are." Gerry read the dates on the front. "This one." She pulled one drawer open and showed a stack of old newspapers.

Ellie looked closer and found the year Baby Sophie had died. As good a place as any to begin.

"It's not the best filing system, but it's all we can afford." Gerry picked up the six newspapers Ellie chose and walked over to a large table.

"This should keep me busy." Ellie took off her jacket and draped it over the chair. "Oh." she glanced at her watch. "How long do I have?"

"As long as you want, dear." Gerry patted her hand. "I've got new book wrappers to put on." She waved airily towards her desk at the front, it's surface invisible under a stack of books.

"Thank you," Ellie said warmly.

"No worries. If you need help, just holler." Gerry hummed to herself as she left Ellie at the table.

With the newspapers in order by date, Ellie started with the issue right after Baby Sophie's death. The newspapers weren't large but were filled with interesting items concerning the town and its people. Ellie caught herself reading articles that had nothing to do with her search and enjoyed them all.

She learned the playground had been installed months before Baby Sophie died, and an anonymous donor had paid for the purchase of the equipment and landscaping. The volunteer fire department had installed the equipment and the Independent Woman's Institute had organized a picnic on the day of the grand opening.

There were pictures of young children playing on the new equipment, happy smiles beaming from their faces, their parents in the background on benches, picnics being eaten, everyone enjoying the day. Ellie searched the pictures carefully for the kind faces of her aunt and uncle. Nope, not there.

Ellie gave herself a mental shake and tried to focus on what she was looking for. But what did she hope to see? "Child Abducted, Family Desperate for News"? It was never that easy.

For the next hour, she flipped through the pages of the five issues that might hold information.

Nothing. No missing children. No mysterious goings on. Not even an announcement of Baby Sophie's death. This part of her search appeared to be a dead end.

Time to switch gears.

Gerry had watched her and noticed how Ellie's shoulders had slumped lower and lower until she folded up the last newspaper and returned it to the pile.

Gerry knew that look; information not found. She put down the book she was covering and went to sit at the table across from Ellie. "Didn't find what you were looking for?"

"No." Ellie shook her head. "And I'm not sure if that's a good thing or not."

"What next then?" Gerry asked. "You appear to be a woman who has a plan of some sort."

Ellie smiled at her. "I have several plans. Next up is—Was there a boarding house in this town at that time?"

"There was." Gerry smiled, holding her gaze intently. "Mrs. Petersen's Boarding House. Mostly for the men and some families who worked around here back then. A few single women, too. The building is still there, empty now, sad to say. It was a lovely building. It's past the Retirement Home, half a mile on the right."

Ellie's face fell at hearing this.

"As a matter of fact," Gerry said, "Mrs. Petersen is still alive. She's at that very same Retirement Home."

"Would she remember that time?" Ellie had a glint of excitement in her eyes.

"Not only would she remember, but she might talk your ear off!" Gerry laughed. "Let me get you the address."

Gerry returned to her desk while Ellie hastily pulled her jacket back on. A ray of sun streamed through the window onto the table in front of her and she turned to see the sun shining brightly outside.

Another good omen?

"Here you go." Gerry handed her a piece of paper when Ellie reached the front of the library. As Ellie took the paper with the directions, Gerry put her old hand on Ellie's and whispered "It gets easier, dear. Be patient and let people help you. Especially that young man."

Ellie knew exactly what Gerry was telling her, but was too surprised to respond. The TV news clips had spread faster than she thought. Did everyone know who she was and her whole life story?

But Gerry only smiled and squeezed her hand. "Good luck with your hunting. And if you need more help, you come find me."

Ellie reached out and gave her a big hug. Gerry's hug was tighter. "Thank you." Ellie turned away before she started blubbering and pushed open the door to the library. She stood on the steps for a minute, in the sun, taking deep breaths and then looked at the directions on the paper.

Another lead. Another possibility.

Chapter Thirty-Seven

Gerry's directions proved to be excellent and Ellie arrived at the Retirement Home five minutes later. A car had followed her from the library and was slowing as she reached the entrance. She caught it in her rear-view mirror but couldn't see the driver.

Ellie pulled into the lot and parked as the other car drove by and out of sight. She shook her head in disgust—now she was being paranoid. She took a minute to clear her thoughts and look around. Everything she'd seen about this town had a welcome feel. The forest was everywhere, and old trees commanded space on the grounds surrounding the large building in front of her.

Shadows danced on the Retirement Home's walls and windows from the sun shining through the branches of nearby trees.

Ellie walked in through the main doors and stopped at the reception.

"May I help you?" asked a small, elderly man from behind the desk. He looked like a resident of the home himself.

"Yes." Ellie checked the piece of paper Gerry had given her. "I was wondering if I could speak with Mrs. Petersen."

The man smiled at her and sighed. "Wish we could all speak with Mrs. Petersen."

Ellie knew a crush when she saw one and smiled as he caught himself and straightened up.

"Are you a relative?" he asked.

"No," Ellie said. "My aunt stayed in her boarding house many years ago and I'd like to speak to her about that. I'm a genealogist," she added, not knowing why that would matter.

"Family history then?" He looked interested.

"Exactly."

"Your name?"

"Ellie McLellan."

"Give me a minute." He got up, headed down a hallway and disappeared into the last room.

Ellie waited.

He reappeared at the end of the hall and waved at her, beckoning her to join him. Ellie met him in front of an open door, and he gestured her inside. "Mrs. Petersen would love to speak with you." Again, he sighed.

"Thank you." Ellie watched as he reluctantly headed back to his post at the reception.

"Isn't he a peach?" called a voice from inside the room.

Ellie stepped in and saw a tiny, elderly lady sitting in a comfy chair beside the window, basking in the sun's heat, her white hair lit like a halo.

"Jed is a dear." Mrs. Petersen smiled.

"He seems quite fond of you," Ellie said.

"Really?" The older woman seemed surprised. "He hardly says two words to me, but he's very helpful."

Ellie sat in the only other chair in the room. "Maybe he's just shy."

"Hmm." Mrs. Petersen smoothed the blanket that lay across her knees. "I never thought about that. Now, Miss McLellan, what can I do for you?"

"Well, I'm trying to find information about a young woman who stayed at your boarding house back in 1990."

"Jed said it was your aunt?"

"Well, my aunt was a friend of this young woman and they were both pregnant."

"Ah," Mrs. Petersen said. "I know who you mean. Only one girl stayed with me who was pregnant and that was Helen. Don't remember her last name. Poor little thing, her husband went north to work and, well, disappeared. She was alone."

Ellie took out the picture of Helen and her aunt and passed it to Mrs. Petersen.

"Did *she* live here?" Ellie pointed to her Aunt.

"No, I don't believe so." Mrs. Petersen gazed at the picture as if it would reveal some long-hidden memory. "Helen had no visitors except this lady here, but she wasn't a boarder."

"That would be my Aunt Jenna."

"Jenna! That's right." Mrs. Petersen smiled at her. "What a lovely woman. How is she?"

"She's had health problems but she'll be okay."

"Such a sad thing when her baby died." Mrs. Petersen's comment hammered another nail in the coffin of Ellie's hopes.

"Yes." Ellie didn't want to reveal too much. "My aunt wanted to get in touch with Helen again. Would you know where Helen went or where she was from?"

"No." Mrs. Petersen shook her head sadly. "She gave birth the day your aunt's daughter passed away. Within days Helen was gone. She left money for a whole week's rent in her room, but her things disappeared, as did she and her baby. A lot of people left that week, including your aunt and uncle. The weather had changed for the better and people were on the move."

Ellie couldn't tell this lovely old woman that her aunt had returned home *with* a baby. She had no explanation for that.

"I remember one thing about young Helen though," Mrs. Petersen added. "She loved to draw. I'd find her drawings on scraps of paper, napkins, anything she could get her hands on. She was very talented." Mrs. Petersen pushed aside the blanket and rose gingerly to her feet. Ellie got up to help her but the older woman shooed her away.

"Here," Mrs. Petersen picked up a framed drawing from the side of her bed, "I kept this when she left. I always thought it was her baby, but I can't be sure."

She held out a small pencil drawing of a sleeping baby. The lines were detailed, delicate, and showed the obvious talent of the artist.

"It's beautiful." Ellie wondered if this was her cousin Sophie.

Ellie handed it back and Mrs. Petersen made her way slowly back to her chair.

"If I were looking for someone," Mrs. Petersen started, "which I'm not, but I read a lot of mysteries, perhaps you could focus on her artistic talent."

"I'll keep that in mind," Ellie said. "I'll probably search for her name first."

"If she hasn't married," Mrs. Petersen offered.

"A lot of women in Quebec keep their maiden names after marriage," Ellie noted.

"Not back in those days."

"Depending on when she got married," Ellie agreed. "When I got married, they wanted $250 to change my name to my husband's. I decided to keep mine."

Mrs. Petersen studied her. "I can only imagine what you went through, dear."

Ellie felt a jolt pass through her. It took getting used to when strangers appeared to know her whole history. "It's disturbing having old news brought up again."

"I can imagine it is," Mrs. Petersen agreed. "But new events will bury the old news quickly these days. So hold tight and you'll weather this just fine."

"Thank you." Ellie reached out and took the old woman's hand. "I've been getting the greatest kindness from complete strangers these days."

"Some of us have experienced similar things in our lives, my dear." She gave Ellie's hand a squeeze. "We are more alike than you know."

"Well." Ellie stood up and gathered her purse. "Thank you so much for your information and suggestions, Mrs. Petersen. This gives me something to work with."

"Wait a minute," the woman blurted as if a thought had struck her out of the blue. "I may have all the guest records still at the boarding house. I'm selling it you know, but my granddaughter is fixing it up for me first."

"You have records that far back?" Ellie felt that elusive discovery-bubble of excitement gurgle through her.

"Oh, most certainly" Mrs. Petersen said. "I'm something of a pack rat I'm afraid. It's part of what Gillian will do for me before the sale. Tidy up, toss out."

She turned to the table beside her and picked up her phone. "Are you in a hurry to get home?" she asked Ellie.

"No, not at all." Ellie sat back down.

"Gilly," Mrs. Petersen spoke into the phone. "Do me a favour, dear. I've a young lady here who is looking for family and I'm sure I have the answer. Can you meet her at the boarding house and let her look through the records on the dining room table? They're in the box marked guests." She paused, listening to the voice on the other end. "Thanks, love, she'll be there shortly."

"This is very kind of you, Mrs. Petersen." Ellie was sure that if the record existed, it might be the next piece of the puzzle.

"Not at all, I'm thrilled to help you." The old woman beamed at her. "Gilly will meet you there, and if you find Helen, tell her I hope she and her daughter are having a wonderful life."

Ellie froze. "I'll do that," she managed to squeak out. "Enjoy your day."

"How can I not?" Mrs. Petersen waved to the window and the sunshine. "Summer is around the corner and I'll spend most of my time in the gardens again. Did I mention Jed is an amazing gardener?"

"No, you didn't. Have you told him that?"

"No." Mrs. Petersen hesitated. "Perhaps I should."

"Perhaps you should."

Chapter Thirty-Eight

E llie noticed the car following her the minute she pulled out of the retirement home parking lot. It looked exactly like the one she'd seen in town.

This wasn't garden variety paranoia. Her emotions rocketed from uneasy to slight fear to downright anger. If the press were pursuing her, she didn't want to give them even a hint of scandal to latch onto. Within minutes she arrived at Mrs. Petersen's Boarding House.

The old sign still graced the front, in need of paint and a few nails to hold it straight but the building itself was still impressive. Buildings always fascinated her. They had a history and feel some people were oblivious to. She pulled into the empty parking lot and waited. She watched in her rear-view mirror as the other car drove by. Before she could glimpse the person behind the wheel, it disappeared around a bend.

Ellie waited to see if it would return. It didn't. Maybe it *was* all in her mind. She grabbed her camera, got out of her car and took a few pictures of the boarding house and sign for Sophie.

The boarding house had four floors in total. Two old wooden chairs still sat on the wide front porch, and a two-seater swing moved slowly back and forth from its rusty chains beside them.

An overgrown rock path drew her around the side of the large structure and the damp grass reached mid-calf, leaving a wet mark on her jeans. As she arrived at the back, Ellie stopped and caught her breath.

A stone patio ran the length of the building. At the end of a stretch of overgrown grass was a large pond. The grass had been cut in a six-foot swath around it, the water was clean and a bench was placed nearby, facing the forest beyond. The woods appeared dense, the trees large and healthy, and the birds abundant and vocal as they flew from branch to branch.

Ellie snapped a few pictures of the pond and forest before turning to face the rear of the house. It was not what she expected.

The lower floor held glass windows that ran the length. Through one on the left, she saw a dining room with tables and chairs set as if expecting the next meal. Swinging doors separated the dining room from the kitchen. The kitchen counters were empty; the cupboard doors all closed, but this room also had a sense of waiting.

She took a few steps backwards, allowing the building to come into better view the further she moved away from it. A balcony ran from one end of the house to another, serving the rooms on the top floor. Those rooms must have cost a pretty penny to stay in.

Two other floors rested below the top, each with its windows gleaming clean in the sun. Ellie figured the building was at least 150 years old. It seemed in amazing condition on the outside, but that didn't mean the inside was still livable.

"Would you be the lady Gran told me about?" The question came in the form of a small voice from behind her.

Ellie swung around in surprise and saw a young woman coming out of the forest towards her.

"That would be me! Are you Gillian?" asked Ellie.

"Gilly is fine." Gillian put on the hat she had been carrying and smiled at Ellie. She wore old jeans, scuffed work boots and a t-shirt spotted with grass and dirt.

"I didn't see your car," Ellie said.

"I live through the woods, past there." Gilly motioned back to the forest and the path she had taken.

"Your Gran said she was selling this lovely building."

"Actually, I bought the place two days ago." Gilly beamed as if this was the high point of her life.

"How wonderful!" Ellie grinned, taking a quick peek back at the building. "I envy you. What will you do with it?"

"Restore it," Gilly said. "My grandmother ran this for years and I played in it before it closed down. Imagine having this as your playground! I'd like to turn it into a B&B."

"Does your Gran know?"

"I haven't told her yet," Gilly replied. "It's a surprise. I want her to help me fix it up, at least give me some suggestions."

"I'm sure she'll be delighted." Ellie loved her gusto.

"Come on then, I know the box Gran is talking about." She unlocked the solid wood door and Ellie walked in behind her, waiting for Gilly to turn on a few lights. "Good thing we never disconnected! Gran asked me to keep the place tidy, for when she sold, but I've been secretly doing renovations. Did I mention I love it here?" She laughed at Ellie.

"I think you did!"

"Here we go." Gilly reached for a banker's box on the table and threw open the lid. "I have to say this for Gran, everything was always organized."

"It's a dying art." Ellie thanked her lucky stars that Mrs. Petersen was one of the organized ones.

"Do you mind if I leave you alone?" Gilly asked. "I have to get back home. Close the lights and pull the door closed behind you when you leave. It locks automatically."

"You trust me with this?" Ellie didn't trust people easily these days and finding it so willing and free in someone she had just met astonished her.

"If you're here because of Gran, I trust you." Gilly walked out. "You obviously love history as much as I do! Happy hunting!"

"Thanks," Ellie called to Gilly's retreating back. And then she was alone with the box wide open in front of her with tidy labelled files waiting for her to dive into.

But what if the records weren't here? What if she couldn't find Helen's last name?

Ellie flipped through the files with vigour, reading the neatly handwritten dates and stopped abruptly at the one dated 1990. The year Helen had been staying here.

Ellie pulled the file out and lay it on the table. She opened it and scanned the names listed.

Halfway through the month of May, she found Helen listed at the bottom of a page.

Helen White.

No hometown noted, nothing more than her name, the room she had stayed in and the notation of having been a guest for over three months. But shouldn't her husband's name be her as well? A Mr. White? Nothing.

Ellie wrote the information in her notebook and put the file back. Her heart raced with excitement and fear. This was something concrete that could move them forward. But to what?

With all resources searched and noted, Ellie decided to continue her photographic spree with a few inside pictures. She didn't think Gilly or Mrs. Petersen would mind. Ellie wanted to see the room Helen had stayed in, so she climbed the staircase to the second floor where the smaller rooms were.

Up here, the air was fresh, as if every window in the place had been opened at once and the stuffiness of years of being closed had flown out. The carpets along the staircase and hallways were vacuumed clean and not a spot of dust lined any surface that Ellie could see. Gilly had been a busy beaver.

She walked the hall and counted three bedrooms on each side and a bathroom at the end. She peeked into each room and noted they all had furniture covered in sheets.

Helen's room was at the end of the hall near the bathroom, facing the backyard and forest. It held one small bed, a chest of drawers and a chair. It must have been nice for Helen to sit by the window and see the woods beyond. Ellie took pictures of the room and headed up to the top floor.

There were only two main doors on this floor and the bathroom. Ellie opened a smaller door at the end of the hall and found closets filled with old towels and sheets.

She opened one of the large doors and saw it connected to another room. She assumed these were for the families. The main room opened onto the balcony and it shared the same view to the forest that Helen would have enjoyed. Ellie snapped pictures as she went, finishing back down in the kitchen where she took a picture of the sun shining through the window and across the huge butcher block in the middle of the room.

Having captured the atmosphere as best she could for Sophie, she turned the light off in the dining room and stepped out onto the back patio, pulling the door closed behind her. When she heard the click of the lock, she took a deep breath. She had a name.

Helen's name. Possibly Sophie's mother.

How could she be happy about finding the information but also have a huge weight sitting heavy on her chest? Sometimes ignorance was bliss and sometimes knowledge had to be acted upon.

Ellie continued her exterior tour around the house and came to a huge enclosed garden. It's crumbling walls surrounded patches of ground waiting to be planted once more. Maybe Mrs. Petersen's Jed would be enlisted for this job.

Ellie ended up back at the front of the building. She climbed the porch and peered through a large window into what would have been the gathering room. More furniture under sheets with a lovely fireplace at one end.

As she started to turn, a reflection caught her eye.

The car that had been following her pulled into the driveway and parked beside hers.

And that weight in her chest became a boulder.

Chapter Thirty-Nine

Ellie refused to turn but recognized Diane Cooper's reflection as she got out of her car.

Ellie carefully backed off the porch with her camera in her hand, gripping it so hard the strap bit into her palm. She stalled and took more pictures of the front of the building.

Diane took her time walking over, and Ellie's shoulders cramped with tension.

"Lovely place." Diane looked at the sign and snapped a picture with her phone.

"It is," Ellie said through clenched teeth.

Diane gave her what she thought was a warm smile. "Is this where your family is from?"

"No."

"What are you doing here?" Diane asked.

"What are *you* doing here?"

"Following you."

"At least you're honest."

"You have no idea, Ellie."

"What do you want?"

"Why *are* you here?" Diane repeated her question and appeared genuinely curious.

"Working on a case for a client."

"They lived in the boarding house?"

"At one point."

"Didn't your aunt and uncle live in this town once?" Diane looked her straight in the eye.

Ellie was stunned by the question. How could Diane have found this out? What else did she know?

"You know, Ellie," Diane took a deep breath, "I'm not a bitch. Really. But I do want this story."

"What story is that?" Ellie wasn't giving her anything.

"About you and Quinn."

"There is no me and Quinn."

"I saw you two together." An unflattering shade of pink embarrassment crawled up Diane's neck. "And how he looked at you."

"Are you interested in him?" Ellie flung out. Was this about jealousy?

"Once," Diane admitted and turned back to the building to gather herself. "But even I know we're not suited. He's too nice." She laughed.

"But you're not a bitch," Ellie reminded her with a tight smile.

Diane stared at her for a moment, deciding which way she wanted to take this.

"Look, I need the story about you saving the boy." Diane turned from her as if keeping eye contact at this point was painful. "It's big news. And who you are, what you went through, all that is icing on the cake."

"You expect me to open myself up to that again just so you can have a good story?"

Diane didn't even hesitate. "No, I want you to open up so I don't have to release the rumour about you and Owen, or," she looked around at the scenery, "go looking for another story—like why you're *really* here."

Blackmail.

Ellie's stomach rolled with nausea. She gripped her camera and held her arm tight by her side to keep from flinging it into Diane's face.

She took a breath. *I'm not a violent person*, she repeated to herself like a mantra. *I'm not a violent person*. But this woman could test a saint.

"I'm working on a case, Diane." Ellie's jaw ached from trying to keep calm. "Nothing more."

"You know what, I don't care." Diane took a step closer. "But I do care about my future, and right now I need something big. And because, *unlike* me, you're not a bitch and you wouldn't put Owen and Lauren through a scandal. And it's the only choice you have." Diane's phone rang. She answered it, stepped away and spoke quietly.

Ellie let the air whoosh from her lungs and headed over to the sign and took a few more pictures. She tried to ignore Diane, hoping she'd leave.

Nope.

"So, here's the deal," Diane said as she pocketed her phone and returned to Ellie's side. "I'll give you till tomorrow to decide. I want an interview about how you've been doing since your family died, what exactly happened when you saved the kid, and what the Walsh family is like."

Ellie opened her mouth but Diane held up a hand.

"Think about it, Ellie, because otherwise, I'll write something, maybe not the truth and maybe not too flattering. Or maybe I'll come back here and look for a better story."

They stood staring at each other like gunslingers in the middle of a dusty town at high noon. Ellie felt like ice, yet beads of sweat trickled down her spine. She was seconds from becoming the violent person her mantra assured her she wasn't.

Diane jammed her sunglasses back on her nose and gave her a tired smile. "I don't always like my job, Ellie, but I've won awards at it, and I want more. I've got nothing to lose at this point." She waited for a dramatic pause and asked. "What do *you* have to lose?"

She took a card out of her pocket and handed it to Ellie.

Ellie refused to take it so Diane shrugged and put it on the ground by her feet.

"Tomorrow, three p.m. If I don't hear from you by then, I'll run what I've got on you and spice it up a bit. Then the stories get worse for you, better for me. It'll be a shame for Owen and Lauren. Be smart."

Diane walked away, not looking back. She slammed the car door shut behind her and left. Ellie couldn't move for a solid five minutes. Her body refused to do anything except hold her upright.

The clouds had returned during their conversation and the first drops hit her heated skin. It eased the fog of anger and frustration slightly, and she raised her face to the light spattering of rain.

She started for her car then went back for Diane's card on the ground.

It was wet, but the telephone number was still large and annoying.

Chapter Forty

The drive home took longer than expected. A jackknifed truck on the highway had stopped traffic for over half an hour, and Ellie was hungry, and thirsty, and pissed off at the way things were unfolding. As she pulled up to her driveway, she felt her shoulders drop in relief to see no press waiting to harass her.

But Quinn's car was still there. She unlocked the gate, drove through and relocked it before heading up the road. The rain had stopped halfway home, but the ground remained damp. When she parked, she saw tracks of what appeared to be a hundred dogs. The minute she slammed her car door Cali came running from around the side of the house. Mud clung to her fur from her paws to her shoulders. Drool hung from her mouth and she had glints of manic happiness in her eyes.

Quinn followed slower. He held a tennis ball, equally covered in dirt. His pants had traces of paw prints plastered to them and his hair was messed and wet, while his t-shirt was plastered to his broad chest. Ellie's heart skipped. She didn't want this picture to be real and yet she yearned for it with every cell in her body.

"Sorry." Quinn grinned at her. "She wouldn't stop playing and the mud came with the fun."

"Looks like the pond for you," Ellie said. With one hand motion and a quiet "pond" she pointed down the path and Cali ran off.

"Me too?" Quinn asked.

"Maybe just a change of clothes for now." Ellie tore her eyes from him and turned to lift the folders from her car.

"I'll take those." He took them from her and waited for her to lead the way. She wasn't used to this. She was usually the one giving the help, not accepting it, but she was so bone weary tired she let him as she made her way into the house.

"How did it go?" Quinn asked. "Did you find what you were looking for?"

"Yes and no." She kicked off her shoes and went to put the kettle on. The healing properties of tea was exactly what she needed. "Tea?"

"Sure."

Ellie busied herself with getting cups and the sugar bowl out.

"What did you find?" he pushed.

"You know what?" she whispered. "I have no idea how this all adds up. I don't even know if I want to talk about it because I don't have all the facts and I refuse to make assumptions."

"Hmm," Quinn said.

"What does that mean?" She brought the teapot and cups to the table and plunked her tired body down.

"It means I'm hurt you don't want to share." He sat across from her. "And it also means I totally understand, but sometimes two heads really are better than one."

"Fine." She threw her hands up in the air, a freeing gesture, as if sending out her frustrations and hoping he would catch them. He waited. "I found a grave marked Baby Sophie, and she was Aunt Jenna's baby."

Quinn sat up with a jerk but kept silent.

"The woman in the photo with Aunt Jenna is Helen White. I learned Aunt Jenna, Uncle William and this Helen White all left town within a day of each other, and Helen White is an artist. That's what I learned."

Silence.

"Okay," he started. "You do know I like you, right?"

Her eyes snapped open wide.

"Right?" he said a little louder.

"I guess so."

"I'll let that go because you're stressed out." He shook his head.

An uncomfortable tingle was starting in her neck.

"I'm going to say something here and you may not like it, but that's tough." He fidgeted in his chair and leaned forward.

Ellie leaned back in *her* chair; arms crossed over her chest for protection. Something was coming, and it was oozing towards her across the table.

"I worked in the Missing Children Division for longer than I should have," he began, nervously brushing his hair back from his face. "It wasn't fun. The one great thing was finding the kids and reuniting them with their families."

"But that didn't always happen," she said quietly.

"No," he confirmed. "But when it could be done, it was the best feeling ever. Imagine having your child disappear and not knowing what happened to them? Not knowing if they were alive or dead? Not knowing if someone was hurting them or loving them? Not knowing if they had forgotten about you or were hoping you would find them? Some people never recover, Ellie."

Ellie took a few calming breaths.

"What would *you* want?" he asked her.

She kept silent for a few minutes. "I totally agree with you, but it's not that simple."

"It's never *simple*, Ellie," he said quietly. "Ever. When children are involved, it rips your heart out."

"It's a fact that Sophie isn't Aunt Jenna's daughter," she blurted out. "I don't know how she came to be with Aunt Jenna."

"Adoption?"

"No one believes Sophie isn't Aunt Jenna's biological daughter."

"You think she kidnapped her?"

"Her own daughter died," Ellie repeated, wanting now to pull those words back. Now they were out there, they'd become alive.

"Sophie wants to find her family, doesn't she?" Quinn asked.

"Yes."

"And this Helen woman is obviously her mother. So, what are you going to do?"

"I'm not sure." Ellie wrapped her cold fingers around her cup of tea. She hadn't taken a sip, and it was cooling in her hands.

"You have to tell her." His voice had become gruff, and he sat back in his chair, watching her.

"But that would mean Aunt Jenna..." she couldn't finish.

"Ellie," he got up slowly and grabbed hold of the back of the chair, his knuckles turning white. "Find this woman and tell her that her daughter is alive and well. You owe her and Sophie that."

"I know!" Ellie gasped out the words. The repercussions of this situation were very clear.

Quinn stepped away from the table, his jaw clenching in anger. "I don't have a right to tell you what to do and this isn't my business."

"I'll find this Helen White first, and we'll go from there." Ellie stood up and held onto her chair for support.

"I said this was not my call, and I meant it." His quiet unnerved her. "But think about this very carefully."

She knew he was trying not to lose his cool over something he believed in from his very core. "But..." she started.

"I can't talk about this anymore." He turned and headed for the door. "I have to go but I'll be back tonight. Talk to Sophie."

The measure of his anger and frustration was evident by how gently he let the door close behind him as he left.

And how he didn't look at her again.

Chapter Forty-One

S ophie arrived for supper with a bottle of wine in hand, expecting the worst and wanting something to ease the pain, if needed. Ellie's raised eyebrows and snort when Sophie walked in and handed the wine to her made her realize she was off base. Alcohol wouldn't help and she didn't like drinking alone.

"I don't think so." Ellie put the bottle on the counter and motioned Sophie to the table.

Supper was ready, and it was a feast. BBQ chicken, potato salad, mixed veggies and a large container of iced tea.

Sophie sat down and looked at her cousin closely for the first time." You look... exhausted."

"It's been a long day."

"You might as well hit me with it now." Sophie took a leg of chicken and loaded potato salad onto her plate. Not much could take Sophie's appetite away. "You're making me nervous."

"Well, I think I found part of the story." Ellie took the smallest piece of chicken and a child's portion of salad.

"You know who my parents are?" Sophie halted in her scooping of veggies and waited for the answer.

"Not quite."

"What does that mean?" Carefully Sophie put the serving spoon down.

"Look." Ellie focused on her cousin's eyes and held her gaze without flinching. "I don't have all the answers, but... Aunt Jenna had a daughter named Sophie... and she died in October, 1990. I found her grave."

"Oh, for fu...!" Sophie let out. "Just tell me." She sat back in her seat, steeling herself for the worst. "Did Mom kidnap me?"

"I'm not sure," Ellie said. "I do know the other woman in the picture was named Helen White. She and her baby disappeared around the same time Aunt Jenna and Uncle William came home, with you."

"Oh, my God!" Sophie's eyes grew large. "Did she steal the baby and then kill this Helen?"

"For pity's sake, Sophie, your mom's not capable of something like that."

"My *mom*," Sophie muttered. "She's not even my mom. She's just some stranger!"

"Aunt Jenna is your mom, and don't you forget it." Ellie slammed her hand on the table. "She's the kindest woman ever, and she was the best mother anyone could have. Don't you ever forget that, no matter what we find out."

Sophie sat stunned by Ellie's outburst. The reality of the situation was slowly dawning on her. It was no longer *just* a possibility. "I could have a whole other family out there, a mother and a father, sisters, brothers!"

"So, you want me to keep looking?"

"Of course!"

"Even if that means your mom, or Aunt Jenna, kidnapped you and may go to prison?"

"She wouldn't go to prison!"

"There's no statute of limitations, Sophie. If this is the case and people find out, it'll get ugly. I won't be able to keep you guys safe from this."

"You have to stop saving people." Sophie stared at Ellie for a few minutes.

"I know," Ellie finally replied, surrendering. "It doesn't always work out well anyway."

"How about we find this Helen woman and take it from there?" Sophie suggested, a gleam appearing in her eyes. "Maybe we can talk to her, see what she's like, not tell her anything and..."

"Yes, we can do that," Ellie nodded eagerly, grasping at straws she knew, but grasping all the same. "Baby steps."

"Fair enough," Sophie cut up her chicken. "And we make no other decisions until you find her."

"Deal." Ellie felt relieved. She didn't have to decide whether to put her aunt in jeopardy yet.

She might not even find Helen.

Helen might be dead.

Helen might not want to be found.

Chapter Forty-Two

Quinn leaned against a large tree by the roadside where the final scenes of Owen's movie were being shot. It was the last night of filming and he couldn't wait to be done with it. He enjoyed watching over his family when they worked in Montreal, but right now his thoughts were focused on Ellie.

He shouldn't have walked out on her like he had, but he needed her to understand how the pain of a missing child tore at his gut. He'd seen too much agony when a child was never found. The parents always wondering, worrying, never letting go.

And now Ellie believed she was involved in a similar situation. It really was none of his business, except that he wanted Ellie to be part of his life. He needed to talk to her, try to help, explain things.

"Fancy meeting you here," Diane's voice interrupted his plans.

Quinn swung around, upset for being so distracted by Ellie that he wasn't paying attention to what was going on around him.

"I'm not talking, Diane," he said as she leaned against the tree he had just pushed away from.

"I don't need you to." She watched the scene being set up and the walkthrough taking place at the end of the street. "Ellie will talk to me. I'm sure I'll get lots of interesting tidbits from her."

"Why are you doing this?" Quinn shook his head as if not having a clue what made this woman tick.

"Because I need a story, Quinn." She gave him a hard glare. "Your family is a good story, and with this saving the kid angle, it'll be juicy."

"But you don't have to ruin Ellie."

"Oh, I have no intention of doing that, *if* she agrees to talk." Diane tilted her head to the side, sizing him up. "Her past is icing on the cake."

He refused to rise to her bait.

"It was big news back then," Diane continued, relishing sharing these tidbits with him. "Texting while driving was just hitting its stride, father and daughter both killed by a texter."

He shifted, sad to his core thinking about Ellie dealing with the death of her family.

"She had quite the meltdown if I recall," Diane said with a shake of her head. "Your Ellie turned into such an avenger, taking it to the media and all. No one paid much attention to it then but look where we are now."

Quinn's Gran had taught him if you have nothing nice to say, don't say anything at all. He had a lot of nasty things to say, so his lips remained glued together.

"Can you imagine this story?" she continued with relish. "A woman who lost her own child saves someone else's, and it's Owen Walsh's son!"

"Don't do this, Diane." Quinn swung back to her. He refused to plead with her, but it was close.

"Sorry, big guy." Diane smirked at him. "This is what I've been waiting for and I'm not letting it go."

"Never thought you would." Quinn looked at her in disgust and walked away.

His gut clenched and he wanted to hit something as the sense of powerless frustration ran through him.

***

Quinn paced back and forth in the small confines of Owen's trailer. Owen changed into his street clothes and eyed his brother from the far end of the trailer.

"What the heck is the matter with you?" Owen asked. "You're like a caged tiger."

Quinn continued pacing, ignoring the question.

Owen walked over and grabbed his arm. "Really, Quinn." He stopped Quinn in his tracks and made him look at him. "What the hell is going on? You're starting to freak me out."

Quinn's eyes focused on his brother and he took a deep breath. "Diane."

"Ah, fer pity's sake," Owen said in his best Scottish accent. His horrible imitation usually got a smile out of Quinn, but not this time.

"She's after Ellie."

Owen sighed. "I didn't realize she meant something to you."

"Neither did I," said Quinn, surprised by the idea.

"What does Diane want?"

"Dirt."

"What kind of dirt?" Owen asked carefully.

"On us, on Ellie, anything she can dig up."

"Why does that woman hate us so much?"

"She doesn't hate us." Quinn gave his brother a brittle smile. "She hates me."

"You couldn't have just bedded her and left?"

"No."

Owen knew his brother better than that. "No, I guess you wouldn't have. So, what are you going to do?"

"I need to convince Ellie not to talk to her." Quinn reached for his phone. "Diane is a sly one and she'll get things out of Ellie that she won't even know she's saying."

"She can't hurt us, Quinn," Owen said calmly. "There's nothing we've ever done that's newsworthy."

"Yes, but we let Gavyn run into the street."

The truth of the statement left Owen feeling sucker punched.

"True. And that's the worst thing I've ever experienced in my life." Owen sat down on the couch reliving the moment he saw the truck driving by Ellie, honking its horn and seeing his son clutched in her arms, inches from harm.

"Diane could make you appear like unfit parents." Quinn sat beside him, his phone dangling from his fingers.

"Let her," Owen said, anger creeping into his voice. "There's nothing else to find."

"Ellie doesn't know much about our family," Quinn said. "But Diane will peel Ellie's past back and she's barely hanging on as it is."

Owen motioned to Quinn's phone. "Call her, tell her to stay clear of Diane. Let the witch do her worst."

"She latched onto that fake story about you and the prop girl pretty hard. I wouldn't want any of us to go through that again. You sure?"

"Quinn, we've had worse than her after us and we're still standing."

***

Quinn punched in Ellie's phone number and waited, his fingers tapping against his leg in an irritated beat.

Owen headed out the door and Quinn stood up to follow, but his brother waved him back. "I'll wait for you in the car."

Quinn sat on the edge of the couch and rested his arms on his knees forcing his fingers to keep still. He was about to hang up when she answered.

"Hello?" she sounded out of breath.

"Ellie, it's Quinn."

Silence.

"Hey." He could tell his call surprised her. "Is this a bad time?"

"Just took Cali for a walk." Her tone was clipped, cautious, closed.

"Look," he said, taking a deep breath, "I'm sorry I was such a jerk."

She waited.

"I don't know anything about your family situation, and I have no right to tell you what to do."

She waited.

"And," he continued, "I saw Diane. She told me you agreed to be interviewed."

"She didn't leave me with much of a choice, but not to worry. I'll give her a good story— I won't say anything about you or your family. I really don't know you."

That hurt. "I'm more concerned with her digging into your past, Ellie. She can get people to reveal private stuff and I know you don't want her in your business right now."

"You think?" Her sarcasm was icy. Her anger was still simmering.

"Look, you don't have to talk to her. She has nothing on us, and you don't need to let her close to you and your life."

"Actually, I do. I've got to give her something, Quinn. I have to lead her astray, keep her off the real story, if there is one."

"Do you want me to come with you?"

"Thanks, but I'm sure I can handle her."

"Don't underestimate her, Ellie," Quinn warned. "Diane is not a nice person."

"She's doing a job."

"You're very understanding."

"Not really." After a moment of silence, Ellie sighed and added, "She's pond scum but I know what she's looking for and I'll give it to her."

"Your husband and daughter?"

"Yes."

"Aw, Ellie."

"Quinn, I've got to run. Thanks for the warning. I'll be careful."

"Yeah, sure." Her abrupt dismissal set him adrift. He'd always known the right thing to say and how to deal with anything life threw at him. But right now, he felt lost.

"Have a good night." She hung up.

He sat for a minute, phone clutched in his hand.

Chapter Forty-Three

After Quinn's phone call, Ellie headed out for another walk. Cali loved her last night romp and two in one night wouldn't hurt either of them. They strolled along the paths, played toss the toy, and Ellie let Cali have a swim in the pond.

"Cali," she called loudly. The dog darted off into the bush to do her nightly ritual before they headed back to the house. Ellie closed the porch door behind them, locked it with a jab of her hand and brushed away the emotional exhaustion tears abruptly filling her eyes. She hated crying for no reason. Who was she kidding? She wished Quinn was here to walk her through all the mess that was coming her way.

Time to go hunting for information. She stretched her arms above her head and worked every tight muscle in her body through a slow stretch. It was a trick Aunt Jenna had taught her when her parents had died. It had saved her emotionally during the first few weeks after her family passed. She'd filled a bag full of tricks learned over the years, and most of them never failed her.

She turned her laptop on and went into her bedroom to get into her pajamas. Comfortable clothes were as good as a cup of tea. She freshened Cali's water, got a glass of juice for herself and sat down at the table. The computer was ready.

But was she?

She opened her file and looked at the name she'd scrawled down at the boarding house. Helen White. And still, she hesitated. She felt caught in a Schrodinger's

Cat situation. If she didn't type in the name, Helen was only a name, but if a hit came up, Helen could change everyone's life.

And Ellie tended to avoid change like the plague. She'd fight tooth and nail if she felt threatened, but this wasn't about her. It was about Sophie, and Aunt Jenna, and yes, even Helen.

Ellie's fingers blurred across the keyboard as she typed into the search engine and smashed the enter key. She closed her eyes and sat back for a minute. There was still time to stop this. She could press the delete key without looking, press it over and over until whatever results came up disappeared completely.

But although Ellie may hate change, she was no coward. She cracked one eye slowly and looked at the screen. Her fingers clenched so hard her nails dug into her palms.

Helen White existed.

The first article revealed that Helen White lived in Montreal and was a well-known painter. Ellie eased forward in her seat and read the information Google had found for her. There were a few articles in local papers and art magazines about her work, her showings, and then there was a picture of her. If Ellie didn't know the truth, she would swear she was looking at an older version of Sophie, red hair, a wide smile, sad eyes.

And that's when she felt the final nail being pounded home like a fully sealed coffin.

Chapter Forty-Four

The next morning was sunny, warm and inviting. The breeze fluttered Ellie's hair across her face as she stood on Sherbrooke Street outside Helen's studio. She pushed it back behind her ear and her hand stayed there as she gave herself a pep talk. *You can do this, nothing bad will happen, just check her out.*

The studio was open and she noticed that one side of the room was a gallery of completed work, while the other side was for works in progress.

Ellie looked through the large glass windows and saw a group of older women painting in a corner. Their easels curved in a half moon, their canvases holding varying degrees of paintings of a lush potted plant that rested on a table in front of them. As the students were painting, a tall red-haired woman walked among them, stopping here to point something out, stopping there to show a brush stroke.

But the woman spun around, as if feeling Ellie there, and their eyes locked.

Ellie smiled shakily but stood rooted to the spot.

Helen smiled back and beckoned her inside.

"Are you here for the art classes?" Helen asked as Ellie walked hesitantly into the large room.

"No." Ellie laughed, basking in the soothing, warm, and non-threatening vibes coming from this woman. "Actually, I'm here to talk to you."

"Helen White," the woman held out her hand, "and you are?"

Ellie took her hand and shook it. It was large and covered in paint, and as they got closer a faint smell of roses came from the woman.

"Ellie McLellan."

"What can I do for you?" Helen raised her eyebrows in question, a sudden wariness coming into her eyes.

"Is there somewhere we can talk, privately?" Ellie noticed the group of painters throwing them sideways glances.

"Sounds serious." Helen took one look at Ellie's pale face and motioned to a door at the far end of the studio. "We can use my office." She led the way and closed the door behind them. The room was small, minimalist with only a single desk, a filing cabinet, and two chairs, but glorious paintings of flowers covered the walls.

Ellie stood transfixed. "Wow."

"Thank you." Helen waited.

Ellie was stalling. The next words out of her mouth would set this ball in motion for good. But that ball had been spinning since she walked in the front door. "I'm looking for a Helen White and I believe you are she."

"And why would that be?"

"I think she knew my Aunt Jenna back in the summer and fall of 1990, when they were in Stellar Heights together."

Helen jerked as if hit by an electrical jolt. "Jenna?"

Ellie hesitated. "Are you that Helen? You knew Jenna?"

Helen grabbed the back of a chair and looked at Ellie. "Yes, I knew Jenna."

"I know this is out of the blue and everything." Ellie felt the panic settling in her stomach, but she pushed forward. Protecting Aunt Jenna was the only thing on her mind. "But Aunt Jenna is in the hospital. Her heart's not good, and her daughter, Sophie, well, I don't think she's Aunt Jenna's daughter, and Sophie wants to know what's going on but she doesn't want to get her Mom in trouble and..."

"Wait!" Helen's hand shot up to stop her rambling. "Wait a minute. Sophie?"

"My cousin." Ellie reigned in her breath and slowed down. "Aunt Jenna's daughter, but not her daughter. DNA says she's not, and looking at you, I agree."

"Jenna's ill?" Helen's grip got white-knuckle tight.

"Heart attack."

"It's time I go see her." Helen's lips went tight and frown lines appeared on her forehead.

"You won't tell the police, will you?" Ellie held out her hands. "Maybe we can fix this. If you talk to her..."

"Police?" Helen looked confused. "I need to talk to Jenna, and I need to see... Sophie."

A knock at the door sounded before a young woman poked her head inside. "Helen? The people from the art gallery are here to see your work. This could be the one!" She threw a quick glance at Ellie and her beaming grin turned into a worried frown. "Is everything okay?"

"Yes, yes," Helen turned to Ellie and wiped her hands on her jeans. "I need to see Jenna."

"Fair enough." Ellie gathered her thoughts. "Okay. Can you come by the hospital? She's at the Queen Mary."

"After lunch, around 1:00?" Helen rolled her neck to ease the pressure, exactly the same motion Sophie did.

"I don't want my aunt hurt." Ellie spoke with more force than intended and Helen looked startled.

"I'd never hurt Jenna," Helen murmured. "She was the only person who cared about me during a rough period in my life."

"But she..." Ellie stopped in confusion.

"I'll meet you at the hospital then." Helen opened the door and paused. "I don't want any problems, Ms. McLellan, but Jenna and I have things to discuss. And Sophie too."

She headed out for her meeting, dismissing Ellie.

Had Ellie made a mistake coming here? She needed to warn Sophie and make sure she was at the hospital when Helen arrived.

***

Ellie sat in her car on the street near Helen's studio. Inside she was shaking. Outside she was shivering with nerves. What had she done?

Even though Helen seemed like a nice woman, was it possible she would harm Ellie's family? Was her concern about Jenna and Sophie real? Would being reunited with her daughter be enough?

Ellie's phone rang, and she jumped. Her heart raced and the feelings of panic she thought she'd beat years ago roared back to envelop her. "Hello?" she said.

"Ellie," came the quick, clipped voice. "Diane here, calling to remind you the deadline is getting close and I need something for the news tonight. Are you ready to talk to me?"

Ellie sat frozen, a twitch in her left eye the only thing that showed things were not right in her world. She knew that if she didn't give Diane what she wanted she'd dig deeper. And deeper meant Aunt Jenna, Helen and Sophie. She couldn't let that happen.

"Yes," she said more confidently than she felt. "I'll talk to you, but only concerning the Walsh family."

"And how *you're* doing since losing your family," Diane reminded her.

"I don't know why that's important," Ellie parried. Maybe if she made that look more important than it was, Diane would search for the story there.

"It all ties in," Diane said. "Everyone wants to hear about the Walshes, especially that elusive Quinn. He's quite the enigma."

Ellie was not ready to throw Quinn under the bus, but a few bits of lightweight information couldn't hurt. She'd clear it with him first. But would he go for it?

"Ellie?" Diane asked. "You still there?"

"Yes."

"I'll meet you at the hospital around one," Diane said.

"No," Ellie said abruptly. "I can't make that, but I'll be in the cafeteria at three."

That should give Helen enough time to come in and do whatever she would do, good or bad. Ellie's shoulders slumped with the stress of juggling everything.

Diane hesitated, as if checking her calendar. "That works. See you then." She hung up before Ellie could say another word.

Ellie glanced at her watch. Ten-fifteen. Enough time to set things up.

***

Ellie dialled her cousin's number. "Sophie, Helen will meet us at the hospital at one."

"That's amazing," she said. "What's she like? What did she say? Is she going to call the police?"

"We... we were interrupted before we could get into details. But the art gallery was full of students. She's an artist, and she teaches and does her own stuff, which is great. I see where your talent comes from!"

"Wow."

"She looks like you, or... you look like her," Ellie marvelled. "And she was adamant about meeting you both. I got some strange vibes from her. Good vibes, but..."

"Maybe she won't turn Aunt Jenna in," Sophie said hopefully.

"Maybe not," Ellie said. "But I'm meeting Diane for an interview at three."

"What? You can't do that, Ellie, she'll bring up the stuff about your family and—"

"Sophie," Ellie lowered her voice, "listen to me." She waited until she could hear Sophie's breathing settle. "I have to do this. It's the only way I can keep her away from you, Aunt Jenna and Helen." No one needed to know about the added blackmail about Owen and Lauren. "I have to give her something, something she thinks is valuable."

218

"Your past is valuable," Sophie reminded her. "Your privacy even more so. Don't you remember how the press hounded you back then?"

"I do," Ellie said with a sigh. "But can you imagine what would happen if dirt turns up about Aunt Jenna, on top of all that? I won't let that happen."

"You can't keep taking care of us, El," Sophie said softly. "You need to think of yourself once in a while."

"You're right. I'm heading over to Quinn's, and maybe he'll have some good ideas."

"Finally! I'm sure he'll help."

"I don't know," Ellie replied with hesitation.

"Go talk to him. You won't know until you try."

"Right." Ellie fastened her seatbelt and put the key in the ignition. "See you at the hospital at one. Sophie, are you sure you want to do this?"

"No going back now."

"No going back," Ellie repeated to herself as she ended the call and started the car.

She pulled into traffic and headed to Quinn's house.

Chapter Forty-Five

Quinn pushed his motorcycle into the garage as Ellie pulled up to the curb. He looked at the car, looked closer at her and smiled. And yet she hesitated before getting out. And he hesitated before walking over to her. And then they both moved at the same time.

"This is a nice surprise." Quinn held her door open for her.

"I was in town," she said lightly. "Thought I'd drop by and say hi."

"I was about to make coffee," he offered, "or tea."

"Sure." She followed him into the house. Once inside, Ellie sank onto one of the chairs at the kitchen table and rested her arms in front of her. She would love to put her head down and nap, but she'd probably stay there for hours.

"So, what's up?" he asked as he got cups and spoons ready for their tea. "If you want to talk, I'm happy to listen."

She sat silent as the water roiled to a boil, it's whistle alerting them it was ready. She watched him move around the quaint kitchen and felt comforted by the bright colours and flowered curtains. "How come you never changed this room?" She was curious.

He stopped pouring boiling water into the teapot and looked around, then smiled. "This house is Gran." He finished pouring. "I loved how she fixed it up. It's pretty high tech for her time and I didn't want to change a thing. Everything works. This kitchen is her."

"Bright, cheerful, tidy," Ellie said.

"Exactly." He laughed as he put the teapot in front of her. He brought the cups, spoons and milk to the table before sitting down across from her.

He poured her tea and she took the hot cup in her hands, cradling it to warm her icy fingers.

"She was tiny, like you," Quinn blurted out. His eyes popped open as he tried to cover up his gaffe. "Not that there's anything wrong with being tiny."

Ellie laughed at him, the first real smile that had touched her face in days. "I have no problem with my size." Her hand shook slightly as she added sugar to her tea. "What was she like?"

Quinn took a deep breath and sat back in his chair; hands wrapped around his own cup. He looked lost in good thoughts if his grin was any sign. "She was the black sheep of the family, but not because she did anything wrong," he started. "She did what she wanted. She never hurt anyone or caused anyone grief by doing it, but she *was* different. After my Grandad died, she was alone but she was ready to do her own thing. She loved it."

"How long had they been married?"

"Close to sixty-five years." Quinn looked at her. "Hell of a run."

"What was their secret?" Ellie held his gaze. Would he know?

"Gran said that they weren't perfect, but they listened to each other." He sipped his tea. "Even if it took a few days for what they were hearing to sink in. They gave each other space but were always there for each other, through everything life threw at them."

"They were best friends." Ellie returned his smile.

"Absolutely."

"Seems that there was a special connection between you two as well."

"She understood me," Quinn said. "When I left the force in Scotland I was burnt, really burnt. She asked me to come and stay with her. I was going to get my own place, but she was getting frail and would have jumped off a bridge before ending up in a retirement home. 'What would I do with a bunch of old people?'." Quinn said in a high-pitched voice.

Ellie laughed at his imitation.

"So, I stayed with her through her last years," Quinn said matter-of-factly. "I have to say she helped me more than I helped her."

"I wish I'd met her."

"Me too." He watched her face. "She would have loved you."

"How do you know?" Ellie shook her head. "She could have hated me on sight."

"She and I have the same tastes."

Well, that shut her up quick.

Quinn watched her squirm.

"Quinn," Ellie began then hesitated, fidgeted with her cup and then pushed it away as if that one action was going to give her strength.

"Yes?" He waited her out while she chewed over what she was going to say.

"I found Helen."

They stared at each other in silence, each realizing the consequences those three words could have.

"Is that good?"

"I *think* so," Ellie said slowly. She held his gaze, almost like a lifeline. "I know I'm doing the right thing, but it could go wrong in so many ways."

"What's she like?"

"She looks like Sophie, or Sophie looks like her. Tall, red hair, quiet-spoken, calm," Ellie said. "Really nice."

"But?"

She was surprised he picked up on her hesitation. "But I'm getting a strange vibe from her."

"Meaning?"

"I can't put my finger on it, but she certainly wants to see Aunt Jenna, more so than Sophie."

"But you don't know Sophie is her daughter," Quinn reminded her.

"I wasn't sure until I saw her. Sophie actually looks like the picture I have of Helen, the one with Aunt Jenna. It didn't hit me before because I hadn't wanted it to be true."

"So, what now?"

"We're meeting at the hospital at one."

"Do you want me to go with you?" Quinn offered. She hesitated and his face fell.

"I didn't want to ask but I was hoping you would."

"Asking for help isn't a bad thing, Ellie." He took her hand across the table.

"I know." She squeezed his hand and held on tight. "But it's kind of new for me."

"We're never too old to learn new things." He had a twinkle in his eye.

***

Ellie left her car at Quinn's and they arrived at the hospital together. She was too nervous to drive. Her mouth was dry, her hands were sweating, and her heart was beating way too fast. She put a hand to her chest and pressed hard, willing her heartbeat to slow.

"You okay?" Quinn watched her. "You're not going to pass out, are you?"

"No worries." She gave him a half-hearted smile. "Not my thing."

"Too tough?" he joked.

"Something like that."

He reached over and took her hand. "It'll be okay."

"I wish I believed that." She didn't want to let go of the safety of his hand but had to when he started to park.

"Come on." He got out of the car and went around to help her out. "It's better to get the hard stuff out of the way. I hate waiting for things to happen."

"You lose control over it, right?" Ellie looked up at him and realized they were more alike than she thought.

"Exactly." He grinned. He closed her door, took her hand in his and headed for the hospital.

***

When they stepped out of the elevator, Diane was waiting for them. And when Diane saw them together, she smirked as if she had just won a prize. Two for one.

"What are you doing here?" Quinn growled at her.

A weaker person would have backed away. But not Diane. "I wanted to finish our interview." She spoke directly to Ellie, ignoring Quinn and his anger.

"It's not three yet," Ellie said, her gaze darting around the hall, hoping not to see Helen walking towards them.

"Who are you waiting for?" Diane asked.

The elevator doors beside them opened and Ellie knew who it was without looking.

A gentle hand touched her arm and the smell of roses wafted to her. "Ellie," said Helen, "is everything okay?"

Sophie came out of Jenna's room at that moment and saw Helen. Helen froze and stared at Sophie. If anyone had trouble seeing the resemblance, they were blind.

"Wait a minute," Diane began, looking back and forth between the two women.

"You really don't belong here." Quinn grabbed her arm and tried to move her to the elevators.

"Let go of me!" Diane raised her voice and he dropped her arm as if it burned his fingers.

Ellie held her ground. She would not show weakness, not in front of this nasty woman, but she had to stop her from getting to Aunt Jenna. She forced herself to speak calmly. "Diane, if you want your interview you'll have to wait."

"What are you hiding?" Diane looked back and forth from Sophie to Helen. "You're her mother, right?"

"And who are you?" Helen asked politely.

"Really?" Diane was both angry and amazed. "You don't know who I am?"

Helen countered, "Do you know who *I* am?"

"I will soon enough."

"Diane," Ellie moved towards her, building steam, eyes like flint and filled with anger. "This is none of your business and you're not welcome here."

"Oh, this is *definitely* my business," Diane said, but she took a careful step back. "I can get the story now, or later, with extras."

Helen looked at Diane, took her measure in seconds and smiled.

Diane shifted her weight from one foot to the other, as if someone had called her bluff.

"You can't hurt us, dear," Helen said softly. "Not with anything you think you have."

"And why would you?" Sophie asked Diane, coming to stand by Helen. "What have we ever done to you?" Her tone got louder and other people turned in their direction.

Helen curled her arm around Sophie's body for a big hug. "She's got a terrible job to do, my dear." Helen leaned into Sophie and smiled. "But let's help her."

"What?" Ellie jerked in surprise. The last thing they needed was Diane finding out Aunt Jenna had kidnapped Sophie to replace her dead baby and Helen White, Sophie's real mother was likely here to call the cops on her. And if Helen didn't, Ellie bet Diane would, for the drama and the eleven o'clock news soundbite.

"Ellie," Helen took her hand and bent in to kiss her on her cheek. "You are a staunch defender of your family and I will always love you for that. But right now, let's go see Jenna," Helen called over her shoulder as she turned with Sophie still wrapped in a hug and headed into the room. "I've missed her."

Sophie looked back at Ellie, wide eyes asking what the hell was going on?

Quinn took Ellie's limp hand and pulled her along behind them.

Diane tried to follow but Quinn stopped her at the door.

"Let her in," called Helen. "This is what she came for. Trust me, she can't hurt us."

Diane's back tightened as if accepting a challenge, and after hesitating a second, she followed them inside. When she stationed herself at the back of the room, near the door, it suddenly occurred to Ellie this might be in case Diane needed a quick escape.

Sophie sat in the seat beside Aunt Jenna and took her hand. Jenna put a smile on her face as she looked at each person in the room. Her heart monitor, however, showed how unsettled she felt.

A nurse came through the door in a hurry, summoned by the sudden shift in Jenna's heart rate. Seeing the crowd inside, she opened her mouth to shoo them all out.

"No." Jenna's voice was surprisingly strong. "I'm fine," she said to the nurse, who checked her monitor and waited until it slowly settled. She glanced at the gathered group one more time and left the room.

Jenna held a shaking hand out to Helen who moved forward quickly and cupped her fingers around Jenna's.

"Hello, dear friend." Helen bent down and gave Jenna a warm kiss and hug. "What have you done to yourself?"

"Gotten old." Jenna laughed, not letting go of Helen.

Quinn picked up a spare chair and brought it to the other side of the bed, across from Sophie, and put it down for Helen.

"Why, thank you." Helen stared at Quinn with a frown on her face. "You look like…"

"Owen Walsh," Diane burst out. Every head turned to her, but she had the grace to keep quiet.

Helen looked over at Quinn. "That's it. Are you an actor too?"

Quinn laughed. "Never!"

"He's a..." Ellie started but turned to him. "What would you say you do?"

"Whatever I want."

Diane snorted from the back of the room.

"Helen," Jenna said, "what are you doing here?"

"It's time, Jenna," Helen said. "Wouldn't you say? Time to reveal the truth."

"Oh, God," Ellie groaned, expecting the worst. She closed her eyes for a minute and took too many quick, deep breaths.

"Ellie," Quinn whispered. "Stop that, you'll hyperventilate."

Her eyes sprang open, and she forced her breathing to slow. Quinn held her hand tight, and they waited.

"I guess there's something I should know?" Sophie looked both happy and scared to death.

"Have you told them anything?" Helen asked Jenna.

"Not a thing."

"Shall I?"

"I'd appreciate that."

Helen looked at Sophie and reached out her other hand to her daughter.

"You're the spitting image of me at your age."

"It is amazing," Jenna admitted. She smiled sadly at her daughter. "I'm so sorry, Sophie."

"What happened?" Sophie whispered, her shoulders edging up around her ears, as if expecting a blow of some kind and trying to prepare herself.

Helen answered. "Your mother and father lived in the same town I did when I gave birth to you."

Sophie's eyes widen.

"Wait a second..." Diane peeled away from the wall and stepped closer. "Do you mean—?"

"I'm serious, Diane," Quinn warned her, "another word, just one, and you're out."

"Fine." Diane's antenna perked up, picking up a whole different story. She took out her notebook and started writing.

"Jenna was the only friend I had then," Helen began. "The only person I really knew. Sophie, your father and I were not married. He didn't even know I was pregnant when he left to go work up north. I waited for him, that was the plan, but I never heard from him. I still have no idea what happened. It was a whirlwind courtship, and we barely knew each other. There is such a thing as love at first sight. I know how silly that sounds but..." She shrugged as if not having any more answers today than she did years before.

Sophie looked at Ellie and her eyes twinkled. Another mystery to solve?

Helen continued. "My parents had died a few years before, and I had no other close family, at least no one who would help me."

Jenna reached up a hand to Helen's cheek and gently ran a finger down it and murmured, "She was so full of life, even under those trying circumstances."

"I'm not dead you know." Helen laughed. "I'm still full of life, only now I'm living a life I can manage."

"Why did Aunt Jenna have Sophie?" Ellie asked the question on everyone's mind.

"Because I couldn't raise her myself," Helen admitted. She stared at Sophie, her expression full of marvel at her daughter's lovely face, red hair and sparkling eyes. "I am so sorry, my darling. I had no way of taking care of you, nowhere to live, no experience, nothing."

Sophie couldn't tear her eyes from Helen's face. "Don't you dare cry," Sophie said, blinking hard as her own tears started pooling.

"Wouldn't dream of it," Helen lied as the tears slid down her cheeks.

"I had just lost our baby," Jenna said, sniffling back her own strong emotions. "I was devastated. Helen kept my spirits up through the last few months and through the birth of my own daughter."

"Her poor little one died the same day, and we buried her the next," Helen said quietly.

"Baby Sophie," Ellie said.

Sophie's head snapped around to her. "Really?" she asked.

"We both loved that name," Helen explained. "Jenna and I were giving our babies the same name, should they be girls."

"You were never second, Sophie, you were Helen's Sophie," said Jenna. "You were the most beautiful baby, so aware even then, quiet, and you slept like a dream."

Helen wiped her damp cheeks. "When Jenna lost her daughter, I thought I'd found the solution to my situation."

"You gave me away?" Sophie's eyes widened in shock.

"Never," Helen said vehemently. "I've known everything you've done your whole life. From your first step to your first kiss."

Sophie looked at Jenna in astonishment. "What does she mean?"

"Your mom had a hard life in the beginning. She wanted to take you back a few times, but we both realized it would have been too rough on you. So, we decided I would keep Helen informed of every single little thing you did in your life. Everything."

"I probably know more about you than you do!" Helen laughed.

Ellie watched her cousin, and she would always consider Sophie to be her cousin even though they were not blood related, and watched the many feelings flash across her face.

But which would last?

"Jenna loved you so much," Helen went on, "I couldn't take you back. She was more your mother than I could ever be, especially when you were young. And you had the added bonus of a great father in William, bless his heart. He took on a lot too. But I was trying to find my way. I wouldn't have been a good mother, Sophie."

"Oh, Helen," Jenna said.

"It's true, Jenna and you know it," Helen said matter-of-factly. "I had nothing to offer a young girl. I've only settled down myself in the last ten years."

"So why not tell me then?" Sophie asked her. "I was fifteen, I could have handled it."

"I was a teen once." Helen laughed. "And believe me, that would *not* have been the time to tell you."

"When *were* you going to tell me?" Sophie looked from one woman to the other. "If Ellie hadn't found you for me, what then?"

"Yes," Helen nodded. "Jenna was demanding it and we were waiting for your exams to be over. I have to confess I've been terrified of what you'd think of me, maybe even hate me for what I did."

Jenna took Sophie's hand and made her look at her. "Helen was desperate when you were born," she told her, her gaze holding Sophie's. "She had no one, no prospects, nothing to give you."

"But I had Jenna," Helen said. Her eyes got watery again, and another tear slipped down her cheek. "I've never had another friend like Jenna in my whole life, from then until now."

"I gained more from Sophie in my life than anything," Jenna reminded her. "I thought I was lost when my baby died, William was so worried. But you gave us a way to heal. And then I found out I could never have another child, and well, the world works wonders sometimes."

Helen leaned in and gathered Jenna in her arms, holding her tight while Jenna cried.

Diane stepped back, uncomfortable with all the emotion.

Ellie beamed; her relief so strong that she swayed. Quinn's arm came around her shoulders and held her close by his side.

Helen pulled back from Jenna and wiped her eyes with the Kleenex Sophie handed her. "Thank you, dear. Well, that's been building for a while."

"Sophie," Jenna asked, "do you remember the clown at your sixth birthday party?"

"Oh, God," Ellie piped up in surprise. "The one Sophie loved and I hated? That clown scared the hell out of me!"

"I'm so sorry," Helen grinned, not looking sorry at all. "Some people hate clowns. Lucky for me, Jenna felt differently than you. We took a risk—we thought it was a good way for me to get close and still be safe. I have never regretted that day."

"You had such kind eyes," Sophie said with amazement. "I remember that so clearly. You looked at me like Mom always did. Did you show up again?"

"No, just that time," Helen admitted. "It was too painful. I wanted to grab you and take you with me, but I was living in a boarding house, like when you were born."

"But she kept in touch with me," Jenna defended. "We wrote every month, and I sent pictures."

Helen took a look at her friend in the hospital bed, hooked up to machines, exhaustion in her eyes. "And now I now why I haven't heard from you this month! You've been lollygagging here in the hospital!" She stood up. "Sophie, will you come with me and talk? We should let Jenna rest."

"Of course." Sophie looked from Jenna to Helen, not knowing what to call them.

Helen saw her confusion. "She's your Mom and I'm Helen. She will always be your mother."

"But how did no one know she wasn't Jenna's daughter?" Diane asked. "I mean she looks nothing like Jenna or Ellie!"

Quinn gave her a dirty glare but Helen stepped forward.

"Are you interested in a human-interest story?" she asked Diane. "This is a good one. Nothing bad happening, no crazy people doing nutty things. Is it too calm and upbeat?"

Diane hesitated, weighing Helen's offer.

"I've got nothing else." Diane looked at Quinn and realized she wouldn't get the juicy gossip story she'd hoped for.

"You keep saying you want out of the trashy tabloid news," Quinn reminded her. "Now's your chance."

Ellie said, "Aunt Jenna, Helen—*no one* has to talk to her. There's no reason for the press to be in our lives or our business." Her body tensed for a fight. She was still angry with Diane, still in protector mode.

Sophie gave her mom a kiss and a nod, then went to Helen. "It'll be fine, Ellie." She nodded at her cousin. "I think this is a great story. I get to have two moms! I've got a lot of questions and the world needs an upbeat ending; don't you agree?"

Ellie shook her head in wonder.

Quinn took her hand and smiled down at her. "It's okay," he said quietly.

"Come on Diane," Helen said as she and Sophie headed for the door. "I believe we need some tea and delicacies to munch on while we get acquainted."

"I know the perfect place." Diane held the door open for Sophie and Helen to pass ahead of her, leaving Ellie and Quinn alone with Jenna.

They all remained silent in the now quiet room. "Well," Ellie let out a sigh.

"Yeppers, as you used to say," said Jenna. Her voice was weak, and she let her head fall back to the pillows. She took a deep breath and closed her eyes.

"Aunt Jenna?"

"I'm fine, Ellie." Jenna smiled. "I feel so much better. But I'm so tired. Take your young man and go home."

"But..." Ellie started.

Jenna opened one eye a crack and waved them off.

Quinn took Ellie's arm and led her out the door. She walked slowly, looking back at Aunt Jenna now sleeping peacefully on the bed.

The heart monitor's regular beep was a soothing sound.

Chapter Forty-Six

"And so, it turns out Sophie is Helen's daughter," Ellie explained to the enthralled group before her.

The nook table was overflowing with her Cozy Seniors. It was Wednesday, which meant it was question night for the genealogy group. But instead of discussing their own research, they were peppering Ellie with questions concerning Sophie, Jenna, and Helen.

It settled Ellie to recount the events of the last week, including the big revelation of that day. The shock was finally wearing off enough that she could share the good news with others—with Sophie's and Helen's blessing, of course. Truthfully, it was a relief.

Quinn sat off to one side. He hadn't left Ellie since Jenna shooed them out of her hospital room. He'd fed her, taken Cali for a walk while Ellie showered and changed clothes, and shared her silence before heading through the woods with her to meet with her seniors. Her hand had found its way into his as they walked, finding a safe haven in their entwined fingers.

Ruth made a slight sniffle sound as she sat with a copy of the picture of her Jeremy in her hands. Ellie had given it to her as soon as she walked in, and she couldn't tear her eyes from it. Everyone turned to her but she smiled and scrunched her shoulders up in delight. They had all seen the picture and everyone, including Lennie, had a little smile for her happiness.

Ellie now looked at the faces in front of her, people who had become another family to her over the past months. They weren't nosy, just curious and concerned, and while they gave Quinn wary glances, they considered everything she had just told them.

"I think it's horrible what Helen did. That's not what a mother does," Shirley burst out, as if expressing a rule written in stone.

"Mother's do the best they can for their children," replied Ruth. Her hands twisted together in her lap as she watched Ellie. "And Sophie turned out lovely," she added.

"She certainly did," said Ellie.

"So, what happens now?" asked Phil, his interest piqued.

Ellie contained her surprise at how Phil had started coming out of his shell. "Well," Ellie dragged out the word, "Sophie and Helen are going to spend some time together and get acquainted."

"But what if they don't like each other?" Phil's brow creased with concern.

"I can't imagine them not getting along, Phil, they are so alike."

Ruth shivered as if a cool breeze had blown across her body. She pulled her sweater closer, her eyes never leaving Ellie.

Phil chuckled at seeing this. "Someone walk over your grave, Ruth?"

"You never know." She shivered again and asked, "And how are you with all this, Ellie?"

Ellie loved this woman. She was so calm and patient, and always concerned for others.

"I'm adjusting," she admitted.

"Did you think your aunt had kidnapped Sophie?" Shirley's blunt question drew a gasp from everyone, but they all waited for Ellie's answer.

"Only in passing," she said.

"Hard not to," Shirley said. "I would never have guessed the truth though."

"But I've lived with Aunt Jenna for a while," said Ellie, "and she could never have done such a horrible thing."

"You never know people, though, do you?" Shirley looked at her sister, a small frown creasing her forehead.

"Sometimes you do, Shirley," Ellie said, "even when they think you don't."

The front door of the Café opened, and Pete stepped inside. He was wearing dusty work clothes, his hair was dishevelled, and he carried a dirty envelope. It was the expression on his face that caught her attention. Something was definitely up, and him coming here during her meeting confirmed it.

He glanced at Maggie as he passed, perhaps longer than would be considered polite. The real surprise was—Maggie blushed when she saw Pete. Ooh... Ellie caught the interaction and smiled to herself. This needed looking into. Maggie *never* blushed.

"Hey, Pete," Ellie called to him.

"Heading out for the night," he mumbled to her, ignoring the Cozy Seniors' faces all gazing up at him. He didn't enjoy being the center of attention. "Found this behind the wallpaper in the bathroom." He handed her a thick envelope, took a last quick peek at the pink-faced Maggie, pivoted on his heel and headed out the door.

"What's that, Ellie?" Shirley asked, her voice unsteady, drawing Ellie's unwilling attention from Maggie's unexpected blushing vulnerability to Pete's shy attention to the completely chalk-white face of Shirley. No longer seated with the Cozy Seniors group, Shirley was on her feet, easing away from the table, her expression unlike any Ellie had ever seen on her face before. The older woman gripped the back of her chair with both hands so hard her knuckles turned white.

"I... I have no idea." Ellie pulled her eyes from Shirley to the envelope. "It looks ancient. It had to have been there for decades." She flipped it over, frowned with confusion and questioningly read the old writing on the front aloud, "It says, 'To My Darling Ruth'?"

Ruth's head snapped up in shock. The colour drained from her face, and as she turned to face her sister, the Cozy Seniors all witnessed Shirley's slow slide to the floor in a dead faint.

About Author

Beth Farrar has been writing stories since her parents handed her a library card and she always took out the allowed five books per week. Her imagination was sparked. Encouragement from English teachers set her on a serious path of learning the craft.

From TV scripts to full length movies (none of which came to screen but were for pleasure and practice), she developed her writing skills by exploring various mediums. Filling notebooks with ideas, sketching characters and locations, and inventing sticky situations for the heroes and heroines to survive, is Beth's happy place (besides walking in cemeteries, but that's another story).

For fifteen years Beth wrote a monthly column, Living Country, in her local English language newspaper, Main Street, sharing interesting observations of living and raising her three sons in the country with her husband.

Having always loved genealogy, Beth melded two of her passions together and created the Ellie McLellan Genealogy Mystery series.

For tips and tricks on how to write your own personal history story, head over to Beth Farrar – Author on Facebook for more information. Also sign up for her newsletter at bethfarrar.com and receive Oral History Questions to help start you writing your own personal history.

Afterword

Would you like to Write Your Own Personal Story?

The seniors in Ellie's genealogy group learned a couple of things during this story that you can apply to your own journey. Also sign up for my newsletter at bethfarrar.com for Oral History Questions to help jog your memory!

1. Find your birth certificate. You may have it already in your possession, your parents could have it, or you can write away to your local governmental body for a copy. When you get it, is there anything interesting on it that you did not know?

2. Start using a Timeline to keep your life in order. You can find an explanation on how to use one at Beth Farrar – Author on Facebook at the link above.

Acknowledgments

No book is written by one person, trust me. I have a lot of people who helped in various ways along the journey that I would like to thank.

Ronnie Roberts, editor extraordinaire, who taught me so much with that first deep dive into my book. Thank you for your patience and guidance throughout. Not only have you helped me with the nuts and bolts of writing, but also the techy stuff that is challenging!

Teresa O'Neil, for your first read suggestions, I am deeply grateful for your time and common sense when plots could have gone sideways.

Karen Kapp and Judy Orenbach, for spending your valuable time reading my work and sharing your thoughts and ideas.

Daphne Petersen, for taking my first born (sorry, first book) on holiday with you and finding those little niggly bits that other eyes missed.

Liam, Connar and Devlin, the best sons a mom could have, always believing and patiently waiting for the book to arrive.

And finally, last, but most important, my hubby, for believing in me even when I complained about the process, cautiously asking how things are going, and never once throwing shade on my dreams. Your belief and encouragement have meant more than you know.

Family Mistakes - Book 2

If you enjoyed following Ellie McLellan and her group of senior genealogists solve their mystery, get ready for the next adventure:

Can you ever go back, make up for lost time?

After finding secreted love-letters inside an old wall during a home renovation, genealogist Ellie McLellan is back in action—still juggling her own demons, of course—while tracking down another mystery, a mystery with the power to destroy a family.

Before Ellie has even started to investigate, her client Ruth appears on her front porch, incoherent and soaked to the skin, clutching the discovered letters. Driven to learn the truth herself, Ruth found concealed diaries in her dusty attic. Diaries kept by the person she trusted most in the world—and is shocked to realize she's been living a lie.

Taking Ruth in, Ellie begins a seemingly impossible search with the help of her weekly genealogy group.

Can Ellie solve the decades old mystery for Ruth?

Can Ruth's family survive this heart-breaking betrayal?

More important—can Ruth catch a falling star before it's gone for good?

Made in the USA
Las Vegas, NV
26 November 2023

81599647R00138